Shrouded Legacy

By the same author

ON A THIN STALK

Shrouded Legacy

A.M. Story

© A.M. Story 2007
First published in Great Britain 2007

ISBN 978-0-7090-8372-6

Robert Hale Limited
Clerkenwell House
Clerkenwell Green
London EC1R 0HT

www.halebooks.com

The right of A.M. Story to be identified as author
of this work has been asserted by her in accordance with the
Copyright, Designs and Patents Act 1988

2 4 6 8 10 9 7 5 3 1

Typeset in 11/15pt Sabon
Printed and bound in Great Britain by
Biddles Limited, King's Lynn

Dedicated to the past, present and future congregations of
All Saints' Church, Westons Juxta Avenum

ACKNOWLEDGEMENTS

I wish to thank Christopher Farmer, my friend District and County Councillor Peter Barnes, and my solicitor, Andrew Bonell, for their considerable assistance with the research for this book – notwithstanding that any factual errors are purely my own; and the Welford and Weston Local History Society for their treasure chest of legends.

CHAPTER ONE

The frail, half-naked figure, invaded by tubes, struggled to reach out – to say something which, judging by the effort he was making, must be important. Did Lord Marston know it was Amos beside him or did he think him a priest, here to give absolution ... or his son Crispin, returned at last? Was he simply sorry he'd neglected to provide a successor, guilty he was leaving them all at the mercy of fate? What provision had he made? Amos needed to know what would happen to the estate, the staff and the villagers of Weston Hathaway when Lord Marston had gone. Was that why he'd been sent for ... in his capacity as district councillor?

Still in his work clothes, he planted his earth-encrusted boots under the bed and lowered himself halfway towards the worn but sturdy brocade chair before collapsing onto it – his knees unable to sustain those last agonizing inches of gradual descent. He held the old man's hand and tried to calm him. What was he trying so hard to articulate?

The shadows lengthened in the great oak-panelled bedchamber as the afternoon drew on, covering the counterpane in gloom, elongating the antique linen hangings draped like waiting shrouds around the bedposts. On the mantelpiece the clock ticked wretchedly, marking the demise of every unwrapped second. Amos sensed the ghosts of Marston ancestors were never far from the bed – come to claim their own.

The latch lifted on the door at the far end of the room, admitting the private nurse. The old man's struggles increased, his skeletal hands clawed strongly at Amos, climbing up his arms, desperate, eyes staring – pleading. Noisily incoherent.

Uncomfortable in his inability to understand what the old man needed, Amos turned to the nurse for help but instead encountered the cold gaze of Lord Marston's private secretary, Sonia Phillips. Amos could have sworn he detected a satisfied smirk cross those pinched features, as if she were pleased to see her employer thus incapacitated.

'I don't know why the doctor called you, Councillor Cotswold.' The emphasis heavily on the 'you', she surveyed him with contempt – staring at his straw-infested checked jacket hanging away at the armholes, his old trousers held up with twine and his filthy footwear. The set of her head suggested he'd be the last person for whom anyone would send. The ghosts had felt warm in comparison.

Amos had no time to respond as Gervaise began to climb out of bed, choking and foaming at the mouth, beating his fists on the covers in anxiety ... or was it anger? The nurse rushed to help and in a moment Lord Marston collapsed back onto his pillows, breathing loudly but otherwise much quieter. Amos turned back to Sonia Phillips but she'd gone.

The old man continued to wander in and out of consciousness, sometimes gripping Amos, sometimes trying again to speak. Each time Amos hoped anew for enlightenment. Once or twice he tried gentle prompting.

'What can I do for you, Gervaise? Is it about the estate?'

But Gervaise just stared at him blankly. As though the words were in a foreign language. What was going on in that once erudite brain?

Presumably thinking it would ease his tortured mind, the nurse brought paper and pen and between them she and Amos propped the old man up, the easier for him to write. But it was useless. Lord Marston had gone beyond writing.

That last fight seemed to have sapped what little remained of his fast ebbing strength. There was so little time. Amos decided to be even more direct. 'How have you left things, Gervaise? Is that what you want to tell me?'

The dying man's eyelids fluttered and his pupils rolled as if in pain but no sound came out. Amos could all but see the answer flickering along some spectral tickertape behind Gervaise's eyes but had no way of plucking it out or interpreting the code.

Amos paced the floor to prevent his joints seizing up. He gazed out of the window across the parkland and the stubbled fields beyond; keen to maintain a solid contact with the living world – fearful lest he too be drawn down into the abyss by the extraordinary power of the old man's mental clutches.

On his second lap of the room Amos spied a figure standing by the gate into the yard. The stranger stared directly up at the window before stooping to pat Napoleon, Amos's pig, busy conducting his own vigil. Someone out for a walk perhaps, the estate was criss-crossed with ancient rights of way, or was it another of the Marston ghosts on guard duty, ensuring Gervaise didn't escape.

At five, Amos phoned Jack Ashley, landlord of the Hathaway Arms in the village and his friend and help-mate.

'Jack, can you do me a favour?'

Jack grunted at the other end. Amos knew better than to interpret this as a negative, more likely Jack was in the middle of one of his crossword clues and was loath to lose his tenuous hold on the solution.

'I'm over at Marston Hall. Gervaise is dying and I'm the only one here except for the staff – I can't leave him like this.'

Another grunt from Jack, then: 'Yes!'

'What do you mean, "yes"?'

'It's an anagram. I knew it was an anagram.'

'Jack, listen, I need you to feed the sheep in the barn and look in on the cattle in the bottom meadow. Will you do that for me?'

'I told you, yes.'

Aware that Jack not only liked solving riddles but frequently conversed in one, Amos gave up and hoped the message would percolate through to him presently.

The evening wore on in misery. Betty Summers, Lord Marston's cook for thirty years, brought Amos some supper on a tray, tutted, shook her head sadly and crept away again. Gervaise lay still now, only occasionally groaning or moving his lips, muttering to himself. Sonia Phillips did not return. Occasionally, in the distance, Amos heard a phone ring, muffled footsteps came and went along the corridor outside the room and once or twice the nurse answered a quiet tapping at the door – but no one else entered.

Amos felt disheartened and exhausted. He'd tried his best to help the old man, done his utmost to understand him. But he wasn't telepathic. Barring a miracle there was little more he could do except keep Gervaise company.

At nine-fifteen in the evening Gervaise Thimbleby, the thirty-eighth Lord Marston, departed this life – without imparting to Amos that which he'd been so desperate to convey; without telling him what would happen to the village.

Bone weary, Amos made his way along the ill-lit, damp, stone passageways to the kitchens. This was the oldest part of the house, once the home farm for the original manor – the ruins of which lay half a mile away. He ducked his head under the lintel into the welcoming brightness of what had been the servants' quarters. Though subdued because the master had just died, nevertheless the latent bustle of the place contrasted warmly with the rest of the house.

Teapot in hand, Betty Summers reigned alone at the oak trestle in the centre of the kitchen. 'Did you know the doctor asked Mrs Phillips to send for you days ago – on Lord Marston's instructions – when the master first took ill? But her didn't do it.'

Amos frowned. 'Why would Gervaise ask the doctor for me

particularly?' He sipped his tea, thinking. 'No wonder he was so put out – must've thought I'd taken my time. Pity is, by the time I did get here he wasn't making any sense at all. I couldn't understand him and neither could the nurse.' The implication of Betty's words belatedly occurred to him. 'You mean the Phillips woman ignored the doctor?'

'Sounded like that to me. Heartless b.i.t.c.h.'

'More than that, Betty,' Sonia Phillips's reaction to him was becoming clearer. 'She did it deliberately so he couldn't talk to me. But why?' His thoughts moved automatically to the man who, in normal circumstances, should have been summoned.

'No word from Crispin I suppose?'

'No-oo.' Betty shook her head dolefully. 'What's going to happen then, Amos? Will I still have a job?' She looked around her. 'I've been here a long time.'

Amos reached across the table to pat Betty's hand. 'Blessed if I know, Betty. But I daresay we shall find out soon enough.'

'I wonder if her knows. Mrs Phillips were the only one that stuck it here – secretary I mean. Loads of them he's had, over the years, none of them for more than a few months. When he were younger he would try it on with them, you know ...' Amos nodded in understanding to save Betty any more embarrassing euphemisms. 'As he grew older he became more and more bad-tempered. Nothing were ever right for him. Didn't suffer fools the Master, never could.' She stopped and considered Amos. 'But then you knows all that, you was around here before.'

'A long time ago, yes, Betty, I was.'

'It were handy her husband being a gardener and all – the old man couldn't keep no gardener neither before they come. No one around here knows them. Some said they'd been in Africa. I suppose the old man must have took up references and the like; I reckons he didn't bargain for the whole family mind. Couple of wasters them sons if ever I saw them. In their twenties they are, supposed to help their father but they're never in the gardens, never do a day's work neither of them. And when they do get up, out they goes at night, comes back at some unearthly hour roaring up the road, shooting and hollering and carrying on.'

'Shooting! Didn't Gervaise put a stop to that?'

'I don't think he heard them, too full of Scotch and pills by that time of night. Oh yes, shooting and whooping and revving them motorbikes and all. Some pretty unsavoury friends they's got as well. You mark my words, Amos, they'll meet a sticky end them two.' She smiled. 'You know, my old Dad used to say that your children display all your own worst faults. Well it's certainly true of hers ...' Betty stopped abruptly, staring over Amos's shoulder towards the passage where Sonia Phillips had materialized in the doorway.

She fixed Amos with her gimlet eyes. 'The nurse tells me you had a wasted journey, Councillor.' The sibilance was stressed. 'He couldn't speak to you anyway.'

Just as he thought. She'd set out to make damned sure he would be too late ... and she'd succeeded. For someone whose employer had just died she looked unduly pleased with herself too. Unlike Betty and doubtless all the other old retainers who were upset and worried, in equal measure, and wondering what would happen to them now. Amos felt he'd let them all down.

Instinctively Amos rose. Unwilling to share the same air as the Phillips woman, he nodded to Betty and strode out through the opposite door into the yard, heading off around the corner of the house to where he'd parked the Land Rover. Napoleon lumbered along behind him. Amos climbed in to the cab but instead of switching on the engine he remained parked, leaning forward in his seat, key in hand, gazing out into the darkness – mesmerized by the day's events. It wasn't as if he'd known Gervaise that well. For a long time, yes, since Amos had been a lad, but not well. In recent years he'd not spoken to him above half a dozen times. So why had Gervaise sent for him at the end?

Witnessing Gervaise's death had resurrected the memory of his own father, something Amos preferred to keep buried. He and his father had never got on.

Squire Cotswold had been a wealthy landowner in Warwick who had treated Amos, his only son, so badly that at fourteen Amos had left home and found a job as a shepherd in Weston Hathaway. Amos's mother passed away four years later. When his father subsequently died, one of Amos's sisters said he had asked for Amos at the end – had seemed to want to tell him something. He went cold as he recalled what had happened to the squire's estate. Was that what Gervaise had planned for here?

Eventually he started the engine but drove slowly, still brooding. As he drew further away from the house down the rutted track towards the river, his headlights picked up the menacing remains of the Old Manor.

Legends were rife about the place and how it had come to be deserted. Amos knew it had been a ruin since the thirteenth century but considered most of the other tales to be doubtful ... except for its tangibly miserable atmosphere. Though with Gervaise having only just passed over, it would be unsurprising to find those centuries of Marstons manning the ramparts tonight.

Desirous of a brighter environment he called in at Jack's on his way home, doubly appreciative of the life and vibrancy in the public bar.

'Why did he ask for you then?' Jack asked.

'Who knows? By the time I received the message to go it was too late – he was incoherent. Ironic isn't it? Man like that, a barrister – used to making himself well understood – but at the last, when it really mattered, he couldn't communicate.'

'What'll happen to the estate now d'you think?'

'How the hell do I know,' Amos replied, keenly feeling his ignorance. It was the second time he'd been asked that in as many hours and it wouldn't stop here. He damned well ought to know.

Undeterred, Jack continued. 'Seems you were popular today. Chap came in here asking for you. I told him you were over at Marston Manor and I was about to direct him but I must have been distracted. Any road he'd gone by the time I came back to him.'

'What did he look like?'

'Middle-aged I'd say, in his fifties. Medium height, if that. Jeans and a jumper. I don't know – I didn't study him.'

'That's probably the man I saw from the bedroom at Marston. He looked up at the window then went away.' Amos supped his beer, mildly curious as to who could be looking for him.

CHAPTER TWO

Early the next morning, Amos managed to catch the doctor outside the paper shop.

'Did Gervaise say anything else to you ... about why he wanted to see me or about the estate?'

The doctor thought for a moment. 'No, Amos, I don't think so. He wasn't much of a one for explanations was he? Come to think of it, didn't he have a son?' Unsaid but clearly inscribed on the doctor's face were the words, *Why didn't he send for him*?

'Yes. Crispin and I were friends as boys; I used to play up at the Manor. Crispin fell out with his old man and left home in his late teens. He hasn't been seen around here for nigh on forty years to my knowledge – we don't even know if he's still alive.'

'Well p'raps Lord Marston thought you knew where Crispin was, hoped you could give him a message – something like that. Maybe he thought you'd kept in touch all these years.' The doctor was in a hurry to be off.

'That's the only explanation, isn't it? That must be it.' Amos straightened, part of his load had been lightened. 'But I still don't know what he wanted me to say to Crispin, supposing he ever comes back.'

Thirty minutes later Amos and Jack were attempting to herd batches of sheep through the makeshift pen they'd made yesterday for inoculation.

'So will you be able to keep the fields you rent at Marston then – and the barn?' Nonchalantly, Jack added: 'Your dad must have had a fair acreage?'

'Two thousand.'

'Christmas, that much! So what happened to it, you've never said?'

Amos stretched. 'Haven't I? Oh that's easy. He left it all to my two sisters who sold it for development and buggered off abroad the pair of them.' Amos couldn't conceal the edge which crept into his voice, time had not lessened the hurt. 'The only thing I inherited from my father was his looks.'

He'd been back in his cottage only seconds when the phone rang. 'Councillor Cotswold?' It was the lady from Social Services. 'There's a man coming to see you. His name's Terry Finn, an ex-vicar. He's on a training scheme for people who are prepared to go out to the Third World and pass their skills on to the farmers out there. We thought you might be prepared to teach him for six months. We'll pay him a subsistence allowance and he would work for you and Mr Tregorran while he's being trained.' Alan Tregorran's farm was on the outskirts of Weston Hathaway.

'I've already sent him over; I've been trying to get hold of you for days. Must go, thanks again.' She rang off before Amos could object.

Now a man stood on the doormat, his back to the light. Just for a minute Amos had a fleeting recollection, but it was gone in an instant.

'I'm Terry Finn,' he said. 'Your new trainee.'

So this was who'd been asking for him in the pub. Jack was right, Amos also reckoned him to be in his late fifties and he was still wearing the same clothes.

'Who lives in the manor house over there then?' Terry asked, as they took a breather from stacking hay in the barn.

'That's Marston Manor where Lord Marston died this week. You remember, you went there looking for me that day, Jack at the pub sent you over. You stood by that gate in the corner you can just see from here – of course I didn't know who you were then.'

'No, I didn't come over here. I managed to find Alan Tregorran and decided to leave you for another day.'

'Oh,' Amos said, surprised. 'That's a mystery then because I certainly saw someone who looked a lot like you from a distance. Must've been a walker after all.'

'I can see a large walled garden. Is that part of the estate too?'

As they looked a figure came climbing towards them across the next field – Richard Phillips, Sonia's husband. He looked uneasy. 'Councillor Cotswold, have you got a minute?'

Terry disappeared into the barn to carry on with his work.

Richard approached Amos. 'I was wondering why Lord Marston wanted to see you the other day ... It's just that I've got some terrific plans for the gardens here but I don't think Lord Marston gave them enough thought. I mean he was ill, wasn't he?'

Amos came alive. Was he about to discover what Gervaise had really wanted him for? 'Why do you think Lord Marston would want to talk to me about it?'

'I thought he might. If he was interested in the idea he might want to test the water so to speak ... see whether he'd be able to get planning permission.'

Richard had uttered the two words guaranteed to strike wariness into Amos's heart. 'I thought you were talking about gardens, not property development.'

'I am, I am. But I'm talking about a garden centre with a difference and a college, a school – for teaching gardening and maybe agriculture too.' He settled into his theme. 'You see we've got eight distinct gardens here, all of them still broadly based on their original designs. They span several centuries – right back to

Elizabethan times. People would like to see these reconstructed – especially if they could see them all in one place. It'd be unique.'

'Yes, yes, Richard, I get the picture and it sounds a nice idea on the face of it but surely, doesn't all this rather depend on what happens to the Marston estate now?'

'Of course it does, Councillor, of course it does,' said Richard, perhaps a shade too hastily. 'Of course it will.' Surprisingly, and in sharp contrast to everyone else, he omitted to follow that up by asking if Amos'd heard what that was.

'What did Lord Marston say when you broached it with him?'

'He said he thought it was unlikely we'd be allowed to do it, muttered something about an ancient monument – I imagine he meant the ruins – and needing all sorts of permissions, oh yes, and why on earth would he want to do it anyway at his time of life. That was the gist of it. Which is why I thought we might get the chance now.'

'Well it's not up to me Richard – even apart from the little question of who will take over the estate. For all I know he's left it to the children's home.'

Richard looked puzzled. 'I wouldn't think so,' he said slowly.

Amos was prevented from pursuing what Richard might or might not know by Napoleon who suddenly took flight and bolted down the hill. Amos yelled and hobbled after him. Hearing the shouts, Terry reappeared from the barn and joined the chase. Amos didn't give much for the chances of Richard's vegetable garden if Napoleon got in there much before they did and he'd soon have that door open, or broken. Terry arrived first but Richard was a close second.

'Don't go in there, I've … er …' – maybe he was stuttering because he was breathless – 'I've … er re-sown all the paths – just re-sown them. I'll get the pig out.' He disappeared through the now open door in the wall and slammed it behind him.

'They didn't look re-sown to me,' Terry muttered.

'Got his mistress in the greenhouse, d'you think?' Amos grinned. Who would blame him with a wife like his.

A minute later the gate opened to allow Napoleon egress but Richard did not re-emerge. Amos wasn't going to discover what Richard knew today. They wandered over to the Manor and finding Betty in the kitchen, Amos introduced Terry Finn.

'They Phillipses are carrying on as though they own the place and Lord Marston not in his grave yet – let alone cold. Giving orders, altering things … you know. They've no right, not until young Crispin is found.'

'Not so young now, Betty, he'll be my age remember. Is anyone even looking for him?'

That flustered Betty. 'Well … I reckon they must be.'

Amos shrugged. It seemed to him the Phillipses had precious little motive to find Crispin. Amos explained to Betty what had happened ten minutes ago.

'Funny, he's like that with me too. I've not been in there above twice myself since he's been here. Wouldn't even let me go and cut the gillie flowers as always grows there, insisted he do it for me – same with the herbs. I thought it were him being extra helpful like.'

Now Amos was even more puzzled. He and Terry exchanged glances.

On the way back Amos showed Terry the church. Like the original manor house, the church at Marston was medieval – although there had been alterations over the centuries. With its back to the Avon and oriented traditionally with the altar at the east end, it boasted the usual collection of knights with pointy shoes and greyhounds; kneeling widows with all their children arrayed in order of height behind them – girls in skirts, boys in trousers, babes in swaddling bands, those who had predeceased their fathers depicted in black – and a selection of brasses and shapes in the floor where brasses had once lain. Amos recalled the young Crispin stretching himself out in the gaps to see how he measured up to his ancestors.

A single bell bore the inscription 'Gabriel, 1210' and had the Marston Coat of Arms etched into it – a bend sinister separating an heraldic pelican at the top from a boar at the bottom.

The most unusual feature All Saints' boasted was a hagioscope; a slanted opening, measuring two feet square, cut at an angle through the outer wall and tapering to a slit, five feet above ground level. It was a remnant of an earlier chantry chapel on the south side of the church destroyed during Henry VIII's purges. Some folk thought it a leper's spy-hole but Amos knew better. He knew its secret.

The Marston family had been buried here from very early times. A mausoleum in one corner of the graveyard housed some of the later ones, but the medieval knights had been buried in the chancel as close to the altar as possible. The more important you were, the closer to God you could be buried – privileged pole position in the race for eternal salvation.

'So what happened? Why did they abandon the Old Manor? Terry asked.

'There are lots of tales, but it was probably something as simple as the lady of the Manor wanting a new house, or the danger of flooding. Mind you I've never seen the church nor the ruins with their toes wet in all my time here.'

'And the tales?'

'As I remember it, apparently an early Baron Marston was murdered by two of his servants who were brothers in order to steal the Manor and the lands, everything. The day before they killed him one of them dressed up as the Baron and lay in bed pretending to die of the plague. They sent for the priest, who because of the plague was only too happy to remain in the doorway, to witness the willing of the Marston estate to the two brothers.

'So no one was surprised when they heard next day that Baron

Marston had died…. But they were astounded to find he'd left the estate to two ne'er-do-wells, thereby disinheriting his son who was away on a crusade.'

CHAPTER THREE

As the procession of mourners slowed to funnel in through the main doors of Holy Trinity church in Stratford, Amos glimpsed Terry on the far side of the churchyard – his familiar sweater and jeans incongruous amongst the black-clad multitude. Amos raised a hand to him but Terry had disappeared behind a horse chestnut. Why had he come, he hadn't known Lord Marston?

It was a cold, official affair. If Gervaise had had friends they were not in evidence. The expected faces were all here, plus some minor functionaries Amos failed to recognize. The estate staff took up most of the rear pews – except for Sonia and Richard Phillips who sat conspicuously in the front along with the Lord Lieutenant and several gentlemen Amos assumed to be Gervaise's legal colleagues from London.

After the service, relieved to make a rapid escape from the indifferent atmosphere, Amos left for Marston graveyard before the hearse. In the back of his mind he had hoped for inspiration by attending the funeral – a bolt from heaven or a divine revelation as to the purpose of his eleventh-hour summons by Gervaise. Because of its very unexpectedness it still seemed important – something unfinished, left hanging.

She was sitting in the little stone porch when Amos arrived at Marston church. But for the single red rose in her hand, he might have mistaken her for a casual visitor. Except they usually came in the summer, not on miserable October afternoons – carrying flowers. She wore a tweed suit with a long skirt and boots, on her head a felt hat and around her shoulders a bright woollen stole. Her dark eyes smiled at Amos as he came up the path.

'I was beginning to think I'd got the wrong day ... or the wrong church ... or both,' she said with evident relief. Amos couldn't place the very slight inflection in her voice – she wasn't local.

'The church will be open; you don't have to sit out here you know.' Amos made towards the door but, when she remained where she was, he changed course and lowered himself onto the stone bench beside her.

'They won't go into the church, will they? I mean, don't they go straight to the grave?' She glanced towards the tarpaulin-covered mound inside a railed area in the corner, by the mausoleum. Why did he feel she not only wanted to stay outside the church ... but wanted him to as well?

'Amos Cotswold,' he said extending an unusually clean hand.

'Annabelle Mainwaring.'

They both heard it at the same time, the low purr of the hearse as it crawled along the lane – Lord Marston's last journey. She rose and walked out of the porch to watch the cortège approach.

'*We brought nothing into this world, and it is certain we can carry nothing out,*' Reverend Whittaker intoned as they entered the churchyard. Pity a few more don't think on that, mused Amos. As the coffin was lowered on its ropes, along with it, steadily descending into the bowels of the earth, went Amos's hope of ever knowing what Gervaise had wanted of him.

'*Ashes to ashes, dust to dust ...*' The harrowing words of the funeral service broke in on Amos's private reverie. The wreaths had been brought from the church and arranged five or six deep in rows around the grave but maybe she felt one person at least ought to remember Gervaise as a man. For whatever reason, it was at this point that Annabelle Mainwaring stepped forward and cast her red rose onto the coffin as the earth showered down on the remains of Gervaise Marston, and the bell tolled in the old church to inform the surrounding countryside of their lord's passing.

Out of nowhere an almighty roar shook the air. One or two of the mourners grasped each other in fear at the shattering intensity of the sound, frightened the day of judgement had arrived. In an instant, what had been an intensely peaceful scene was transformed into an ear-splitting cacophony. Two unsilenced motorbikes roared up the lane at full throttle, in through the lych gate and around the graveyard.

The riders showed total disrespect for the holy ground – rode over the graves, toppled statues, knocked edgings awry and clipped the corners off crumbling ancient headstones – as they careered across it. The group at the graveside stood transfixed, unable to believe their eyes and ears – aghast. Reverend Whittaker crossed himself in mid-sentence.

Being the first to recover, Amos and the undertakers started towards the bikers but they accelerated away out of the gate and down the lane, revving their engines in mockery as they retreated. It had been like a scene from some demonic film where the graveyard is defiled by aliens – now all it needed was for the other graves to open and yield up their corpses and Amos would believe he had indeed died and gone to hell with Gervaise.

Almost more shocking was the lack of reaction from Sonia and Richard Phillips who remained impassive throughout their sons' desecration of the cemetery. They behaved as if a flock of irritating starlings had flown across at an unfortunate moment, and made no attempt whatsoever to stop them.

Reverend Whittaker finished the short service at the gallop, visibly anxious lest the aliens return. Still in shock, the group turned hurriedly away. Some peeled off towards their cars, others took the track to the main house where the bulk of those from the Stratford service had already gathered.

Although the manor was crowded with people, numbers which befitted Lord Marston's position, nevertheless without a host the house felt empty. Gervaise's departure had left a hole, but it was the uncertainty of whether or not his son was alive, and would reappear, which caused the real vacuum. Without him the estate was rudderless and as far as Amos knew there were no other close relatives to step into the breach, more's the pity.

'I tried to wave to you but you ducked behind a tree,' Amos said as Terry, ever helpful, filled his glass. 'At Holy Trinity this morning, just before the service. You were in the churchyard.'

'Not me Amos, sorry.' Terry moved on with his tray.

Amos felt he was being watched. Turning to determine the source of this intuition he locked eyes with those dark ones again. She was standing in a corner of the hallway, by the hunting prints.

'Mrs Mainwaring …' He'd noticed the wedding ring earlier.

'Annabelle, please.'

'I must say I'm curious.' Though now he thought about it, no one else had shown surprise at her presence, or her action.

'You'd like to know what I'm doing here – you're wondering what the connection is?' She smiled at him. 'I'm an archaeologist. Lord Marston commissioned me to do some digging in the old ruins – to discover more about them.'

'Oh I see.' But he didn't. Lord Marston had never shown any interest in those ruins – certainly not when he and Crispin had played in them. 'I'm a bit surprised.'

'So was everyone else.' She indicated the room. 'I mean people here. They were suspicious, wondered why I was suddenly poking about down there.'

'And is there something special about the ruins?'

'Well anything over a few hundred years old is special to me, Mr Cotswold.' She nodded when he mouthed, 'Amos'. 'But I specialize in architecture, how buildings were built, why, what was where … that sort of thing.'

'Ah so it wasn't buried treasure he was after?'

'Not if you mean gold doubloons, rubies as big as ripe plums … pieces of eight!' She laughed. 'No it wasn't, at least, he never mentioned that to me. Actually he wasn't terribly specific, simply said he'd like me to try and piece the old place together, figuratively speaking – understand where the gatehouse had been, the main courtyard and the Great Hall.' She looked away for a second, no doubt distracted by Terry who'd just come in carrying a large tray of coffee cups.

'What had Gervaise been trying to do? Why such belated curiosity about the lay-out of the original manor?' Amos desperately sought a link in his mind with this new puzzle and what Gervaise might have wanted from him, his District Councillor. There was one obvious. 'Do you think he intended to rebuild it?'

Annabelle looked serious. 'Honestly, Amos, I don't know. Whenever I managed to work out some of the design he was always very interested. Particularly when I proved, to my satisfaction at any rate, the location of the Great Hall. The next step would have been aerial photography, he even wanted to go up in the plane himself, but he died before we could arrange it.' Her mouth turned down. 'I grew quite fond of him you know. The staff here were wary of him but he was always very kind to me.' She stopped on an upbeat, as though about to say something else she'd thought better of.

'No reason not to be,' Amos said, thinking how Gervaise had never lost his liking for the ladies.

John Wilkinson, Amos's solicitor, approached. 'Monopolizing the fair sex as ever I see, Councillor.' He grinned at Annabelle.

'Mrs Annabelle Mainwaring, John Wilkinson. There, what else do you want?'

'Councillor?' asked Annabelle.

'Hiding your light under that rough exterior, Amos? That's not like you, I smell at least a mouse,' John teased, wrinkling his nose.

Several others joined them and Amos lost Annabelle in the press; for which he was sorry, he'd have liked to know more about her work for Gervaise.

John Wilkinson was still beside him. Amos drew him into a corner. 'What do you know about Gervaise's will, John? I know you weren't his solicitor but you might have heard something.'

'All I know is his solicitors are in London, as you might expect. My guess is they're also his executors. I imagine they'll be busy estimating the value of the estate – for inheritance tax as much as anything – and applying for probate.'

'Can they do that without finding his son?'

'Of course they can. His son may not figure in it at all ... except of course, if he *is* alive he'll inherit the title.'

'How can we find out what the will says? Livelihoods around here depend on it.'

'Well, once probate is granted the will becomes a matter of public record. Then you can send the probate registry your fiver, I think it is, and they'll send you a copy.' He punched Amos sympathetically on the shoulder. 'Until then, old son, you'll have to be patient.'

No one lingered – the atmosphere wasn't conducive to it. The proprieties had been observed, they'd all done their duty, and paid their last respects. Amos helped to clear up. Sonia and Richard Phillips had disappeared immediately after the last dignitary.

Down in the kitchen, Amos turned on Betty. 'Why didn't you tell me Lord Marston asked this lady to come and research the old ruins?'

'Professor Mainwaring you mean? Because I rarely sees you, Amos Cotswold, and this last couple of weeks it didn't cross me mind. She'd gone back to Oxford.'

Professor indeed. Now he was even more impressed. 'Why was Lord Marston suddenly so interested in those ruins after all these years? Had he mentioned them before? He certainly didn't when I was a boy.'

'All I can tell you is that the master seemed excited that day she told him she'd found the Great Hall. Comes rushing through here he does, yelling and cursing, looking for his gumboots. Said he were going down there to have a look.'

'Was she with him?'

'No, I don't think so. I think she'd gone off home by then.' Then Betty remembered. 'He went down there again after that. If you ask me that's what started that last bout he had, going out on a day like that – he were gone ages.'

Terry came in from the back yard with Napoleon at his heels. 'I've found out what's in the walled garden. When I heard they'd ridden all over those graves today it got me thinking, reminded me of something I'd seen before. So when the Phillipses were occupied with the reception I nipped across there.' He paused for effect. 'If you'll excuse the expression, it isn't crumpet – it's cannabis! And ripe for harvesting before the frost comes if you ask me. Looks as though they may have started already.'

*

Lindsay, Betty's sister and a village goodwife who did Amos's housework, was earlier than usual and making more noise – bashing saucepans onto the scullery table, throwing cutlery into drawers. Amos struggled downstairs. It was five o'clock, time he stirred anyway. He hobbled into the kitchen running his hand through his grizzled hair and almost tripping over Napoleon who lay sprawled in the doorway, singularly untroubled by Lindsay's mood.

Amos subsided into a kitchen chair as she put a mug of steaming sweet tea in his hand. 'I should drink that, Amos, you're in for a shock.' Such melodrama wasn't like Lindsay, apprehensively he took a sip or two. 'Them Phillipses have got the estate.'

'What!' The tea slopped onto the table as Amos dropped the mug back down. 'What on earth do you mean?'

Lindsay joined him at the table, sat up straight, squared her shoulders and took a deep breath. 'Our Betty come knocking at the door at gone midnight – in a right state she were. She'd walked all the way from Marston, across them fields. Said Mrs Phillips had called the staff together late in the evening and told them Lord Marston had left his entire estate, including the manor and all its contents, to her and her husband.'

There were so many questions Amos knew not which to voice first. What about Crispin, had they found him yet? Would he challenge the will? What sort of hold had the Phillipses had over Gervaise – was that what he'd been trying so desperately to tell Amos the day he died? Amos could easily believe Gervaise had had a sufficiently murky past for someone to blackmail him if they had wanted to – and his position as an eminent barrister meant his reputation was paramount. But would he have submitted to such threats when he himself would soon be well out of it and he had no one else to protect? That surely was stretching credibility too far. He hadn't been that sort of man.

So what on earth could have driven him to give the estate away like that? Or had he done it out of spite – a last laugh from the grave at the village's expense? No. Amos couldn't believe that of him. Whatever else he may have been, Gervaise had always been a local benefactor. So why then do what he'd done? Like Lindsay, he could hardly believe it. Would that he had given his money to the children's home – how infinitely preferable that would have been.

What else did the will say? What would the Phillipses do with the estate? They weren't farmers – would they try to build all over it? Had the Phillips woman asked the staff to stay on?

However he looked at it he couldn't believe Gervaise would have left everything to the Phillipses. Maybe he'd known Crispin was dead ... was that it? Even then it didn't make sense. Why the Phillipses of all people? Yes, Gervaise had been a nasty individual himself at times, certainly not someone you'd want to cross, but even so .... Amos couldn't believe Gervaise had actually liked Sonia Phillips. And from what Richard had told him last week it sounded as though he'd had little time for her husband. Surely if Gervaise had left the estate to the Phillipses he'd have told Richard to get on with his gardening school. None of it made any sense.

By lunchtime Betty and Lindsay were both sitting at Amos's table. 'The worst of it is, it were me and the estate manager who witnessed the master's will! I had no idea what it said mind. If I had I'd have refused to do it, really I would.'

'I suppose a man has a right to leave his money to whomever he wants,' mused Amos, unsure of the veracity of his statement.

He returned to the witnessing subject, his memory suddenly ignited. 'You're sure it was Gervaise, Betty?' She frowned not understanding. 'When you witnessed the signature. Did you see Gervaise himself write his name or did somebody bring you the document already signed?'

'I saw him sign it all right. Near as I am to you now, he was.'

There was a tap at the front door, too soft for it to be Napoleon. The doctor put his head round the door. 'It's all over the village. It's true then, that he's left everything to the Phillipses. I must say, I'm more than surprised.' He sat down, flashing Lindsay a grateful smile for the mug of tea which appeared in front of him. 'If I didn't know better I'd say he'd taken leave of his senses.'

'Can't we challenge it?' Lindsay asked.

'That's what I want to ask John Wilkinson,' Amos replied. 'My guess is you have to be a relative or a dependant. Otherwise all sorts of people could go around challenging other people's wills and holding things up just for the hell of it, couldn't they?'

'You know, I've been thinking. It's strange how I said he must have been deranged – well, ironic really.' They all looked at the doctor, fully aware Lord Marston had been in perfect control of his faculties right up to that last afternoon. 'Only he asked me to prepare a short report, testifying to his sanity ... ooh, only a month or so before he died.

'I've done it before, usually for solicitors. Nowadays a solicitor has to be able to prove he has taken steps to ensure that his client, especially an elderly one, was sufficiently in command of his senses when he made his will, just in case there's a claim. They call it the golden rule I believe. Usually that "proof" consists of a letter from their doctor – more work for GPs.'

'But this is nonsense – we all know he was quite sane....' Then Amos realized. 'Oh no, that's the point isn't it? You mean, if he did his own will he'd still covered himself by asking you for that written opinion. In other words, Crispin couldn't challenge the will on the grounds of his father's not having had full possession of his wits!

'Which brings us back to the same question – where the hell is Crispin?' If Gervaise had disinherited him, had he then repented at the last minute? Was that what he'd been trying to say on that final afternoon – that he wanted to change his will? Taking brinkmanship to the extreme, wasn't it? And now look what Gervaise had bequeathed the community – a couple of con merchants and two hooligans. The real tragedy was, there seemed little he or anybody else around there could do about it.

The talk in Jack's bar that evening consisted of nothing else. It was really none of anyone's business as Amos kept pointing out, receiving unpopular glares for his pains. He felt the same as they did of course – something was wrong.

He'd tried suggesting to himself that they were all jealous. Which one of them hadn't dreamt of winning the lottery or the pools or benefiting from the millions left by an uncle who'd struck it rich in the diamond mines? It's what kept them all going on cold, wet, boring mornings. After all, the local people were far more deserving of inheriting the Marston estate than these incomers were. Even if the Phillipses had been really nice people he suspected the villagers would still have felt aggrieved – if not nearly so worried.

Many villagers had friends or relatives who worked on the estate or rented farms there – what would happen to them? The Phillipses had no more idea of how to run an estate than they had of how to fish. No wonder the estate manager had left as soon as he'd guessed – he wasn't going to hang around and toady to the likes of them!

'They can't inherit the title though can they, Amos?'

He must have answered this one at least five times today. He wished he'd managed to get hold of John Wilkinson – to ask him again about that. 'No, I'm sure they can't.' Uncomfortably in the back of his mind he knew people could buy the title of 'lord of the manor'; that the lordship of the manor had often been divorced from the land itself when the manors had been leased out, as long ago as the fifteenth century. But surely this didn't apply to the hereditary title the Marston family held?

'Presumably they'll try and find Crispin,' he said, wondering just exactly who the 'they' are who do these things. 'Then, as I understand it, they look for the next male relative. With a family as old as theirs, who've held the title for hundreds and hundreds of years – I mean you've only got to look in the church, that title's been theirs since at least eleven something – there's bound to be a male descendant somewhere, poor so and so. Probably means he'll inherit a load of responsibilities without, in this case, any money.'

'Do you think his son's still alive?' Jack asked. 'Lord Marston died three weeks ago – why hasn't he come forward? What's he like, Amos?'

CHAPTER FOUR

'It's been over forty years Jack.' Amos stroked his stubbled chin. Crispin's face, as smooth as it was when Amos knew him, shiny and laughing, appeared vividly in his mind's eye. 'He's probably changed beyond all recognition – I'm sure I have.' He glanced down at himself, seeing only an older version of the teenage ragamuffin he'd been when he last saw Crispin. 'I probably wouldn't know him.'

'What was he like though? Was he like Gervaise?'

Amos realized what Jack was getting at. He couldn't see Lord Marston letting someone else inherit what should have been his, even if he had walked out and never come back until now. He remembered the soft-hearted boy who seemed the antithesis of his father – mild, a lover of every kind of animal, interested in the land, history, the natural world, but most of all, people.

It had happened during one Christmas holiday when he and Crispin were thirteen. Fighting their way along the riverbank one afternoon, they'd been trying to beat the weather back to the manor. Without warning, a bitterly cold, but sunny day, had turned to a swirl of freezing fog; their breath hung outside their bodies, mingling with the mist, increasing its impenetrability. It was all they could do to make out the tow path in the gloom, let alone the river beside them.

They'd have missed him entirely if he hadn't been sitting right on the corner – on the old stone which marked the turn as the path changed direction. They'd been keeping an eye out for it –

didn't want to miss it in the fog and end up in the graveyard. He'd looked about eight or nine but was so thin and drawn he could easily have been older. He'd no shoes, and only ragged pyjamas – no coat, no sweater, no comfort of any kind. Amos remembered thinking the kid wasn't going to last long out here like that. At first he didn't speak, his pale eyes just looked at them – hopelessly.

'You can't stay here like this, you'll freeze to death. Come with us.' Crispin had commanded.

The boy had shaken his head violently. 'They's after me. They knows I'll tell what they did to me.'

Although it meant losing important minutes, Crispin had crouched on his haunches next to the boy and coaxed the rest of the story out of him. He had run away from the orphanage at Branchester, fifteen miles away. He'd been running all day, but he wouldn't come back to the manor for fear he'd be caught. His father was in the navy he said and he was determined to get to Portsmouth to try and find him. It had been too cold to stand there arguing, and in a few minutes it would be dark, too.

With an understanding way beyond his thirteen years, Crispin had made a decision. Taking the runaway back to the manor would have been the easy solution, would have salved Crispin's conscience ... at the boy's expense. Instead he had helped in the way in which the boy wanted. He'd stripped off all his clothes down to his underpants and thrust them at the boy along with his gumboots. 'I'll say I fell in the river. Stay here, I'll bring you some food and money.'

Barefoot, Crispin had run the half-mile back to the manor while Amos stayed with the boy. Within twenty minutes he was back, carrying in a holdall whatever he'd been able to lay his hands on in the kitchen, plus the contents of his money box and a pair of shoes. They never saw the boy again.

The escapade had cost Crispin six month's pocket money plus

a caning for theft and for lying to the police when they came searching for the runaway a day later.

Back in the present, Amos shook himself. Jack was staring at him, waiting for an answer. 'I really couldn't say. He was no firebrand, but show him an injustice and he'd be there, trying to right it. He and his father had that much in common I suppose.'

'How come you knew him? Were you at school together?'

'That posh school didn't do me much good, is that what you're thinking?' Jack looked sheepish and Amos grinned. 'Only kidding. No, we weren't. Crispin went to a prep school then to Winchester. I only saw him in the holidays after that.

'I don't know how it came about, but my father and Gervaise were acquaintances, not surprising, I suppose, as they were both major landowners – but how Crispin and I met I don't know. I'd just always known him. We hit it off and after that, well I used to pester my parents to let me come over to Marston – as much to get away from my old man as anything else. I'd stay whole weeks at a time in the holidays. My father was as pleased to get rid of me as I was to escape, maybe more so.' Amos took a sip of his beer. 'It's funny, but thinking about it, I can remember him suggesting it – more than once – as though it were some sort of punishment for me.' He shrugged. 'Who knows, maybe I'd played the "Don't throw me in the briar bush" trick on him – you know like Brer Rabbit in that story.'

'You mean you told your dad you hated it at Marston?'

'Probably. I can't think why else he kept sending me here. He never gave me anything else I wanted.'

'So why did Crispin leave home then?'

'I don't know, I'd gone myself by then.' Amos caught Jack's old-fashioned look, so he downed the remainder of his pint out of devilment – to prolong the suspense. Putting his empty glass pointedly in front of Jack he went on: 'But if you asked me to guess, I'd say it was because his mother died.'

Jack returned with an overflowing pint. 'You'd think he'd

feel duty bound to keep his father company for a while after that.'

'Oh no! Crispin hated his father almost as much as I hated mine. Loathed him. That was one of the things we had in common. Oh no, I can imagine he couldn't get out of here fast enough with his mother gone. He'd have blamed Gervaise for that anyway. The real reason he hated his father was Gervaise's womanizing. It broke his mother's heart every time.'

Jack went to serve other customers and Amos sat with his eyes downcast, pondering on the past. He exchanged a few words here and there with people as they came and went from the bar, but his mind dwelt on those two boys all that time ago; as though he were a detached observer – watching a film. A film which finished with the first reel, and no satisfactory ending. It surprised him that he felt it so sharply now, after all this time.

After his own mother died, Amos had left Warwickshire altogether. Neither he nor Crispin being the sort of eighteen-year-olds who wrote letters, Amos had thought little of it when their paths had failed to cross for a few years. He'd been busy, young, and anyway he'd thought Crispin was away at university. But on returning to the area after his father's death, Amos had been surprised to find that not only had Crispin left Marston, but no one seemed to know where he'd gone. Again, for a year or two he'd thought nothing of it but as the years had stretched into decades he'd felt sorry he'd not made more effort to stay in touch originally. Even then he thought Crispin would come back when he'd sown enough wild oats and grown up. But he never had.

Amos felt reluctant to think the worst but this continued non-appearance increasingly pointed to one inevitable conclusion – that Crispin was dead.

*

John Wilkinson was crossing the street in Stratford. Amos waved, 'Hope you've got a couple of minutes, I've been trying to get hold of you about this Marston Estate business.' John looked patiently at Amos. 'I know you weren't his solicitor, I just want to understand what the situation is ... from a legal point of view.'

'You mean, is there anything anyone can do to stop the Phillipses inheriting the lot?'

'Yes.'

'No.'

'But there must be! What if the son, Crispin, is still alive? Surely he can contest the will?'

'Yeees,' John said, very slowly '... but you have to understand, Amos, a will has no obligation to be fair. No one has a right to inherit anything – except perhaps a title. Remember the poor old second, third and fourth sons, let alone any daughters. They frequently got absolutely nothing under the law of primogeniture – everything went to the eldest son. So even Crispin would have to prove that either the old gentleman was not in full command of his actions when he signed the will, which sounds unlikely in this case, or that he was misled by others – given false information on which to base his views and opinions – which is even more far-fetched from what I knew of him.'

'The doctor says Lord Marston asked him to certify his ability to make his will a little while ago. Made him put it in writing. The doctor says it's quite common these days.' Amos was interested to see whether John agreed with that.

'Yes it is – it can be tricky where the old folk are concerned. But that sounds to me as though Lord Marston knew exactly what he was doing – knew the will was likely to be disputed and made sure he closed that loophole.' John looked at his feet. 'I rather wish you hadn't told me that, Amos. Like you, I'd hoped this was all a bad dream or Gervaise's idea of a joke. What you've just told me confirms it isn't. Unless he was murdered ... or the will is a forgery.'

'Did I tell you Annabelle Mainwaring is an archaeologist he hired to study the ruins? What was all that about?'

'He was always interested in the ladies, you know that as well as I do.'

'I've thought about that but she didn't come here asking to look at the ruins. According to her, he commissioned her to come and investigate. OK, he could have met her somewhere and when he found out what she did, used the ruins as a lure ... but I don't think so somehow. Besides, by then he was a bit old to go chasing after a woman thirty years younger, surely.' Amos went on: 'Between you and me, if he hadn't gone to the trouble of getting the doctor to certify him as being fit to make his will, I would seriously think now, that he'd begun to lose his senses. Trouble is, the very fact he knew to do that means he must have been sane – he knew he was doing things which were out of character and didn't want them stopped or overturned on the grounds of his insanity. He thought of everything!

'So what do you think?' Amos asked.

'I've just told you.'

'No, what do you really think? You knew Gervaise, albeit not well. Do you think he'd have left everything to the Phillipses?'

'I was afraid you'd ask me that. No, I don't.' He took hold of Amos's sleeve, preventing him from flinging his arm up in triumph. 'But neither do I see how we'd ever prove it. The police would need something more than our surprise to go on. Surprising things happen every day – I can hear them saying it. And anyway, the fact that Crispin hasn't resurfaced would give them even more reason to drag their feet.'

'But what if he did, has ... and they've, you know ... got rid of him.'

'Now you're making it up, Amos.' John lowered his voice. 'Look, I'm as angry about it as the next man, but to take action we'd need evidence and most of all, we'd need Crispin Thimbleby.'

*

Amos drove out to inspect the sheep he kept in the Marston field; the one which had its own barn. As he approached he saw the barn doors were closed. He always left them open unless he had lambing ewes in there. His first thought was that Terry, in a fit of over-efficiency, to which he seemed prone, had come up to put the tractor battery on charge and thought the doors ought to be closed. It was possible and yet.... As he drew nearer he saw the padlock.

Had Terry seen fit to secure the barn and forgotten to give him a key? He felt sure Terry had done no such thing. Neither had the estate manager – partly because he'd never done it in the fifteen years Amos had been renting the field and partly because the estate manager had left. No, this had the smell of Sonia Phillips about it. Well he'd soon stop her from interfering with his barn. He turned abruptly and drove straight to the manor.

Seeing no reason why he should stand ringing the front door bell for an eternity only to be told to go around to the back, he marched straight through the deserted kitchen, along the passageway and up the stairs into the main house, cursorily wiping his boots without breaking stride. He flung open several doors, hollering as he went. The dining-room looked unused; the back parlour, with its unmade grate and still, cold air, had acquired an even gloomier appearance than on the night Gervaise had died. The billiards room was strewn with empty beer cans and cigarette packets. Then he heard the noise. Distant but definitely an argument. He backed out of the hall and set off into the east wing which held the estate offices. Amos stopped hollering and, whilst incapable of tiptoeing, his curiosity was certainly aroused when he realized who was doing the shouting:

'You stupid little man. Did you really think I was going to let you have your gardening college!'

'But I thought—'

'No, you didn't! That's the point. You never do.'

'Sonia, I ...'

'That's the land which will fetch the real money. Big houses with river frontages – it's a perfect spot.'

'But you can't destroy those old gardens!'

'Can't I? You watch …' She whirled round as Amos appeared in the doorway.

'What the hell are you doing here?' Sonia Phillips turned her anger on Amos.

'The barn on my field has been padlocked,' Amos replied, none too happy himself.

Richard backed away into a far corner of the large office, doubtless grateful for the respite. Sonia reassumed her reptilian demeanour. With her lank greasy hair, shapeless sludge-coloured trouser suit and sharp white features her resemblance to a serpent struck Amos afresh.

'My sons require it for their equipment.' She turned her back on him.

'But that's my barn, I've rented it for years and my hay is in there.'

Turning back she looked him up and down as she had at Gervaise's bedside. 'Do you have a contract?'

Amos realized then that the world at Marston had changed. 'Of course not. We had an agreement.' One look at her face told him it would be like explaining morality to an adder. 'You can't steal my hay like that.' Amos retorted, sounding to himself like an outmanoeuvred schoolboy, about two inches tall, yet it was he who was in the right. What could he do? If he forced the door she'd have the police on him, he couldn't afford that in his position – a councillor's behaviour had to be exemplary. On the other hand if he complained to the police about what she'd done it would seem so petty. Glancing across the room at Richard who was sitting at a table gazing fixedly at some large drawings, another option crossed his mind. Should he mention the cannabis? But perhaps she didn't know about that – in which case it wouldn't help him and would make things worse for

Richard. Despite himself he was beginning to have a deal of sympathy for that man.

'And you can remove your sheep from my fields too – before I turn them loose.'

Amos wondered afterwards whether, if he'd been less hasty, not gone striding in there complaining but had just ignored it – if that had been possible – would he still have had those fields? Would she have even bothered about it? Not for the first time in his life he kicked himself for failing to handle the situation more diplomatically.

One thing Amos was sure about – he'd best make haste: she was probably ordering the gates to be opened this very minute, and clearly cared nothing for the animals' welfare. Of course he could have argued with her – could have insisted she get a court order. But how could he prove he'd been paying the rent when it was paid in hay and lambs and the estate manager had already left? Or he could have asked how she intended to keep that land under control without the sheep? Trouble was he was afraid he knew the answer – she intended to develop the lot. Well she'd got another think coming. Marston was a designated category four hamlet, which meant the planners would avoid any further building, except ... Amos also knew that government pressure to build houses almost anywhere was increasing weekly.

He drove straight from Marston to see Alan Treggoran, taking the turn into Alan's yard without braking and juddering to a halt outside the old milking parlour where Alan fattened turkeys for Christmas.

Alan and Terry emerged from the shed. 'What's up with you, Amos? Any further and these daft birds would've died of fright.'

Seething with rage and impotence, and unable to restrain himself any longer, Amos poured out his pressing problem to the two men.

'You can have the finished sprout fields. If you can get hold of that big trailer you sometimes borrow, me and Terry'll come and help you shift them all this afternoon. And you can have this turkey shed after Christmas if you like – you'll be needing somewhere for the lambing.'

He'd counted on their support and they'd willingly given it. During the afternoon several of the Marston hands came to help as well, though Amos was afraid if madam caught them they'd be looking for another job. 'Don't 'ee worry,' said one. 'We'm all lookin elsewhere anyways, Amos.' And Amos realized his little hiccup was nothing compared with the lot of these stalwart labourers who faced certain redundancy.

He would no longer have a legitimate reason to be on the Marston lands. No more popping in for a cuppa with Betty and no way of keeping an eye on what was growing in the walled garden. It seemed his almost lifelong links with the estate were being torn out by the roots. Is that what Gervaise had been trying to explain, forewarn him about, for old time's sake? No, Gervaise had been more disturbed than that would have warranted.

After church on Sunday when everyone else had gone, Amos strolled around the churchyard with Terry. The path which ran along the riverbank, forming the eastern boundary of the churchyard, was an old right of way. He smiled to himself remembering the snatch of row he'd overheard between Sonia and her husband '... big properties with river frontages ...' and wondered how her prospective buyers would take it when they discovered that any Tom, Dick or Kevin had the right to walk straight through their garden. And he'd make damned sure the local people suddenly fell to exercising that right – literally.

They paused at the lych gate where the road bent sharply to the right up to the manor. In front of them slept the medieval church, solid, and enduring. Over to the right lay the ruins of the Old Manor. And between them, hidden from this angle by the church, was the ancient boundary stone where the young runaway had sat all those years ago in the fog. While Terry poked around the churchyard, Amos strolled across to it. He and Crispin had taken turns to sit here as boys. He lowered himself onto the stone and sat staring out over the river.

A soft voice said: 'Penny for them. Or can I guess?'

For a suspended second he thought ... Crispin? Turning slowly he saw Terry regarding him strangely. And again Amos felt he'd known him somewhere before. Whatever had engendered that feeling was indefinable, subliminal even, but there nonetheless.

They walked back towards the church and as they rounded the corner the porch door opened, startling them. Out stepped the Reverend Whittaker whom they assumed had left much earlier. He turned and locked the door behind him muttering, 'Can't be too careful after that business at the funeral,' and nodding to them both, marched away to his waiting car.

Terry was still engrossed in gravestones. 'I've found quite a few Tregorrans and Summers's, but no Cotswolds,' he called.

'You wouldn't. The family lived in and around Warwick, at least our side of it did.' Amos straightened up. 'Come to think of it I don't know much about them either – my father and mother, of course, my mother's maiden name was Lawrence – but not before them. My grandparents died soon after I was born.'

They were interrupted by a buzzing sound, a whining and buzzing sound, penetrating, harsh – like an enraged hornet. Without a word they moved swiftly across the churchyard to stand in front of the lych gate, blocking the entrance; Amos wished he'd had time to move the Land Rover across. What could he and Terry do if a horde of bikers decided to rampage around the churchyard again – except get run over? But he had to do something, and fast. He had to stop this. He scrabbled for his mobile and dialled Stratford police.

Suddenly the hornet was joined by others until the air in the churchyard was thick with their noise. They must be coming down from the manor, one after the other – he couldn't see up that road from here. The dust thrown up by this phalanx of mechanical insects rose in great clouds above the hedgerows; the drifting fumes threatened to choke him. Terry had his eyes closed as Amos braced himself for the onslaught.

CHAPTER FIVE

The onslaught didn't come. They continued to swarm round and round, up and down, but they hadn't broken out of their cluster. Terry opened his eyes slowly, breathed deeply then closed them again – this time in thanksgiving Amos reckoned.

He and Terry left the churchyard and started to climb up the track towards the manor, away from the river. The dense, overgrown hedgerows prevented their seeing into the fields, but the noise was shattering, making conversation impossible. Terry held his hands over his ears. Increasingly frustrated by his inability to see through the hedge, Amos hobbled as fast as he could from clump to clump in the hope of soon finding a suitable gap. Suddenly the sound acquired a new two-tone addition. Below them on the track appeared the welcome sight of a police car swooping round past the churchyard. It must have spotted the two figures further on for it barely hesitated at the lych gate, before accelerating up the hill towards them. Amos and Terry flattened themselves against the hedge to let the squad car pile past but it screeched to a halt beside them. There was little likelihood the hornets would have heard it above their own noise.

'Jump in, councillor.' Terry and Amos scrambled into the back. 'You can hear this row the other side of Weston Hathaway,' volunteered the driver. The car sped on towards the manor. At the top of the rise they pulled in where they could look down over the hedge onto the scene below. Hundreds of bikes were whirling around a roughly marked out circuit, like some demonic gathering whipping itself up into a frenzy before spilling out over the countryside and committing God alone knew what mayhem. To Amos, their presence juxtaposed with the church and the sleeping Marstons increased the sense of defilement.

'What the devil...?' Amos was almost speechless. 'How the hell did that lot get there?'

'Must have come along the towpath from Stratford, last night maybe. Just got up, I shouldn't wonder,' the policeman answered, obviously trying to take it in himself. Their eyes were drawn to the mess strewn haphazardly across the area of grassland behind the ranks of old tyres and straw bales which marked the course. Small tents, tarpaulins, trailers, and sidecars also dotted the area ... 'Maybe they didn't want to disturb the good citizens of Weston Hathaway.'

Amos turned his wrath on the hapless constable. 'If you think that, then I'm a frigging Dutchman. More like they didn't want to ruin the element of surprise.' Watching that abandoned spectacle, Amos had a fair idea of what would come next. He turned to Terry. 'You tell me, are they in the state I think they're in?'

'We-ell at this distance I'm not sure.'

'Can't you feel it, man?' To Amos the atmosphere was unreal, out of control – evil. He turned back to the constable.

'Get on to your people fast! We've got to stop them going back through Weston – God knows what damage they'll do!' Amos shouted this over his shoulder as he hastened back to the car. 'Then get this heap back to the churchyard. Now!'

Whether they'd been heard, or whether the clouds had parted signalling the appointed time or whether it was just one of those things, Amos would never know. The policeman pulled the police car across the entrance to the churchyard just as the first bikes came haring down the road. A few idiots leapt their machines over the stone wall but most were going too fast and veered round the bend when they saw the car, speeding on towards Weston. Amos had no time to reach the Land Rover and drive off in pursuit. He, Terry and a solitary policeman were marooned inside the police car until the legions had passed. The policeman was on the phone.

'Urgent assistance requested. Approximately two hundred motorbikes headed north from Marston through Weston Hathaway.'

Amos sat with his head in his hands, buzzing inside and out. Seldom had he felt so helpless. And what could the police do? They couldn't catch them now before they got to Weston and if they attempted to arrest them there the hordes would just spill out through people's houses and gardens ... running over children. His mind was in overdrive. Neither could he warn anyone. He held his mobile in his hands, gazing at it. If he were to ring Jack at the Hathaway Arms now, and all the Sunday lunchtime crowd turned out into the road, there'd be carnage. Even if they managed to build a quick roadblock the result could be disastrous. High on free cannabis, the riders were beyond reason. No, much as he itched to use that phone – falsely tempted in order to exonerate himself, to show he'd tried – a warning this late would actually do more harm than good. They were in the hands of the Almighty. He glanced across at Terry, thankful to see he had his eyes closed again.

It seemed to go on forever. How long did it take for 200 bikes to pass? He was to blame. If he hadn't called the police and gone snooping, might they all have stayed peacefully in their field not bothering anyone? He knew part of that was nonsense, the peaceful part. But might they have stayed put? He doubted it, their behaviour had definitely been unnatural, trance-like even, so surely it was better to round them up until the effects had worn off. Yes but they could have been rounded up quickly and easily where they were – now they were loose in the countryside and it was his fault.

The constable was still on the phone. 'Well haven't you got someone to slow them down at the junction?' Amos guessed he meant the junction with the main road, the other side of Weston. From there the swarm could wreak havoc in Lower Farthing, or Broad Farthing or Stratford – not to mention along the highway itself.

He grabbed the phone. 'This is Councillor Cotswold. You have got to stop these people! Block the road at the junction and turn them all into Smith's field on the left there. At least that'll contain them until you find some reinforcements!' He threw the phone back at the policeman and as the last bikes passed the churchyard he struggled out of the car and made for the Land Rover.

'Come on, Terry, we've got to see what we can do to help.' He feared what they might find in Weston; feared what might have happened if Napoleon had been snoozing in his favourite afternoon spot, on the road outside the cottage, when those bastards had ridden through. Then, above the noise of the bikes whose echo still resounded in his ears, he could just make out the wail of the police sirens coming from Stratford. He slowed as he came out of Marston lane into the village. Ahead in the distance the hornets still buzzed but the sound was stationary, no longer receding.

The main street and the entrance to the Stratford Road were mercifully deserted. Despite himself he glanced to the right as he passed the cottage. No sign of blood in the road, no mangled black flesh. Suddenly they heard a galloping and splintering as a magnificent bay hunter catapulted through the fence from Tom Dutton's pasture, caught his feet in the timber and crashed headlong in front of them. Amos braked hard, at risk of causing the police car, which had followed him from the churchyard, to cannon into the back of him.

He thrust the mobile at Terry. 'Get the vet, 26 66 14!' he yelled, leaping down from the cab. The horse was struggling to get up, its eyes frantic, its front legs splayed at right angles to its body. Other doors opened and Amos held up a warning hand, the animal had enough to contend with. In seconds Tom Dutton himself appeared, carrying his gun. Amos looked at Tom's face as the man saw his horse; he'd guessed anyway – hence the weapon.

'Do you want me to do it? I've sent for the vet.'

Tom couldn't answer him. Tears welled up in his eyes as he shook his head, unable to get the words out. Amos turned to the small group of neighbours who'd been summoned by the screeching brakes and the shattering fence:

'Give him some space, folks, just go away now. You can help later.'

Before he backed the Land Rover away and around, Amos turned to see Tom lying in the road, his head against the horse's, sobbing. At least it hadn't been a child – but to Tom it amounted to the same thing.

Amos and his police tail arrived at the junction with the main road in time to see the vet negotiating his way past the road block. The hornets were considerably quieter, pity it wasn't they who were being put down. They'd been undeniably the cause of the horse's fright and then its mad final jump.

He glanced across the paddock into which the bikers had been herded. Most sat by their bikes looking dazed, a few looked furious, others defiant. Amos registered the arrogance emanating from Colin Phillips as their glances met.

A police sergeant came up to Amos. 'We're doing what we can, councillor, we can do some for possession but these days I'm afraid they'll get a warning, that's all.'

'What about dangerous driving, speeding, disturbing the peace, killing a valuable and much-loved horse, putting children in jeopardy ... they're even growing the stuff up there you know! How much more do you want?'

The sergeant looked sympathetic but powerless.

A.M. STORY

*

Even Jack was subdued. 'We're regressing that's what it is. Regressing back to a lawless society.'

'Yes but in those days the lord of the manor himself was the law, or at least the man who meted out justice,' replied Amos.

'So where is he then, when we need him?' Jack polished a few more glasses vigorously. Amos had long been convinced that the shine on Jack's glassware was in inverse proportion to his peace of mind. 'You know I still can't believe Lord Marston meant this to happen. He obviously didn't realize they'd get away with murder up there and we'd be the ones to suffer? I mean in his day the police could take yobbos like them and give them a good birching. If you ask me that's what we need here – some good old-fashioned discipline. That'd soon sort them out.' Jack had found his theme for the evening.

'They've put up posters in Stratford advertising motorbike meetings up at Marston Manor.' There was no gentle way to break this to the village, but Amos had half expected Jack might already know. Apparently he didn't.

'They can't do that! What about all that noise ... and then they'll come down on Weston like the Assyrian hordes again. Oh no, Amos, you've got to stop it!'

Amos subsided onto the barstool. He might have known it'd be down to him. 'They'll have to get permission for change of use if it's to be a regular occurrence but more importantly they'll need a public entertainment licence for each event. That's our chance.'

'I'll bet it's on the "net" then,' said Marion, Jack's wife. 'That's how they'll get thousands of visitors – like they do for those May Day riots in London every year.' Marion was right, Amos had wondered how they'd managed to amass that many layabouts at Marston the last time.

'They came in here you know, the pair of them bold as brass, day before yesterday,' Jack said suddenly. 'The Phillips brothers. I wouldn't serve them, told them to clear off.'

'Good for you, Jack!' But Amos was worried, he wouldn't put it past those two to get their own back on anyone who crossed them. He turned to Marion. 'Were you here, Marion?' She shook her head. 'Well I'd be careful all the same. No point in taking any chances.'

'Oh surely they wouldn't do anything really ... well you know. They just want to do their own thing – think they've a God-given right regardless of how it affects others,' Marion argued.

Amos was thoughtful. 'Let's hope that's all it is,' he muttered into his beer.

Like malicious genies unwittingly conjured up by his thoughts, the sound of motorbikes coming quietly up the lane engendered a raised eyebrow from Jack who moved swiftly towards the phone and held his breath.

Seconds later the door burst open and seven leathered and helmeted figures strode down the steps into the bar; their chests festooned with chains, their gauntlets with spikes – the skull and cross-bones fetchingly etched in white rivets wherever space permitted. 'Seven pints of your finest ale, landlord,' the leader called over his shoulder as he swung his helmet onto the nearest coat-hook, revealing tangled black tresses Charles II would have coveted. He turned and grinned at Amos.

'Well I'll be ... Marty Singleton! What brings you all the way over here on a wet Wednesday night then?' Amos struggled off his stool to shake the giant by the hand. Jack visibly breathed out and the atmosphere in the Hathaway Arms returned to something resembling normality. Amos knew it would – if he rated the men as all right, they'd be accepted, after all he himself looked more like a tramp than a councillor most of the time.

The gang grabbed chairs from neighbouring tables so they could all sit together, except for Marty who moved a stool next to Amos's, heaved himself up on it and gently used Napoleon's ample back as a foot-rest. Napoleon didn't stir.

'Don't usually see you this way except for the rally,' Amos said, still surprised.

'Well we've got a couple of problems we thought you might be able to help us with.' Marty sipped his pint appreciatively.

'Not the licence again. I wasn't aware ...' although he did know the bikers had to plan their annual event nearly a year in advance.

Marty held up his hand as he finished his swallow. 'No, not exactly. Thing is, we've heard the Ministry of Defence are putting the airfield up for sale.'

'That's been on the cards for years Marty, whoever buys it will make a fortune out of events like yours.'

'Ah, well – that's what might have changed.'

Amos had that sinking feeling, he could guess what was coming, though hadn't heard as much locally – yet. 'You mean they're going to grant planning permission to a developer ... so it will be built on?'

'You've got it.'

'I'm sorry Marty but surely there must be other ...' He saw Marty's face.

'Yes probably but you know what it's like. We don't have the money some of these big impresarios have with which to buy our way into a different venue.'

'But your reputation is so good here. There's never any trouble from the rally and you're always very generous to our local charities.'

Marty looked down into his beer then straight at Amos. 'Our reputation's being ruined by another group of bikers who think it's clever to get high on drugs and cause trouble. People have already started lumping us together. We're all getting blamed. We heard two of the ringleaders are over at Marston Hall so that'll put paid to us in these parts unless you can explain to people ...' Marty stopped in mid-sentence as he registered Amos's expression.

'I see what you mean; I confess I hadn't made the connection. I'm afraid it may have already happened. They killed Tom Dutton's hunter and scared half the village out of their wits before I could stop it.'

Marty looked over his shoulder at the other people in the bar who, despite Amos's assurances, looked wary, keeping a close eye on Marty's friends. He inclined his head in the local's direction, underlining his point.

Amos was silent while he thought. 'I don't think we should give up on the airfield just yet, I'll do some ferreting on that for you. Your organization's been so good, if it's close on timing I might be able to persuade the Council to hold off the permission until after next August's rally – reckon we owe you that much. As for this other lot ...' Amos finished with a sigh, he had no answer.

Marty looked relieved. 'Would you Amos, that really would help. I don't think they understand how far ahead we have to plan these things – it's no good springing it on us a month beforehand – people come from all over the world you know.' He turned, and addressed Jack. 'Another pint for my friend here landlord if you please ... and Amos, if there's anything we can do for you in return just sing out, man.'

*

Jack was gesticulating to Amos and Terry from outside Alan Tregorran's house. Even from this distance Amos could see he was excited about something. They drove over to him.

'They're going to hold one of those all night raves – in your barn, or rather, your old barn. That's what she must have wanted it for. I heard some of the kids talking last night but only caught snatches – I thought they meant somewhere the other side of Stratford. But when I bumped into Sergeant Wilson at the garage this morning I thought I'd mention it. Seems he already knew, his own daughter told him.'

'I trust he's going to stop it then – no licence and all that.'

'He said so, yes, but I wonder. Isn't that part of the attraction of these things, that they're illegal? The courts are so full it would be months before any prosecution – supposing it even got that far.'

'I'll talk to the licensing people and the enforcement committee. Just because we're short of resources doesn't mean people can flagrantly break the law and get away with it.' Yet Amos secretly feared it did.

Whilst in Stratford, he called in to see John Wilkinson on the off-chance something – anything – might have changed the situation. 'So when can we get a look at this will then, John?'

'Not until it's gone through probate – and that'll take a while yet with an estate that size. Unless of course you wish to contest it, then I could write to the executors asking for copies. But you don't have any grounds for contesting it so....'

'So they could tell me to get lost.'

'Unless you apply a caveat so it can't go through probate until you release the caveat or they take you to court. Then again, where are your grounds? That it's not right or not fair or not what you think he ought to have done won't cut much ice, I'm afraid. And it's likely to cost you thousands too.'

'There must be something we can do. He's not cold in his grave yet and they've already started rampaging about Weston. Now I hear they're going to stage a "rave" of all things – in *my* barn!'

'I heard about what happened the other Sunday. We can only hope the police will prosecute.'

'Do you know where these people have come from? I mean where did they get the idea they can just do as they like?'

'No idea, Amos. No respect for anything or anyone, think they're God. Last time I saw that kind of behaviour was in South Africa.'

'Funny you should say that, Betty Summers muttered something about them having been in Africa. I thought she was just guessing.'

After Gervaise's death he'd thought it would all die down, become a 'nine day wonder' and then fizzle out. The old order had passed on, a new order of sorts would be established and folks would soon forget how it used to be and accept the change as though they'd known it that way all their lives. But he hadn't bargained for such radical change – and neither had anyone else in the villages. The Phillipses' actions and intentions so far were intolerable – would ruin Weston Hathaway and its tranquil countryside. Every day his constituents appealed to him to do something about it.

He had alerted the licensing committee, but the district authorities had so far received no application. It looked more and more as though the Phillipses simply intended to carry on as they pleased and wait for the law to catch up with them – if it ever did. Apart from the dire consequences of their activities, to Amos this cavalier attitude indicated another unhappy conclusion – that they intended not to be around for long. They would sell to the highest-bidding developer and then clear out.

Building at Marston would make the hamlet double or treble the size of Weston, which would overload the school, dissolve the values, and turn the whole area into a suburb of Stratford – urban, and impersonal.

Nothing had really changed though. It had always been the prerogative of the lord of the manor to decree what happened locally. Why was this any different? The Phillipses would decide that Marston should become a development area. So much for democracy. The trouble was, Amos's supporters wouldn't understand. They'd think he'd failed – and so would he.

At midnight on Saturday the phone rang in Amos's cottage. It was nasty weather, the wind howled down the chimney and all sensible dogs were tucked up in their kennels. He'd been dozing by the fire, his feet propped up on Napoleon, the whisky bottle, as yet unopened, beside him – knowing he ought to summon the energy to go to bed. Or perhaps, deep in his subconscious, he'd been expecting trouble.

Amos picked up the receiver: 'I was just locking up when Lindsay's Ted drove past on his way back from Stratford. He says the roads are full of youngsters, walking, driving – hundreds of them, all going the same way. Says it's like something out of one of those zombie films where they've all got out of their beds and are wandering across the moors to the mineshaft, hypnotized.' Jack stopped for breath.

'I imagine even the police can't have failed to notice if there are that many – or was it simply turning out time at the Indian restaurant?'

'No, no, no. He said they were all along the road. Amos, I think they're headed for Marston. I think this is it. This is the rave.'

'Well the police can sort it out; I'm going to bed, other people's teenagers are not my responsibility – thank goodness. Good night, Jack.' Amos hung up.

Now wide awake he sank back into his chair and groaned audibly. Napoleon twitched but otherwise remained inert. There was nothing Amos could do about it, this was police business. Still, he'd better just check. He got up again and dialled the station.

'Sergeant Wilson? Oh Constable Johnson. It's Councillor Cotswold, I've just been told there are multitudes of the nation's youth headed for Marston as we speak and I ...'

'Yes, we know, councillor. Sergeant Wilson's out there now.'

'Oh good. Have you got enough men to get this organized?'

'Don't you worry, Councillor, it's all in hand. Goodnight to you.'

Amos looked longingly at the Scotch, made a cup of tea and

settled back into his armchair. 'Don't worry', at the very least there'd be broken ankles and bodies in the river when a lot of drunken youngsters, high on whatever they could lay their hands on, went for a walk in unknown territory in the dark. What did the police know about those fields – not much was the answer; they'd need an army to round up that crowd. Amos hoped Wilson had had the sense to head straight for the barn and seal it off before the masses arrived.

Awoken from his slumber he thought for a minute it was an earthquake, they'd had mild ones before. The china on the dresser was rattling and Napoleon was on his feet at the door, whining with pain from the noise. The cottage shook with the bombardment as if a tank brigade were pulled up in the street outside shelling it with mortars ... boom, boom, boom. Amos struggled to his feet, then came another noise, someone was pounding on the door. Before he could answer, it burst open admitting Lindsay, her husband Ted, Tom Dutton and several other neighbours.

'Amos, Amos, you've got to do something!'

Boom, boom, boom, boom, boom, boom. He couldn't hear himself speak. 'Ted, have you got some rubber boots?'

'Yes, they're in the truck, but it's not that muddy.'

'Trust me, go and fetch them. We'll take my Land Rover.'

Amos and Ted rode out across the fields from Weston Hathaway, Ted opening gates and Amos negotiating his way across the rutted terrain – without headlights. He'd known these fields since boyhood, he could get right up to that barn at the back without anyone seeing him, as long as the Land Rover didn't shatter with the noise.

Amos wished he'd brought earplugs – though through some quirk of acoustics the volume of noise in Weston was as high if not higher than it was out here. The barn was ill-lit, part of the atmosphere they were trying to create, Amos supposed. No one would hear their engine with that row going on. Boom, boom, boom. Amos was afraid to think how many animals had run amok this time, unable to bear the sound in their sensitive ears – literally frightened out of their lives.

'What do you think, Ted, have they got a generator out here or have they run a cable across the field from the manor?'

'These people usually use generators, don't they? I mean they set up in all sorts of out of the way places where there wouldn't be access to a local electricity supply.'

'Pity they didn't do that this time,' Amos said grimly. 'But I expect you're right, and they must have brought it in through Weston Hathaway. With all the big farm trucks that go through the village no one noticed.'

Amos stopped the Land Rover behind a small rise, yards from the back of the barn yet sufficiently well concealed to give them a chance to escape before anyone realized where they were ... or what they'd done. 'We can get into the barn on this side, there are some boards missing ... hang on, look at that. It's our lucky night.' There'd be no need to go in after all. Parked against the back wall of the barn was a large generator on a trailer.

There was no sign of anyone about only the boom, boom, boom and the noise of a large crowd contained behind closed doors, gyrating, dancing, yelling ... and no sign of the police either. Ted and Amos could have sung at the top of their voices without fear of detection. Boom, boom, boom went that relentless beat. Jack had been right, it was hypnotic – mesmerizing, demanding.

The armoured cable must run from the generator's engine, through the gap left by the missing slats Amos knew about, to the amplifiers inside the barn. From his poacher's pocket he pulled a large, two-handed hacksaw and two pairs of the rubber gloves he kept for dagging sheep. He handed Ted a pair.

'There's no fear of anyone hearing us. I want to be sure they can't restart this thing. But you can run faster than me so here are the keys. The minute the music stops run for the Land Rover, I won't be far behind you.'

Boom, boom, boom, boom. With Ted on one side of the cable and himself on the other, they hacked through the steel armour; Amos felt the jolt as it gave way. As they continued sawing Amos shot Ted a look, they both knew they'd be fully through the cable any second. As they sliced through the last strands, Boom, boom boo ... The music stopped. Sweet peace, beautiful peace, amazing peace. Silence. Absolute silence – for a second.

'Run!'

The crowd started shouting: 'What the hell!', 'Put the music back on!', 'Where's the f***ing music gone?' Lost in the music they'd been happy enough in the dark but now the voices sounded anxious, frightened, wondering what was going to happen to them. Several youths were groping their way around the corner in the dark, one or two had torches. Without stopping to watch, Amos made his way as fast as he could towards the Land Rover.

Ted already had the engine started and was wheeling the vehicle round. Less certain of his way than Amos, he flashed the lights as Amos clambered aboard the moving vehicle, and in that split second illuminated a figure propped against the barn wall, watching them. It was Richard Phillips.

CHAPTER SIX

Was this a recurring nightmare? The hammering wouldn't go away. Amos buried his head under the pillow but the pounding continued – bang, bang, bang. Had he dreamt it? Had it been in his mind all along.... Surely he'd stopped it, him and Ted?

Bang, bang, bang! He shook his head in the vague belief it might help. The whisky bottle stood half empty beside the bed ... oh yes, no wonder it hurt. It was in his head then. Bang bang ...

'Councillor Cotswold!' The voice was male and vaguely familiar. Not Ted, not Jack, not Terry and definitely not Lindsay. She'd have marched in anyway. He looked at the clock, half past five. He climbed slowly and agonizingly out of bed, the doctor had told him often enough that drink made arthritis worse but at the time of imbibing Amos perversely convinced himself of the opposite. Throwing up the window he could make out the shape of the police car drawn up at the curb. Sergeant Wilson was looking up at him.

'Sorry, councillor, thought you were normally up by now.'

Without a word Amos pulled the window back down, fumbled for his trousers and half stumbled, half ricocheted down the narrow stairs – his feet unwilling to bend, his knees only too keen to. He threw open the door then turned and staggered into the kitchen, leaving Sergeant Wilson to admit himself.

'What do you want?' Last night came back to him. 'And where were you?'

'Actually I've come to ask you that question.' Sergeant Wilson followed Amos through and sat down at the table while Amos ran cold water into the kettle. There'd be no hot until the stove was lit.

Amos was fully awake now – and wary. Guessing who'd shopped him was easy, Richard Phillips. Although he hadn't attempted to stop them at the time.

'Look here, sergeant, I don't know what you're driving at but I rang the station at some unearthly hour and spoke to your Constable Johnson who assured me you had this so-called "rave" well under control. I distinctly remember him telling me not to worry. An hour later, the noise was so indescribable we thought the village was being shelled.' Amos paused for breath but only for a second. 'Took you long enough, didn't it?' Another pause, this time for effect. 'God knows how many animals have gone crazy this time – let alone people.'

The sergeant looked uncomfortable. 'Our hands are tied, Councillor. If it's private property and they're holding a private party then ...' They stared at one another across the table.

'The reason I came to see you was ...' The sergeant shifted his feet, he looked awkward. Here we go, Amos thought, any minute now I'll be accused of criminal damage. His mind was racing – it would only be his word against Richard Phillips's. Should he deny it? Or brave it out as having been the right thing to do in the interest of the community?

'I don't know how to put this, councillor ... but the Phillipses say they had nothing to do with the rave.' Amos poured the boiling water over the draining board instead of into the pot.

'Well if you believe that you're more of a fool ...' Amos was in no mood to be diplomatic, or even kind.

'You haven't heard the rest of it yet, Amos.' Sergeant Wilson stood up, took the kettle off Amos and put it back down on the hob. The sergeant's sudden and unusual use of his Christian name alarmed Amos. 'They're saying you've rented that barn for years – so the rave must have been your doing.'

Amos laughed. He sat down and laughed until it hurt. Criminal damage was a serious offence, so was trespass – especially for a councillor. Proving he was not the impresario behind a teenage rave would be the proverbial child's play in comparison. His laughter was so infectious even Sergeant Wilson was forced to smile – visibly relieved that Amos had taken it so lightly.

'Oh that's rich that is, really rich!' Amos slapped his thigh and guffawed some more. 'Immediately after they inherited the manor, the Phillipses threw me out of the barn and off those fields. Said I didn't have a written agreement. Ask anyone! Now I see why you came round at this hour – thought I might be going to start again, in my cottage, did you?' Amos couldn't help ribbing the sergeant, he was so thankful he wasn't facing serious charges – the possible magnitude of which had only just struck him. And he could have got Ted into a lot of trouble too. One day his impetuosity would cause him real problems.

The sergeant's phone rang. He listened and looked gravely across at Amos.

'They're sure who it is?' He listened again. 'Yes ... thanks.'

Napoleon heard the footsteps first and shuffled away from the back door in time; without stopping to knock, Jack walked straight in. He exchanged glances with Sergeant Wilson.

'You'll have heard then ...'

'That they're blaming me for the rave ...' Amos saw Jack's face. 'No, what?'

'Tom Dutton was found dead in his car on the Alcester Road this morning,' said the sergeant. 'That's what the phone call was about. He cannoned into a tree on the wrong side of the road at high speed. Sounds as though he fell asleep at the wheel; it's a common problem.'

Amos sat down. He'd been fond of Tom who'd always been willing to help, always friendly. 'He had a daughter in Hertfordshire, used to visit her once a month. I bet that's where he was off to so early.' Then he realized. 'They killed him. First his horse, now Tom himself! Sure as I'm standing here that's what this amounts to!'

'Well I don't think we can—' began Sergeant Wilson.

'Oh can't we? Who was it woke us all from our beds with their infernal row? Enough to drive anyone crazy it was. I dread to think what some of the old folk must have thought. No, they killed him all right. He sets off without having had his night's sleep and look what happens. I pray to God we don't hear of more in the next hour or two.' Amos remembered Tom Dutton's as being amongst the faces in his front room pleading with him to stop the noise.

The phone rang in the other room. Amos went to answer it.

'Amos, could you come quickly! All the turkeys are dead and Alan's so upset he's gone striding up the yard with the key to the gun cabinet. I don't know what he's going to do!'

'I'll be right there, Madge.' Leaving Jack and Sergeant Wilson in the kitchen, Amos grabbed the Land Rover keys off their peg and left through the front door, collecting his boots from the step on the way.

As he drove into the Tregorran yard, he met Alan crossing to his truck, a twelve bore held loosely in his hand.

'They've killed all the turkeys, Amos, every one of them. They're all in a tangle of black feathers and twisted necks from their panic. They couldn't stand it you see …' His face distorted at the memory. 'What worries me is what else I'm going to find – sheep caught in barbed wire, cattle with their horns caught in one another, trapped or maimed. Thought I'd take a drive round, put them out of their misery.' He glanced down at the gun, not needing to voice the thought he shared with Amos … about who he'd really like to use it on.

'I saw you cross Long Barrow Bottom last night; guessed it was you. No one else would know to go that way – not without lights. Then this morning the cows were that jumpy I had to get Ted to help with the milking and he told me the rest. Thank goodness they were all locked in the barn or Lord knows what would've happened to the dairy herd.' He paused, upset. 'Can't you get these people stopped, Amos? Somebody's got to!'

By the time Amos and Alan returned from inspecting the damage – despatching livestock and wild life which couldn't be saved, moving carcasses and deciding the fate of others with the vet – it was dusk. They'd managed to catch one runaway pony but knew of five others still missing. Old Mrs Sampson's chickens had flown their coop in terror – only to find a worse fate among the cars on the Stratford road. She had known every one by name; they were her pets.

If only he'd done something when they'd first heard about the rave, when Jack had told him, instead of leaving it to the police. Even last night he could have cut the generator feed earlier, before the rave started, instead of burying his head in his cosy cottage, pretending it was none of his business. If he'd shouldered the responsibility he should have done, Tom would still be alive ... along with a myriad of innocent beasts.

The Hathaway Arms looked more like a public meeting than a bar-room, Jack had opened early to accommodate it. He came from behind the bar, nodded to Alan and whispered to Amos. 'I tried to phone you earlier. Amy, who works at the Council Offices ...' Amos nodded, he knew Amy well, she was secretary to the chief executive, '... well, she says that some big promotions company has just applied for a licence to hold an all-night concert out at Marston. The folks here want to know what you're going to do about it.'

Amos turned with his back to the bar and the room fell silent except for a lone plea.

'You'm got to stop this, Amos. It ain't right.'

Amos smiled reassuringly. 'There has to be a licensing committee meeting to decide on this and I'll attend that. I'm sure when the committee realize how much this will affect us here at Weston they'll refuse permission.' This was greeted by a loud cheer and the hubbub of voices started up again. At least now it was out in the open – going through official channels. He felt confident local feeling would prevail.

*

Deep in thought Amos missed the turn he usually took into Weston so was forced to carry on and turn down the much narrower Featherbed Lane instead, which would bring him out on the track behind the Hathaway Arms. It was a long narrow lane bordered by blackthorn and hawthorn hedge interspersed with the occasional hornbeam tree.

In the distance he could make out another car, few used this route because there weren't many passing places. Luckily this one was going in the same direction, towards Weston – but as he gained on it in the dim light, he realized it must be stationary, or almost. Some lady driver had probably stopped for a pheasant or a hedgehog. Amos began to slow. He saw the figures, three of them, two on one side and one on the other, leaning in through the car windows. Were they pushing it? Then he saw it was Marion's car.

Something about the scene felt wrong. Alarm growing inside him, Amos accelerated until he was close – the car was actually crawling along the road. What on earth? As he approached, three lads detached themselves and started to move nonchalantly away towards Weston. Amos hooted to show Marion it was him and struggled swiftly out of his vehicle. Ignoring the lads he went directly to the driver's door. Inside, shaking and close to tears was Lucy Poulton, the young student who cleaned the bar for Jack at the Hathaway Arms.

'What on earth's the matter, sweetheart, are you hurt?'

She shook her head. 'Oh Mr Cotswold, thank goodness you came along, I was really frightened. They wouldn't let me pass, then they wanted to get in the car. I feel so foolish. They're village lads, I recognized them, but they kept leering at me and saying things. It was horrible.'

Amos looked up, the boys were running down the lane now. 'Move over love.' He hadn't time to fetch the Land Rover if he was to catch them. Lucy scrambled across to the passenger seat and she and Amos set off down the lane. He knew the boys couldn't get through the dense thorn until the lane reached Lower Bottom, which was why he was racing along. Stupidly they tried to remain in the road, but had to leap for the hedge as Amos tore by, hoping they'd be badly scratched. Then he reversed back at speed and extending a large rough hand through the open window, caught hold of the nearest by his ear. The other two fled.

It was Kevin Sanderson. 'What the hell do you think you've been doing?' he yelled at him. The boy said nothing, not so brave without his pals. Amos gave him a hefty clout round the other ear and shoved him back into the hedge. 'Let's see what your parents have to say about this.'

Amos collected the Land Rover and escorted Lucy back to the Hathaway Arms only half a mile further on. Jack phoned the police but got their answerphone.

'It all sounds so silly now, but it was scary I can tell you.'

Jack made her sit down and poured her a brandy. 'Marion had to take one of the villagers to the hospital in my car, you know, they have a rota for giving lifts to people – but it's her day to go over and see her mum,' he explained. 'Well I'd got a chap coming about the Christmas wines so Lucy said she'd be happy to pop over and make sure Mum was all right.'

Lucy took up the story. 'That's right so I borrowed Mrs Ashley's car ... even when I saw the boys I thought nothing of it, in fact I felt sorry for them, thought they were out killing time until their parents got home. When they waved me down I wound the window down without thinking and it was, we-ell ... like they were drunk. I knew I shouldn't be scared but there were three of them and some of the things they were saying ...' She blushed and stopped.

'You know who it was, Amos?' Amos nodded. Jack was putting his coat on. 'Let's go.'

As Amos and Jack marched up the front path, Mrs Sanderson came out of the house towards them. 'I've just come home and I hear you've attacked my son.' She rounded on Amos. 'He's got a big red weal across his ear and scratches all over him.'

'Has he told you what he and his friends were up to?' Jack interjected. 'Intimidating a young woman, that's what. They stopped her car in Featherbed Lane and made lewd remarks and frightened her with their suggestive behaviour. If Councillor Cotswold here hadn't come along when he did, goodness knows what might have happened. How dare you accuse Amos of hurting your boy. Lucy's father'll give him more than a thick ear if he catches up with him. You need to get that boy seen to before he does something worse!' Amos and Jack both knew Lucy's dad was abroad.

As they spoke her husband drove up and heaved his suit-carrier and briefcase out of the boot of his car. The man looked tired.

'They're saying Kevin and his friends held up a woman in her car in Featherbed Lane ... and made intimidating remarks.' His wife recapped as he walked across to them.

'A bit more than that! When I arrived they were leaning in through the windows in a very threatening manner!' Amos said.

'Oh so that gives you the right to hit Kevin, does it?' countered Mrs Sanderson.

'That's not true – you must be mistaken, Councillor. Our Kevin wouldn't do a thing like that.' Mr Sanderson was clearly in denial. He looked at his wife. '... And if you don't stop accusing my son I'll go to the police.'

'They didn't do anything. They weren't even where you say, they were over at Marston Manor. They often go there after school,' his wife added.

When they went for a drink later, Amos and Terry were waylaid by Jack.

'Amos, am I being paranoid or are you thinking what I've been thinking ... about this afternoon? It wasn't an accident was it? I mean it wasn't an accident they picked on Marion's car and you did say to watch the Phillipses after I banned them from here. I distinctly remember you saying it. If these kids have been up at Marston then ...'

'Well there aren't too many other cars that go down that lane.' Amos had no more comforting remark to offer – because he'd come to the same conclusion.

'Any chance of getting served down this end, landlord?' Jack had to go.

'Why don't you get Marty and the boys to sort out the Phillips brothers?' Terry asked. Jack must have told him about Marty's visit.

'Don't think it hasn't crossed my mind!' Several times lately Amos had been tempted to at least discuss the situation with Marty – he'd half meant to phone him tonight, especially after what had happened to Lucy Poulton. 'But I'm afraid it would start a gang war and God alone knows where that would lead.'

'I don't have to tell you how impressionable kids are at that age. Nothing to do when they come home, mum and dad both out. Then they suddenly find they can go traipsing all over the Marston land, sampling fast bikes and interesting substances ... which they certainly wouldn't have been allowed to do in Lord Marston's day.' Terry straightened his back and took a swig of his beer.

'Do you really think the Phillipses are luring the local kids over there, where they can run riot, and then filling them up with cannabis and sending them out on their own evil errands? I mean it beggars belief, doesn't it?' Amos exclaimed, astounded.

'You want me to say yes, it beggars belief, don't you? Well, I can't. Do I really think that's what's going on? No, not exactly. If you ask me, I think the kids did what all kids do given half a chance, they went exploring. But the Phillipses didn't stop them, may have even encouraged them to try the cannabis. Then maybe the kids overheard the Phillipses moaning about Jack – or maybe they did suggest to the kids that they should pull some stunt, as they did with Lucy. Maybe they even offered them a bribe, like they could ride the bikes. Or more likely they taunted them, dared them, said they were too chicken to do it – then offered them illegal courage. Who knows?'

Terry looked at Amos before he went on. 'All I do know is it's a very short distance from one to the other and it's got to be stopped. If the Phillipses haven't yet realized how much more disruptive they can be by using the local kids, it won't be long before they do. The more I think of this carry-on the more unreal it seems – like some maniacal Pied Piper!' Terry had really wound himself up now. 'And you can't blame the kids; at that age it's exciting, illicit. You know, you've been there. We'll be guilty ourselves if we stand by and watch them corrupt the youngsters like that – no matter how unintentionally.'

'Well there's not much we can do,' Amos said hopelessly.

'Except cast out the tares.' Seeing Amos's puzzled expression, Terry waved a hand impatiently. 'Never mind, it's an old word for weeds that infest cornfields – remember the parable? But that gives me an idea. At least we could sabotage the bulk of this year's drug crop, before they finish harvesting.'

CHAPTER SEVEN

The police car screamed through the village and took the turn up to Marston as Amos arrived back from feeding the sheep. Now what? Maybe the Phillips brothers had gone one step too far this time and the law had finally decided to act. He thought immediately of Marion and phoned Jack.

'What's up? Are you and Marion all right?'

'Yes, fine. I was about to ask you the same question. And now there goes the fire brigade.' Sure enough, a fire engine went rattling through the village, the echo of its clanging lingering long after it had turned down towards Marston.

'What do you ...' Jack's voice was drowned by a second fire engine tearing through the village.

'Maybe they've set the barn alight,' Amos said. 'Hang on, Lindsay's just come in.'

Lindsay stood in the open doorway of the cottage, gesticulating to him. Amos held the receiver wide so Jack could hear too. 'Our Betty says it's the garden, the walled garden – says there's a dickens of a blaze. All she knows is that Sonia Phillips came running down the slope into the kitchen saying the garden was on fire. Because the wind's blowing that way they were afraid it might spread to the house.'

'Well if that's all – who cares. Got to go.' Jack rang off.

Amos decided to give Napoleon a treat – a walk along the riverbank towards Marston church; though he knew he wouldn't be able to see much from there he could at least be on hand, not just sitting indoors like the other night. Taking his walking stick he set off at as brisk a pace as he could manage, Napoleon cantered on ahead.

About half way along, the hedgerows thinned and he could see the smoke in the distance – and taste it. It had an acrid smell, like that of burning stubble – which farmers weren't allowed to do any more. Perhaps that was it – the Phillipses had harvested the cannabis and decided to burn the evidence, hence the fire. No, that didn't make sense, why draw attention to something they'd rather people didn't know about? A bonfire might have got out of control, of course, like so many other of their enterprises, and one of the staff had taken fright and called the fire brigade. That seemed more likely.

Amos was surprised to find himself alone out here on the towpath. Though the children would be in school and many of the adults at work, there was usually a rambler or a dog-walker about and he'd expected there to be several others as curious as he to know what was going on – the fire engine followers. Not today.

He slowed to a stroll. It was peaceful out here. With the noise of the fire crews dampened by distance, the fire gave a surreal touch to the landscape; drifting smoke mingled with the mist and clouds to mask the definition between earth and sky, and the scent evinced by winter's damp, turned to incense over the river.

Amos hadn't come this way for years, except in the Land Rover to his fields. He hadn't walked here nor meandered around the churchyard since those holidays with Crispin – now it seemed he couldn't keep away. Common sense told him it was just circumstance – yes, it was circumstance which had brought him back here now, reintroduced him to an area he'd disregarded. But why should he feel so drawn ... so compelled by this land. Lord knew, he'd plenty else to occupy him; he had been neglecting his council work lately.

Following Napoleon, he wandered through the churchyard, looking idly at the headstones as he went; battered by the elements most were unreadable, as abandoned as the lives they commemorated. As he reached the old marker stone for a sit down, Napoleon, who'd been contentedly nosing around a grave or two, suddenly pricked up his ears and grunted. Now Amos could hear it, someone or something was running their way, fast. A figure careered round the corner and came belting along the path towards them as if he'd seen a ghost, so out of breath he could only point.

Terry bent double trying to catch his wind enough to speak. 'Richard Phillips,' he wheezed, '… he's dead.' Terry pointed. 'Over there. In the ruins.' He straightened up. 'Have you got your phone … must call the police.'

Amos pulled out his phone. When it was answered he kept his voice steady.

'Constable, Councillor Cotswold here. We've found a body in the ruined manor at Marston.'

He listened then corrected. 'No not in the fire. In the Old Manor, the one by the church.' Satisfied they'd understood him he hung up. What else could he have said?

Meanwhile Napoleon had set off at the gallop towards the ruins. Amos realized he'd got to stop him quickly before he wrecked any evidence. What was he thinking about, 'evidence'? He was making it sound as though Richard had been killed. Why should he think that? Nevertheless he began walking towards the Old Manor, taking Terry with him.

'What happened, did he fall?'

'I don't know, I didn't see. He was just er …' Terry swallowed and breathed deeply. '… just lying there.'

'But had you been speaking to him, I mean what were you both doing there?'

Amos wondered why Terry had been running quite so fast when Richard was already dead. It wasn't as though quick action might save him. And why hadn't he run towards the manor? Maybe he hadn't wanted to break the news to Sonia, or maybe he thought Richard had indeed been murdered and the perpetrator was still around – that could explain the running. On reflection he might have done the same himself in similar circumstances.

And what about the fire? Or was that it? Was that what Terry had been doing at Marston? All sorts of black thoughts crowded in on Amos. Had Richard caught Terry in the act and chased him down the path? Had Terry turned on Richard when he knew he couldn't out-run him? Had Terry been escaping from whatever had ensued – when he'd had the misfortune to run straight into Amos? Is that why such a show of catching his breath – to give himself time to think? This was horrible.

'What were you doing here anyway?' Amos repeated, sharply this time.

Terry regarded him with a hurt expression. 'When I saw the smoke I was on my way to the graveyard – you know I often come here – so I started up the hill to see what it was and whether there was anything I could do.'

'You'd no need to go via the ruins though?'

'No, of course not. In fact I'd only just started out when I heard the police and the fire engines so I turned back – not wanting to be accused of trespassing – when …' Terry looked lost. '… I know this is going to sound odd but I had this urge to go over to the ruins.' Amos looked at him doubtfully.

'So I just wandered over and when I got to about here …' Terry stopped and indicated the north side of the ruins which were in shadow. 'I felt something really bad had happened. Then I saw him.' Amos looked where Terry was pointing.

A booted foot was projecting from behind a pile of large boulders in the corner. 'I thought someone was having a snack or just a rest or had found some interesting lichen.' Amos looked at him. 'I don't know what I thought! I didn't want to think it was a dead tramp or somebody who'd crawled in here for shelter and died of hypothermia. I didn't want to go through that again.'

Richard Phillips lay inside the old building, half propped against a boulder; the leg they'd caught sight of at a distance was stretched out in front of him, the other beneath him, his head crooked as though his neck were broken, eyes staring in surprise. For once Napoleon stopped when Amos called him and trotted obediently back outside to where Terry had remained, fixed to the spot by his own horrors. Now Amos understood why Terry had run, he too wanted to run – away from this sinister place and whatever had happened here. No, he hadn't liked the man – but this was such a lonely place to die.

Could he have fallen off the wall of old stones behind him? It was possible, though surely he'd have been more likely to have fallen face down – and it begged the question of what he'd been doing here. He had on his padded windcheater, corduroy trousers tucked into thick socks and gardening boots – his outdoor clothing. Was it suicide? Would he have bothered to wrap up that well if it had been? Amos cast around the area, no obvious sign of a poison bottle or a gun of any sort. From this distance he couldn't see any blood either. Perhaps he'd suffered a massive heart attack?

Amos felt reluctant to approach any closer – nothing could help the man now, and the police were on their way. He imagined the Marston ghosts ranged overhead in the smoke clouds which were now billowing towards the river – watching, victorious.

He forced himself to look again at Richard's lifeless body, at least at this time of year he'd been spared the flies. How long had he lain here? And how long might he have lain, undetected, in this forsaken spot? So long that no one would be sure exactly when he'd died? Should he touch him, find out if he was cold? Why should it be he and Terry who had found him like this? But above all, why was he, Amos, mixed up in this? What had made him come and investigate that fire when he could just as easily have let well alone?

He also realized how little he knew about the dead man which in turn made him feel strangely guilty ... and all the more convinced that Lord Marston had not intended any of this. Was he, too, up in those vile clouds, looking down, blaming Amos for not understanding him.

The police car came swiftly around the corner and stopped. Two policemen alighted leaving the car doors wide open and jogged across to them.

'Don't touch him, sir.' One policeman approached and for a few seconds felt for a pulse on Richard's neck. He looked at his colleague and shook his head then pulled out a phone and began to speak into it while his colleague shepherded Amos and Terry away from the ruins.

More police cars arrived, blocking the lane with their paraphernalia. Terry, being the person who'd found the body, had to go down to the station to give a statement. Once they'd taken Amos's address he was free to go. Sergeant Wilson was just arriving.

'What's this got to do with the fire then?' Amos asked. 'Is it bad?'

'Looks like arson, definitely. Whoever did it left the petrol can there,' he looked at his feet. 'I expect you knew it was cannabis did you?'

'I distinctly remember telling you people that on the day Tom Dutton's horse was killed.' Amos looked towards the ruins. 'What do you think happened to Richard Phillips?'

'We don't know yet, councillor – heart attack perhaps?'

'Are the two things linked?'

Sergeant Wilson shrugged.

'I have to ask you. Between us ... did you set fire to the cannabis?' Amos demanded. Terry and he were in Amos's cottage. At five in the afternoon the police had finally let Terry go.

Terry sighed. 'I did suggest it, didn't I?' Looking Amos straight in the eye he said, 'But no, I didn't. I would have done mind, I was going to.'

'Do you think somebody overheard you in the pub the other night?'

'What, and deliberately did it so I'd get the blame?'

'Not necessarily – maybe someone else just thought it was a good idea and beat you to it. I can think of a number round here with enough reason – including me.'

There came a tap at the door; Lindsay entered followed by Betty Summers. Amos pulled a chair out for Betty next to the table and she sat down heavily. Lindsay bustled into the kitchen to fetch tea.

'What happened then, Betty?'

'I don't know I'm sure, Amos. Comes rushing down the path she does. I didn't even know she were in the garden ... then I don't know much of what goes on up there any more. If I moves from the kitchen I gets accused of slacking. Right nasty atmosphere since the master went, I can tell you.'

Amos could imagine this from the little he'd had to do with the Phillipses. 'Could you see the blaze then, Betty, what did she say? Did she say how it started? Did you see anyone strange about – anything suspicious earlier?' He could hardly contain himself while Lindsay handed round the tea.

'No, nothing like that. I didn't see no one strange, no ...' Betty glanced at Terry, as if afraid her answer might be repeated elsewhere, and stirred her tea thoughtfully. Amos had the feeling she was hiding something. Was she shielding someone from the village who she thought had fired the cannabis?

'Was it the kids who set light to it, Betty?'

'Wouldn't kill the goose that lays the golden eggs now, would they?' She sipped her tea. 'Perhaps Richard Phillips committed suicide. He'd looked pretty miserable lately. Whenever I'd seen him he'd been very down like, never managed a word or a smile like he used to. They didn't include him in things you know – she and he didn't even eat together; used to have his meals in his room.'

The phone interrupted the conversation. It was Sergeant Wilson. 'I thought you'd like to know, councillor, about Richard Phillips. Apparently he was hit on the head with something very heavy – a rock or something most like.'

'So it's murder.' Behind him Amos heard Betty and Lindsay gasp.

'Well I suppose it's just possible he fell and hit his head that hard,' Sergeant Wilson went on. 'We won't know for sure until we've had the autopsy report, but we're treating it as a murder enquiry.'

Betty shook her head and tutted. 'I always knew they'd come to a sticky end, them Phillipses.' It was a standard remark in the circumstances; he was thinking much the same himself. As if reading his thoughts, Betty continued, 'Especially there.' Amos wasn't sure what Betty meant by this though and it must have shown.

'You know, Amos ...' – she looked impatient with him – 'about the old legend. Ever since that Baron were murdered, in the Middle Ages, weren't it, they's always said that anyone who gains improper ownership of the manor will meet with certain disaster.' She sounded pleased, whether because she'd explained Richard's murder or because she was glad he was dead, Amos wasn't sure.

'Are you saying Richard gained "improper ownership" then, Betty?' Amos asked.

She glared at him. 'No-oo, but he weren't the rightful heir, we all knows that.'

Silence. Betty had voiced what they'd all been thinking.

Then Betty remembered. 'Right distracted he was this morning. I had to ask him three times to fetch me cabbage for dinner.' Poking a finger into Amos, she went on, 'And he sent one of the trainee gardeners for it. Didn't go hisself. Now that were unusual.'

Lindsay and Betty drank up their tea and left, anxious to impart the latest news to the rest of the village.

'What is it they say? It's likely to have been because of something he'd done, something he'd seen ... or something he was standing in the way of,' Amos mused. 'All I know is it wasn't a smart move. If someone around here thought to solve the problem of the Phillipses by murdering Richard – then they picked the wrong Phillips. For my money his was the only half-decent influence, I think Richard Phillips may have had a conscience.'

Terry sat on the edge of a hard chair and leaned towards Amos. 'I was in the graveyard yesterday as well.' He stopped and anxiously cleared his throat. 'I think I saw someone hanging around the old ruins then. I didn't tell the police because, well, I couldn't identify who it was. I just know there was someone there.'

Amos was worried about Terry. He looked dreadful – though he looked like this so often now Amos had almost stopped noticing. Even before the murder he'd seemed preoccupied, as if something was eating away at him. And he'd reacted more strongly than most to the Phillipses' outrages – especially for a newcomer.

Police cars milled around the village for days. The murder was talked about at every lane end and Jack was no exception.

'*Cherchez la femme*, that's what I think,' he expounded. 'I wouldn't have blamed him if he'd had a bit on the side. Who knows, maybe she wanted a slice of the fortune he'd been left? It might explain why he was down in the ruins – a perfect trysting place I'd say, out of the wind.'

'Well, I can't see it changing anything,' Amos said, ignoring Jack's theory. 'It isn't as though Richard was the driving force over there. I don't think his death will stop their plans.' In fact, the more he mulled it over, the more he concluded that the rest of the Phillips family were likely to be mighty pleased Richard had gone. Maybe he'd become a nuisance. Had he threatened to stop the concert for instance? Amos still didn't understand why Richard had let him and Ted sabotage the generator that night without trying to stop them. In his more fanciful moments he even thought Richard had come close to helping.

Then there was that conversation he'd overheard between Richard and Sonia where she'd certainly sounded keen to scotch his renovation schemes. Maybe they'd had another argument.

'I keep thinking about all those victims; all those people and animals which've died or suffered at the hands of the Phillipses: Tom Dutton, his horse, mine and Alan's livestock, Alan's turkeys, Lucy, those local kids … and Richard Phillips himself. Then of course there's the effect on people like Betty and the rest of the staff. It seems it's not just the Marston usurpers who have to pay – we all get caught up in it.'

'You can't really believe this is all to do with some ancient curse.' Jack eyed Amos sideways. 'You do, don't you? Well, I wouldn't be surprised if Crispin has already come back. Come back and exacted his revenge.' Jack leaned towards Amos and said into his ear, 'You admitted you probably wouldn't know him these days so why couldn't he have returned and none of us be any the wiser – least of all Sonia Phillips and Co?'

'Whatever gives you that idea?'

'Because I think there's an obvious coincidence you've ignored,' Jack looked expectantly at Amos then announced proudly: 'Terry Finn.'

From the moment Terry had come through his cottage door, to the day Amos had been sitting on the stone way-marker, as well as on several other occasions he couldn't immediately recall, he had felt there was something familiar about Terry.

'And what makes you think that? Surely he'd have told us,' Amos retorted.

'What ... and risk being bumped off by the Phillipses!'

Jack had a point there. 'Surely it's not that bad.' It sounded so melodramatic, but ... Richard Phillips had been murdered by someone. Amos went on, 'Richard may have been killed because of something in his past. They haven't been here very long after all. In fact it's highly likely his death has nothing whatsoever to do with Marston. Or he could simply have been in the wrong place at the wrong time. But what makes you think Terry is Crispin?'

'Well, according to you he's always hanging around Marston; whenever you go to the churchyard he's there, wandering about. Why? And from what you told me he's about the right age.'

And he has the right personality, too, Amos thought, that is, Terry and Crispin share certain traits – compassion, a way with animals, a determination to right the wrongs done to other people.

'So what do we do – confront him with it?' Amos reconsidered what he'd just said. 'In a way I've already done that – once or twice when I thought I'd seen him somewhere he's denied it. So he can't want me to know what he's up to.' He paused. 'Thinking about it, I remember when he first came he was asking what the manor was, and about the church – Crispin would have known all that. Which means, if he is Crispin then he's gone out of his way to deliberately conceal his identity.'

Amos fell silent. Just because Terry might in fact be Crispin – still didn't mean he'd murdered Richard. 'We keep wondering why Crispin is staying away since his father's death. He may not have heard of course.'

'Or he may have come back and, if he isn't posing as Terry then maybe ...' Jack looked at Amos aghast. 'You don't think he actually did return here and the Phillipses have murdered him, do you?'

*

Ten days later, coming in from the fields, Amos saw a police car go by with Sonia and Colin Phillips in the back – he imagined on some official errand, maybe they had to formally identify the body. Stopping only to grab a couple of dead rabbits by way of excuse if he needed one, he drove up to the manor. He wanted to get a look at that garden – see for himself what might have happened.

Betty saw him coming and waved to him from the kitchen window. He held up five fingers to her and strode up the slope towards the burnt-out garden. Most of the wall was still intact but the gate had gone of course. What lay inside would have broken Richard's heart. Amos hadn't considered the timing before – only that both events had occurred close together. But Richard surely must have died before the fire broke out, otherwise he'd have been on the scene trying to save the garden.

The three-acre plot lay smouldering like some burnt-out lunar landscape of tangled black vegetation, stinking of wet charcoal. One of the young under-gardeners raked disconsolately in a corner. Amos strolled over to him as Betty Summers picked her way across the garden holding a large mug.

'Have you told Councillor Cotswold about how you helped Lord Marston?' she asked abruptly.

The young man looked from one to the other. Amos struggled to keep the curiosity he felt from showing on his face.

'I only carried some tools for him – a spade and trowel and a bag which were quite heavy. I don't know what were in it, it were tied up. Oh and water, a jerry can of drinking water.'

Why was that remarkable Amos wondered? 'What was he doing – planting something?'

'I don't know, sir. He just told me to leave them down outside the old ruins, a few weeks afore he died.'

The ruins? Now Amos was interested.

'The same week Mrs Mainwaring told him she'd located the old hall and he'd gone rushing off down there catching his death of cold,' Betty added.

'Then I has to go and collect them again, the next day,' the gardener went on, 'which was easier this time because the sack and the jerry can was empty.'

Amos thanked him and left him and Betty chatting while he wandered around, thinking. Had Richard known about Gervaise's expedition – is that what he'd been doing in the ruins himself? But in that case why leave it so long after Gervaise's death? Unless, failing to find anything he'd gone for another look? Terry had said he felt certain there'd been someone in the ruins the day before Richard died ... this person could have been Richard himself. They'd not considered that, only that it might have been Richard's murderer. He wandered back to Betty and the lad.

'Did Richard Phillips know what you had done for Lord Marston?'

The young man's forehead creased in thought. 'He might have done. I didn't tell him, but that doesn't mean he didn't know.'

Wishing to elicit the truth rather than the evasion which he expected, Amos assumed his most benign expression before he asked, 'And did you ever go down there yourself afterwards ... after Lord Marston's death? To find out what he'd been doing?'

The gardener looked genuinely horrified. 'Not me, sir. You wouldn't catch me down there in a month of Sundays. I just put the tools outside and collected them. It's haunted that place.'

Betty and Amos wandered back to the kitchen. Amos was extremely tempted to have a root around in the ruins himself – assuming any sign of digging would still be obvious. Then he remembered that Annabelle Mainwaring had been hired to dig there, so anyone else would have a hard job distinguishing between her earthworks and any that Gervaise might have created.

He wondered if he should try and contact her, she shouldn't be too difficult to find at the university in Oxford. She might still be the one best placed to know what the old man had been looking for, even though she'd denied any knowledge of his real interest in the Old Manor. What was it she'd said? 'He wasn't terribly specific ... wanted to piece the whole thing together ... understand where the entrance had been etcetera.' That was it, he'd asked her if Gervaise had wanted to rebuild the Old Manor and she'd said: 'Honestly I don't know.' Did he believe her? He had at the time. But he hadn't then known what the gardener had told him this morning.

He still felt there had to be a link between what Gervaise had been trying to say to him, or ask him ... or tell him, and this unprecedented interest he'd shown in the Old Manor so late in life. There had to be.

'What do you think Lord Marston was up to, Betty?'

'It was certainly out of character is all I can say, Amos,' she smiled mischievously. 'Maybe he were hiding someone down there – a fugitive from the law p'raps!'

'Can you imagine it, Lord Marston, a pillar of society, Queen's Counsel – hiding a runaway criminal? I don't think so. And why the spade – for the man's lavatory, was it?' While he scoffed at this idea, Amos was acutely aware that Lord Marston had done a number of irrational, out-of-character, things in those last few weeks. Was this just one more? Was the hiding of a fugitive that far-fetched?

'Is he still there then, Betty? You did see somebody that morning didn't you ... the morning Richard was killed?'

'Don't miss much do you, Amos Cotswold. Actually I seen two people – one was her, Mrs Phillips.' Betty looked towards the door before she continued, 'I seen her before she come down from the fire in the walled garden. I only noticed because I was up on the landing, not that I was s'posed to be, and I saw her going across the fields towards the Old Manor. I'd never seen her out walking afore.'

'Did you tell the police this?'

Betty hung her head. 'Not yet, no, Amos. I haven't because' – she looked up at him – 'she's that vindictive, I knows I'd get into trouble if she found out I'd said anything – and I don't suppose it's important anyway. Why shouldn't she walk across the fields? They're her fields.' Betty was trying hard to justify her actions.

'I know what you mean, Betty, why cause trouble for yourself when you don't have to eh? I wish I could remember that sometimes.' He looked across at her; she looked frightened. He couldn't blame her – thinking there was a murderer at large. 'Betty I think you should come and stay with Lindsay until this is sorted out. Go on, go and pack your bag, I'll take you over. Leave madam a note – say Lindsay's sick and you've had to go and look after her, she won't know any different. Quick now, before she gets back.'

When they were safely in the Land Rover and driving down the road to Weston, Amos turned to Betty. 'So who else did you see?'

'I thought you'd guessed that: Terry Finn.'

'Do you know, there are more sightings of Terry Finn than there are of the abominable snowman! Are you sure it was Terry? Let me guess, he was by the walled garden – before the fire started.'

'Not when I saw him he weren't. He were down by the Old Manor.'

'After the fire started, yes I know – he was on his way to help.'

'That's as maybe, Amos, and I like Terry, he's a good man, which is why I haven't said anything because I'm sure he meant no harm; but I saw him down by the ruins before the fire started and before I sees her.'

Amos didn't want to hear this. She must be mistaken. At her age it could be difficult to recognize people from a distance.

'Hey look, Betty, look up there! I haven't seen a buzzard round here for years. Look high up there, above those yews. Can you see him?'

Betty craned her neck to see up out of the windscreen. 'You'm losing your grip, Amos Cotswold, that's no buzzard, that's a red kite. Can't you sees its tail?'

There was nothing wrong with Betty's eyesight.

He couldn't concentrate. He got up to look for Napoleon, it was time he came in or the good citizens of Weston Hathaway would justifiably complain about tripping over that black booby-trap in the dark.

Amos raised the latch on the front door and swung it open. A man stood there with his fist raised – whether to knock or to hit Amos wasn't clear in that split second. Six foot six or more, stooped under the porch, burly, bearded, his skin tanned like Amos's armchair, he advanced into the living-room forcing Amos backwards and slammed the door shut behind him.

CHAPTER EIGHT

'Are you Amos Cotswold?' Amos nodded, noticing the accent – South African?

'I need to talk to you about Crispin Thimbleby. McKenna, Ian Mckenna.' The giant extended a hand. Amos shook it, willingly accepting Crispin's name as a passport into his home.

'You'd better sit down.' Except between beams, the man had difficulty standing upright in the cottage anyway. He perched on the edge of a chair, jumpy, ready for flight – his size dominating the little room. He had on clean jeans and a voluminous anorak. Amos noticed his hands, large, tough and calloused – a working man's hands.

The phone rang. 'Amos, there's a man on his way down—'

'He's already here, Jack. Good thing I'm not the nervous type is all I can say! Thanks anyway.'

Amos returned to his chair, hopeful that here at last was someone who knew where Crispin was – else why had he come? 'You know Crispin?'

Just then, tired of waiting at the front, Napoleon barged his way in through the back entrance in his customary manner, sending the door smashing against the kitchen table and causing McKenna to leap out of his chair and crack his head on a joist.

'Don't worry, it's only my pet pig, he won't hurt you ... well, not intentionally.' The man continued glancing nervously towards the door, as if he half expected the devil himself to come through it at any moment.

'What's the matter?'

McKenna studied Amos as though trying to judge whether or not he could trust him. 'They killed a man you know!'

Amos digested this. Did he mean Richard? Who were 'they'? And who was this man mountain who seemed scared out of his wits and knew Crispin? Whatever the answers Amos was determined to find out. Here was the first link to Crispin he'd had in forty years. He eased himself out of the armchair and walked across the room to fetch the Scotch bottle and a couple of glasses. He poured McKennna a good measure and handed it to him, employed the bolts on both external doors, and returned to his seat. 'Why don't you start at the beginning?' he said encouragingly.

McKenna relaxed a little, letting the amber nectar warm his throat. He struggled out of his coat. 'You're a friend of Crispin's?' he asked.

Amos leaned forward. 'I used to be.' Relenting he added, 'We played together as kids. He left here when he was nineteen or twenty and I haven't seen him since, but I'd be very keen to see him right now. Does that help?'

Crestfallen, the man ran huge fingers through curly hair. 'They said to see you so I thought …' His disappointment visibly deepened the lines in his already ridged forehead. 'I have to explain to Crispin. You see it's all my fault. I didn't realize … and then today, well … I'd no idea.' McKenna looked as though he was suffering from shock. Amos wondered if he should substitute brandy for the scotch.

McKenna gulped his drink and helped himself to some more. 'I used to work with Crispin.' Amos was wary. Had this man simply heard of Lord Marston's death and thought his ex-workmate had come into a nice fortune and might look kindly on his old pal – was that it? Even so he might still lead them to Crispin.

'We both worked for an outfit called United African Aid – UAA for short. We were sent all over Africa wherever there was famine, usually due to war. You get to know people pretty well after a while – out there in the bush or the desert. There's nothing much else to do at night, except talk.

'Public school, Crispin was, but then you'd know that. He talked about his ancestors, and his old man – not in any bragging sort of way, in fact the opposite – he hated his dad. He never said exactly why but I guessed it might be the usual father and son thing. Said he'd left when his mother died and had no intention of going back – wanted to do something useful with his life, something to help other people.'

So far this sounded likely, Amos thought, but anyone could have picked that much up listening to Jack Ashley's recounting of what Amos had told him, well, almost – with a little embroidery here and there.

'I was fascinated. I'd never been to England. My mother was Dutch and my dad a second generation South African. I grew up in an ordinary part of Johannesburg, so I could only imagine what it must be like to be a lord of the manor, part of the "landed gentry" with acres of English land, and a mansion ... well I couldn't understand how he could possibly leave it.' McKenna gulped more Scotch. 'I felt privileged to know him – proud, you know.' He grinned for the first time. 'He used to get into a lot of trouble, always siding with poor people against authority, standing up to the bullies, stopping beatings. Took a few himself in the process, I can tell you – and got me into some along with him.'

McKenna was beginning to sound more like a man who really did know Crispin – and liked him. 'Said he'd done that to a friend of his back home, too.' Amos kept quiet.

'I didn't entirely believe what he said, mind. I thought when he'd had enough swashbuckling he'd go back home, settle down at Marston Manor, inherit the title from his dad, find himself a nice English wife. It stood to reason. But he was always adamant, said he'd no right to a comfortable life while others were starving.'

That's our Crispin, should have been christened Quixote! Well-intentioned, hot-headed, defender of the down-trodden. Amos wondered if he'd inherited the trait from his crusading forefathers.

'After a while I chickened out. Running convoys across Ethiopia, Sudan ... all those places – never knowing when you'd get ambushed, or who by, or what they'd do to you; I couldn't take it any more. So I went back to Jo'burg, the urban jungle, the one I felt at home in.'

Amos had begun to doubt that McKenna knew where Crispin had been lately or might even be now ... until he said, 'But I have heard about him. From someone else who'd been with us in UAA – oh I forgot to mention, it was broken up and swallowed by several other agencies soon after I left. This guy tipped up in Jo'burg and we had a few beers one night, got to reminiscing. Said he'd last seen Crispin in Afghanistan.'

Amos had been patient long enough. 'But you came to this area looking for him?'

'Oh no, I'd no idea his place was round here.'

Amos found that hard to believe, and made no attempt to hide his feelings.

Seeing his expression, McKenna added hurriedly: 'I came to see Richard Phillips.'

There it was! A definite connection between Richard Phillips and Crispin – and he was sitting in front of Amos right now! Amos had to have a refill. He topped up McKenna's glass and looked ruefully at the rapidly depleting bottle while trying to fathom this new conundrum. McKenna had stopped talking, almost as though his coming to see Richard Phillips required no explanation. What had Amos missed? He raised an enquiring eyebrow with a great deal more nonchalance than he was feeling.

'I'm a gardener see, like Richard. We met when we worked as foremen for the same landscape contractors in Jo'burg. Always got on well, shared interests I suppose it was. And again, there was always plenty of time for a chat.' He drank some more Scotch; Amos noticed how little affected he seemed by it. 'That's where the trouble starts. I told Richard all about Crispin.'

Here it was at last, here was the corroboration of what Amos and others had suspected. Somehow Sonia Phillips had tricked Lord Marston – deliberately. They were fraudsters. Here was the connection! Now he was sure. Amos sat back in his chair, even Napoleon had the sense to keep quiet.

'The Phillipses came from England, hadn't been out in South Africa all that long I don't think – come to make a quick buck they thought, like so many others did around that time. Richard was always thinking up new schemes – trying to keep that wife of his happy; money, money, money was all that mattered to her. Why he stayed with her I don't know, but Richard was never one to stand up to people.

'We used to daydream, sitting there in the shade, watching the sun wilt the flowers and parch the lawns. One day when we were fantasizing about how nice it would be to have an English country house with acres of lush green garden I remembered about Crispin and what he'd turned his back on, and told Richard all about it. He was incredulous, couldn't believe anyone would give up that lot. "What will happen to it when his father dies?" he would ask. He made me repeat the story over and over. He became obsessed by it. I thought no more of it.'

It occurred to Amos that McKenna might not know. Gently he said, 'You do know Richard's dead don't you?'

McKenna looked up and answered very slowly. 'I found that out today.'

He went on. 'They had these two sons, Richard and Sonia, called, Colin and Paul.' Amos pulled a face. 'I see you've met. Bad lots those two were, evil bastards if ever I saw them. Of course South Africa was perfect for them, ran wild they did with a mother like her and a dad who couldn't stop them. As teenagers they rampaged round Jo'burg, got in with the rough gangs – you can probably guess the rest – thought the world owed them a living, treated everybody like dirt. One day they ambushed this black guy who'd gone onto their land after his goat, which they'd probably stolen anyway, and just shot him in cold blood. They would have got away with it too, except the local chief witnessed it and said he'd get them. So the Phillips family left South Africa – sharpish.'

McKenna stole a glance at the front door – as though afraid the Phillips brothers were about to come after him? Amos still couldn't piece it together. 'And came back here?' he enquired.

'To England, yes. It was the only place they were allowed to go in a hurry. Somewhere in Manchester, I think. Richard and I stayed in touch – once e-mail came in it was easy. We swapped notes on plants, he'd taken quite a few with him. I knew he was keen to get further south, Lancashire wasn't warm enough for what he wanted to grow.' Was it too cold up there for cannabis? Amos wondered.

'Over the last few months the e-mails from him increased; he didn't tell me much but he was obviously very unhappy. More than that, I'd say he sounded ... worried. I assumed either his wife or his sons were playing him up again, though Lord knows those two should have been long gone from home by now.

'Then I got the opportunity to pay him a flying visit so to speak. The company I work for are exhibiting at a winter show in Birmingham this week and they wanted me to look after the blooms – so I jumped at the chance. I e-mailed Richard suggesting we meet.'

'So then you knew he was at Marston?'

'I know this sounds stupid, but no, and I'm not sure I'd have connected the two at that point even if I had. He said he was near a place called Weston Hathaway and to ring him when I got to Stratford station, he'd come and pick me up. To tell you the truth I wasn't keen on bumping into his family so it suited me fine to meet him in Stratford.

'I rang and rang, no reply.' Amos could understand that, he'd seen Sonia and Colin go out, he'd taken Betty away himself and Paul Phillips had either been too idle or too high to answer the phone. 'Well I'd come all this way and today was my only chance of seeing Richard, so I took a cab out here and asked the cabbie if he knew where Richard Phillips lived. He said there was a family called Phillips who owned Marston Manor – he'd taken a load of kids to a rave out there one night. Well, of course, Marston Manor rang a loud bell; not that I understood at that moment quite what it meant – it's a common enough name. Richard might even have adopted the name for a smallholding of his, he was a bit Walter Mittyish like that. And at that point I simply thought he'd forgotten what day it was.

'As soon as we turned off the road and started up the long drive I realized. I said to the cabbie: "Is this all Marston Manor?" "Oh yes, sir", he says. "Stretches for miles the estate does, with its own church and everything". That's when I knew it must be *the* Marston Manor – but how had Richard come to know Crispin? And of course I thought the cabbie had got it wrong and that the Phillipses simply lived here, not that they owned it. It was quite likely Richard might be head gardener or something. I was intrigued I can tell you – and hoped I might see Crispin too.' He looked sheepish. 'In fact it even crossed my mind that they'd deliberately not met me at the station or answered the phone so that I found out this way – I know it sounds ludicrous now, Mr Cotswold, but at the time I was quite excited.' He paused. 'In fact I was so convinced it was something of the sort I paid off the cabbie and away he went. Crazy, wasn't I?

'Paul opened the door, out of his head he looked, so I don't think he recognized me at first, not until I asked for Richard. Then he stared at me and scowled – it must have been my accent.

'He just yelled it at me. "Richard's dead and if you don't eff off I'll show you what we do to trespassers", and slammed the door. Well, I knew what that could mean so I didn't hang around, Mr Cotswold. I just made off down the road I'd been driven up as fast as I could – kept imagining him coming after me with hounds or something, or lying in ambush like they had with that other poor sod in Jo'burg, for a laugh.

'I must have run for half a mile or more, down past some old ruins, then a church before I dare ease up for a rest. There was an old boy working in one of the fields I passed, he must have seen me running because he came over and asked if I was all right. When I asked what had happened to Richard, he told me Richard had been murdered and they didn't know who'd done it. I asked about Crispin and he said he didn't know where he was and that Crispin's father had left Marston to the Phillipses.

'Well I didn't know what to think – or do. I'd set out that morning to have a nice drink with an old friend only to find he'd inherited the estate of a man I'd told him about … and then been murdered.'

Amos made sympathetic noises then looked at the clock. 'That must have been hours ago?'

'Aye it was. I've been sitting in that church porch, the church itself was locked or I'd have taken sanctuary inside I can tell you Mr Cotswold. I needed to think. And the more I thought the worse it got. If only I hadn't mentioned Crispin and his estate to Richard – why, oh why, had I done that? Truth was I was boasting. Boasting that I'd known someone who was heir to a title. That's the truth, there's no getting away from it, so you see it really was my fault – I can't even say it was just one of those things that was bound to happen anyway, because it wasn't. And look where it's led! And to top it all, by now they will have remembered who I am and they must know it was me who originally told Richard about Marston Manor and Crispin abandoning his birthright – so I'm a real threat to them, because

I'm the one who knows their coming here, to Marston, was no accident. And I know what those brothers did in South Africa ... and now Richard has been murdered!'

Again Amos topped up McKenna's glass to calm him.

'I waited until it was dark then I ran here and went into the pub to phone for a taxi. The landlady's a good sort, isn't she? She could see I was wound up, asked if she could help. I asked her where I might find Crispin and she said to come and talk to you.' He swigged his drink.

'So you see, Mr Cotswold, I'm a marked man – they'll try and kill me for sure, just like they've killed Richard!' He stopped abruptly, realizing he'd actually said what he'd been thinking. He shrugged. 'Well I'm sure they have, it all fits.'

Yes Amos thought, but here was one very overwrought man, jumping to conclusions which were too easy to say and difficult to prove.

'So where can I find Crispin, Mr Cotswold? I've got to explain.'

Amos was taken aback. He'd felt sure McKenna knew that far better than he. 'I thought you'd know.'

'I've no idea. It must be twenty years since I met the man who'd seen him in Afghanistan.'

Amos felt leaden. He'd thought McKenna meant a few years ago, not twenty. He was back where he'd started – Crispin could be anywhere ... or dead. 'I was banking on your knowing. No one here has set eyes on him for forty years!'

McKenna blinked at this further surprise and took a moment to assimilate the unwelcome revelation. He'd obviously thought Amos knew where Crispin was, even if he hadn't seen him. Then he relapsed into silence, frowning. Amos kept quiet, lost in his own disappointment.

After a while McKenna ventured: 'If he's still alive and he's not here then I reckon he's still in Africa, most likely the Sudan; he loved it there.' He hesitated. 'But I still can't believe he meant it, about not coming back – not after his father died. So either he doesn't know or …' McKenna looked beseechingly at Amos, soundlessly begging to be excused his guilt and knowing he couldn't be. 'Or he has come back and they've done away with him, too.'

Amos ran McKenna back to his hotel at the airport. On the way they chatted desultorily but Amos learned nothing more of relevance.

Sure enough, the labourer was still cutting hedges near the church the next day. By the time Amos reached him, Napoleon was busy demanding a majority share in the man's lunch.

'I hear you helped that South African chap yesterday.'

'Oh aye, councillor, looked fair done in he did, must have done the four minute mile down yon track and he wasn't no youngster.' He stooped to rescue his apple. 'Mind you I daresay I'd feel like that if I'd had to speak to one o' them.' He took up his shears again.

So McKenna had been telling the truth.

'We'm all been given our marching orders any road. Them's bringing in Chinese labour I heard, cheaper I suppose – though not by much I'll be bound.'

'Chinese? Odd, isn't it? I could've understood eastern European – just, but Chinese? What do they know about farming in this country?'

'Only one thing if you ask me.' The old man stroked his chin and looked at Amos. 'Poppies I shouldn't wonder. I've seen it on telly – makes a nice profit out of it they does.'

Amos walked back past the bottom meadow, where he used to graze his sheep. So what was the difference? His father's fields were now a housing estate, Lord Marston's would soon be growing poppies or some other illicit drug if the Phillipses had their way – all because he and Crispin had shared the same fate; they'd both been disinherited.

Maybe that's what their fathers had wanted – change. Amos didn't understand, but he knew what it felt like. Deep inside he knew what rejection was. Oh, he tried not to think about it, wouldn't have dreamt of ever talking about how he felt, wasn't supposed to care. But it still hurt. Not the loss of property or land or status, not that, he'd learned to do without those; no, it was the loss of love. Weren't fathers supposed to love their sons – regardless?

He tried to think of something else. Why was he raking all that up again now, he'd buried it hadn't he, a lifetime ago ... so why was it nagging? Nagging like the memory of Gervaise's death and what he'd been trying to say. Had Gervaise chosen him because he knew Amos had suffered the same fate as that which he'd been about to inflict on Crispin? Had he wanted Amos to explain it to Crispin? Well, if so, tough. He could no more explain it to Crispin than he could explain his own father's actions to himself.

Wanting some comfort and support, Amos fancied one of Marion's splendid all-day breakfasts. Over his food he confided to Jack his conversation of the previous night with McKenna.

'It won't do you know, you can't just let things go on like this, you've got to do something! People round here are really worried.'

Amos was well aware of that. For weeks now, and increasingly since Richard's death, the villagers had been concerned about what was going on up at the manor. Not that they cared about that in itself – but with the Phillipses there it was bound to harm the village. Quite aside from making the fieldhands redundant and serving notice on those with tied cottages – which seriously affected fifteen households in Weston Hathaway – they were worried sick about the murder, in case there was a random killer on the loose. The horrors of the concert and motorbike events that the Phillipses seemed intent on inflicting also loomed large. Hardened as they were to the occasional tragedy where animals were concerned – they couldn't stomach wanton slaughter.

'What do you suggest?' Amos queried.

'Well you could get off your backside and start looking for Crispin!'

'I thought you were convinced Terry Finn is Crispin.'

'Well if he is, he's not admitting it, is he, so either way you've got to flush him out! Pity Terry wasn't in the other night when that chap McKenna was here, maybe he'd have recognized him.'

'Don't forget McKenna hasn't seen Crispin for twenty odd years either,' Amos said. 'Anyway, I presume the London solicitors have been doing their best to find Crispin.'

'Why should they? What do London solicitors know about someone they've never met who left home forty years ago? Even if they had been looking they've probably concluded he's either dead, or doesn't want to be found. Neither will they relish having to tell him he has the title but his father has given Marston to some "johnny cum latelys". No, I don't think they'll be looking too hard for him, do you.' Jack wasn't pulling any punches. He'd even stayed more or less on the subject without any of his usual digressions – in itself an indicator of his strength of feeling.

'What's got into you?'

'You! Now we know it was no accident. The Phillipses arrived here fully aware the son and heir was not at home so to speak. Yet still you do nothing.'

'What do you want me to do? Nobody's going to listen to me.'

Jack leaned across the bar. 'Never mind about listening to you! All I know is everyone around here is bloody counting on you.'

'You know very well I can't challenge the will.'

'No, but you know the man who can! Find Crispin Thimbleby, Amos!' Jack stalked off.

That night the Marstons haunted his dreams. In and out of his room they sailed – calling, beckoning, goading ... and they all looked like Gervaise; Gervaise through the centuries, Gervaise telling him what to do ... but he couldn't quite hear him. Nor was Amos in his cosy room in the cottage but in a great medieval chamber open to the sky where the wind howled and the spectres travelled through paneless windows.

He tossed and turned, half awake, half somewhere else. Gervaise was relentless. On and on he went, by turns pleading, angry, scoffing ... saying he should have known better than ask Amos to do anything. Useless Amos, hopeless Amos – couldn't even manage this much. Gervaise had trusted him, trusted him to do something, but he wasn't doing it. That wasn't chivalrous, that wasn't how a knight would behave.

He woke abruptly. The wind had stopped howling and the moon lit up his room with amazing clarity. The cracked mirror above his chest of drawers reflected the night sky through the open curtains and he could even make out the hands on the wall-clock opposite – 2.45. He felt sharp and alert. Why had it taken so long? What Gervaise had been trying to say seemed so obvious now; what else could it possibly have been? Why had he been so dense? Gervaise did want him to find Crispin.

Amos was out of bed, pacing the room in the moonlight, talking aloud to himself. 'That's why me. He thinks Crispin might respond to me whereas he'd ignore everyone else.' He stopped pacing. 'Gervaise knew what was going to happen didn't he, knew what the Phillipses were like. He knew what would happen to the staff, to the village. In which case, why leave the estate to them? The only explanation was a fit of pique – and at the last minute he had regretted it. Why have I been so blind? That's what he wanted me to do. There was no one else he could ask, yet what have I done besides sit mithering like some old woman, losing precious time – watching instead of acting.'

Too keyed up to sleep, Amos dressed and went downstairs. 'We're going to find Crispin, that's what we're going to do, boy,' he said to Napoleon, adding a playful kick. It was the middle of the night but he felt as if Jack had slipped cannabis into his beer. Even his joints had forgone their creaking to allow him to concentrate on his quest.

Where to start? He'd go and see John Wilkinson in the morning – it crossed his mind to ring him now but he stopped himself just in time. John would know the legal avenues down which to search – newspaper ads, more of what the London lawyers must have been doing. John could check with them first to see what progress they'd made.

Either through wishful thinking or because his face had not shown up in the dream, Amos did not believe Crispin was dead. For whatever reason, perhaps just irrational certainty, he felt convinced Crispin was alive – somewhere. Whether he knew about the situation at Marston was a different matter, he might not. Amos felt confident Crispin could be found, the question he still had doubts about was whether he could be persuaded to come home. That's why Gervaise had chosen Amos. That was the task he'd been given.

It wasn't so unlike the tasks everyone gave him – something was wrong – send for Amos; someone had been hard done by – Amos would straighten it out. What was it Jack had said to him? 'You've got to do something!' It was one of the things he and Crispin had had in common, championing those in trouble. He hoped Crispin hadn't lost that quality because Amos was relying on it to help persuade him he was needed at Marston. Without Crispin this whole area would soon be wrecked and countless more lives ruined.

Amos sat at the kitchen table, mug in hand, thinking. He'd wasted enough time. He must do something no one else had done, something more positive. He could look on the internet, find out all the Aid Agencies and contact them. He could put a notice on one of those electronic noticeboards for missing persons he'd heard about – someone who'd seen Crispin in recent years might just reply. What was it McKenna had said, try the Sudan? He could write to the head of the Red Cross there or Oxfam perhaps. Terry! It suddenly struck him, Terry was due to go out there!

Later that morning he found Terry Finn at Alan's, clearing out the turkey hutches and stacking them in the barn out of the way – hiding the reminder. Over a mug of Madge's tea, Amos explained about McKenna and his own determination to find Crispin, the only man who could challenge the new order.

'I looked for Crispin on the internet,' Terry said. 'I found his birth certificate, of course, but no marriage certificate, no census information.' He paused. 'And no death certificate either. Which could mean he's still abroad.'

'Thanks, Terry, at least it confirms what McKenna said – if he's anywhere it's not England – which is what I really came to ask you. I'm writing to the major agencies in Africa but the next step would be easier for someone who's out there, someone working in a similar field, so I thought maybe ... when you go out, I mean if we haven't found him by then.'

Terry still seemed down. 'Of course I'll help, whatever I can do – if I ever get out there that is.' Amos decided not to pursue that, then Terry, sounding more positive, added: 'I'll put some feelers out anyway. I know a few of the clergy out there.'

They thanked Madge and walked back outside. Terry continued: 'By the way, since you said you didn't know much about your family, I looked you up too. I didn't have much time, but I think I've found one set of grandparents for you. They all lived near Warwick, which won't surprise you. If I'm right your paternal grandmother was a Lawrence.'

'Yes, I think I knew that.' He tried to look pleased because Terry had obviously put effort in on his behalf, but the less he had to think about his family the better. It always upset him, even now. 'Thanks, Terry.'

*

'When are the Licensing Committee hearing the case for the concert at Marston then, Amos?' Marion asked at opening time.

'Next week, Marion, don't worry I'll be there, we'll get this stopped. Though I had hoped it wouldn't come to this, that I'd find Crispin and it would all go away.'

'I've been thinking about Richard Phillips. He could have been killed simply because he disturbed someone or was in the wrong place at the wrong time ... which means we're all vulnerable.' Marion looked scared.

'And what about that McKenna chap?' Jack said. 'What do we know about him? We've only got his word for it that he came here after Richard had been killed. What if he had some grudge against Richard? Yes, that's it! To start with they were in this together, McKenna was to have a share in Marston – but then Richard and Sonia tried to cut him out so he decides to come over here and kill Richard.'

'But why come back in that case?'

'Because he still hadn't got what he came for, so he came back to get it from Sonia.'

Amos chuckled. 'You should write for TV, Jack. The old labourer said McKenna looked scared stiff and saw him run the half mile from Marston to the church. Not the action of someone brave enough to tackle Sonia Phillips I wouldn't have thought – unless he's a damned good actor. No, I believe his story; it's bizarre enough to be true.'

What could he say in a letter to Crispin? 'Please come home, your father's dead so the coast is clear, but by the way he's left the estate to some strangers,' or 'Urgent you return home – strangers have stolen Marston'? And Crispin was now a lord, so was that how the letter should be addressed, or would that frighten him off altogether?

Amos sat gazing into the fire, the writing pad Lindsay had provided propped on his knee. How could he appeal to him? By telling him the truth. Amos started to write. He began with the motorbikes in the graveyard, the killing of Tom Dutton's horse, the rave, the dead turkeys and sheep, Tom's death through lack of sleep. He moved on to the supplying of drugs to local youngsters and their incitement to harm others, and the sacking of the estate workers and the turfing of them out of their homes – some of whom Crispin would remember as lads not much older than him when he'd left. He finished with the prospect of the Phillipses growing opium poppies at Marston before selling to a developer and, finally, spelled out what that would mean for Weston Hathaway.

He tried to imagine how it would all sound to someone who'd abandoned Marston forty years earlier and made his home in the African desert. How unimportant it might seem amid all those homeless, starving wretches. But Amos was relying on two things: that Crispin hadn't abandoned Marston, just vacated it whilst his father lived, and that he had retained his strong principles. As lord of the manor he had a duty to protect his own and he was currently reneging on that duty. What was it the spectre had said: 'Not what a knight would do.'

Terry had discovered that there was a central co-ordinating aid agency in Sudan to whom all such communications could be sent, so Amos would use them. He signed the letter 'Gabriel's Keeper, Amos Cotswold,' to remind Crispin of the bell in Marston church they'd read with such interest as boys, thereby providing some proof of his own identity. He sealed it, wrote a covering letter explaining the urgency of finding Crispin Thimbleby, addressed it to the agency whose address the ever-efficient Terry had provided, and put it on the table ready to post in the morning. He found himself picturing its arrival, this small white envelope that held their future in its grasp; he pictured Crispin opening it, reading it ... and then what?

And if Terry Finn really was Crispin? Then Amos must trust that the man knew what he was doing.

*

A few days later Amos encountered Jack in the paper shop.

'Have you seen Terry, Jack?'

'Not for several days, p'raps he's busy over at Alan's.'

Amos's phone rang in his pocket. It was John Wilkinson on the line. 'I'm duty solicitor this week, you know, if some felon demands legal assistance I have to attend. I've been at the nick most of the night. That's why I'm ringing. I thought you'd be interested in something I picked up when I was leaving. They've just charged someone with Richard Phillips's murder. Someone you know.'

CHAPTER NINE

'Sonia Phillips. I don't know much more, Amos, she didn't request my services. All I know is they've actually charged her, she's not just "helping police with their enquiries". I hear they've got a witness but they're not saying who it is.'

Amos was having difficulty assimilating this information. Not that he thought her innocent. All along he'd considered that of all people the Phillipses had a strong motive for killing Richard. But he hadn't seriously thought.... Even when he'd heard how the brothers had killed the black man in South Africa, he'd wanted to think it had been exaggerated. He'd have found it much more comfortable if they'd discovered Richard had been killed by a stranger, that it was a fluke. Whereas cold-blooded, calculated, murder – by a man's own wife – fell outside Amos's comprehension.

'John, I wanted to talk to you anyway, I've decided to try to get Crispin back. Will you get on to those solicitors of Gervaise's down in London – see if they'll tell you what they've done to try and find him.'

'They'll think I've got a bloody cheek asking; accusing them of incompetence. Some of these fellows can be very touchy.'

'Especially first thing in the morning when they've been up all night – yes I know. See what you can do though, eh? And thanks John, I appreciate the news, very much.' He hung up.

'Didn't I tell you – weeks ago! I was right, *crime passionnel*!'

Jack attempted a French accent with limited success. 'She found him with his mistress and bumph! Jealousy, rage, a woman scorned … all that! I told you so!'

The relief in the village was tangible. The murder itself had shocked the neighbourhood, but now Sonia had been arrested, they were accepting it as the neatest solution. It was nothing to do with the village or its inhabitants – 'good riddance to a bad lot' seemed to be the general consensus. And best of all, surely it would mean the entire Phillips family would clear out now, and leave Weston Hathaway in peace.

No one doubted her guilt. The supposed motives varied from Jack's mistress theory to the widely held view that Richard had had an attack of conscience and started resisting Sonia's plans. This made sense to Amos – especially after what McKenna had told him about Richard, how he'd dreamed of being lord of the manor and owning a large English estate. He could see why Richard would want to prevent it being turned into a racetrack or a rock concert venue or a massive housing estate; that would never have fitted with his rural idyll.

Amos remembered the night of the rave and how Richard had stood in the shadows watching as he and Ted nobbled the generator. Now it made sense – Richard had no more wanted raves at Marston than they had.

His family must have played him along while it suited them; doubtless feigning interest in his schemes to restore the old gardens, establish a gardening college. Perhaps they'd originally thought all that might help endear them to Lord Marston – until he rejected the idea as well. By that time though Richard must have known too much about their scheme, so he either had to be with them … or dead.

As soon as Lord Marston had died and their plans came to fruition it must have become all too evident that Richard's desires were not going to be met. Met! They weren't even going to be considered. Amos disliked thinking ill of the dead but suspected that whilst Richard had believed he was going to accomplish his dream he'd been prepared to ignore, or even actively assist in, whatever underhand business had gone on in order to acquire the estate. Only when he'd seen he wasn't going to achieve his aims, had he suffered his attack of conscience. Richard had become a rich yet unfulfilled man who had suddenly realized he'd sacrificed the hereafter without gaining his heaven on earth, the classic Faustian pitfall. No wonder he'd started having second thoughts. Had the rest of his family feared his next step would be the police?

Had Sonia lured him onto those rocks? Or had he too seen someone lurking down there, as Terry had, gone to investigate and Sonia had seized her chance? Maybe she'd even calculated that whoever had been around would get the blame. Which is why the witness could only have been someone who'd seen her from the house – Betty, or one of the other staff. Surely if she'd been aware of someone else near the ruins, Sonia would have taken particular care to ensure she wasn't observed by them. The problem was ... from as far away as the house no one could possibly have seen Sonia actually strike her husband.

And why the fire?

*

Amos was on his way to the licensing committee meeting which he often attended when there were licences being discussed which affected his electors. At least it would be short today as they would no longer have to cover the proposed rock concert gathering at Marston – not with Richard Phillips dead and Sonia Phillips in gaol awaiting trial for his murder.

Arriving at the third floor, Amos was heading for Committee Room One when the district council's solicitor called to him from behind. 'Councillor Cotswold, wait a minute will you, I need a word.' The man hurried up breathlessly. 'The applicants are insisting the licensing committee still table their application for the concert at Marston Manor. We'd taken it off as you know.'

'What on earth for? Surely with what's going on up there they don't really think …?'

The district solicitor shrugged. 'All I know is they laid it on thick. Said we'd no right to remove the application and insisted the committee chairman reinstate it.'

'He didn't let them dictate…?' Amos could see the answer on the district solicitor's face. 'Oh, for heaven's sake!' He turned sharply on his heel and marched towards the committee room, thoroughly disgruntled.

The meeting had already started, mostly licence extensions for pubs and clubs over Christmas and the New Year, plus one or two relicensing applications from landlords. The room cleared as these cases were swiftly dealt with. Sitting against the far wall was a phalanx of strangers, lap-topped, sharp-suited and smug. From London, Amos guessed. It transpired they comprised the production company's legal team, from a fancy firm in the City. Well he'd soon see about them! He was pleased he'd come, he nearly hadn't.

Amos felt unsure what they were up to; maybe they thought they could go ahead regardless of the situation at Marston. If they were trying to pull a fast one by assuming the local people had lost interest and would be looking the other way, then they had another think coming. They might be able to intimidate the council's officers but they weren't going to get past Amos Cotswold. Oh no. He couldn't afford to let them, the whole village was depending on him.

The chairman of the licensing committee, one of Amos's fellow councillors, announced the application for a concert to be held at Marston Manor in April. Next, one of the officers from the licensing department read out the details of the request '… through their extensive national advertising the promoters expect up to fifty thousand dedicated clubbers to attend, and will have the backing of national radio stations; as well as featuring live acts, world famous DJs and other dance festival attractions....'

'Whatever that's a euphemism for,' Amos muttered under his breath. Even conceiving of 50,000 people traipsing through the surrounding country roads, lanes and pathways was an absurd proposition in his opinion. They had absolutely no idea what chaos and yes, death, that would cause. They were out of their tiny city minds. But through his many years' experience of such meetings, Amos had learned to keep quiet until the moment was right to speak out. He sat, impassive, knowing this nonsense would not succeed. He'd only to point out the traffic problems – that would soon stop it.

The officer then briefly mentioned a petition and that some letters had been received from local people. Much to Amos's surprise he did not read them out, which was the usual procedure, nor even paraphrase their contents which was occasionally done in the interests of time if the correspondence was overwhelmingly large. Amos coughed loudly and the officer shot a glance at the district council solicitor and hung his head. What was going on here? Maybe he shouldn't have stormed off as he had in the corridor, what had they been trying to tell him?

A representative from the production company stood up next. 'Mr Chairman and Committee Members, we've held several of these concerts elsewhere and they've been hugely popular, brought enormous amounts of extra business to the surrounding areas and provided a welcome addition to the attractions of the locality, including ...' he looked meaningfully at the chairman, '... considerable donations to local organizations.' Did that mean the coffers of the district council's ruling political party, Amos wondered ... or assistance with helping them plug that big hole in the budget? 'We've already spoken to the police and the fire brigade.' He waved a sheaf of papers. 'Subject to the usual sensible precautions they see no reason....'

Amos could take no more. He leapt to his feet.

'Are you saying the police have OK'd fifty thousand people coming and going from Marston – after what happened the last time?'

One of the smarties, a young female lawyer, interrupted. 'Mr Chairman, a point of order.' Everyone turned to stare at her. 'Because this gentleman is the ward member for the area in question I submit that he therefore has a vested interest and must not be allowed to speak at these proceedings.'

'What! What utter nonsense! That's the whole point! The ward member represents the people of the area concerned and it's their views which are the most important.' Amos couldn't believe such a ridiculous remark; where had they got her from?

She turned to the district solicitor. 'May I remind you that it is the human rights legislation which has priority here and that legislation dictates that we have the right to hold our concert without prejudicial influence by local bodies being unfairly brought to bear.'

'And what about the human rights of my constituents then?'

The district solicitor held up his hand. 'Mr Chairman, Members of the Committee ... Councillor Cotswold, my advice is that we should heed the human rights legislation here or it will cost the ratepayers considerable sums in High Court fees.'

The chairman looked around his committee, shrugged and turned towards Amos. 'I'm sorry, Councillor Cotswold, but we've been overruled on this. I'm afraid I have to withdraw your right to speak at this meeting.'

Amos wasn't the only one who was stunned, the murmurings around him told him that – but the council was afraid. They'd obviously been threatened before the meeting; yet it was evident they hadn't realized that the ward member would actually be prevented from speaking. Amos simply couldn't believe what was happening here. Democracy had been dealt a knock-out punch.

It was all over very quickly after that. In a daze Amos heard the chairman do his best but – with the opposition quashed and the threat of an expensive court action if they refused – the committee granted the licence.

The room cleared around him but Amos remained, too wretched to move. He certainly didn't want to talk to any of them, couldn't trust himself to be civil – which would certainly have landed him in trouble. He suddenly wondered what Crispin would have done had he been in Amos's shoes this morning – the young Crispin that is, Amos didn't know what he was like now. Something more positive was the answer. Then he remembered Jack's words: 'They're counting on you ...' What was it he'd said to all of them that night? 'Don't worry, I'll attend the meeting and we'll have no trouble putting a stop to this.'

He'd failed to realize how clever these people were, failed to be properly prepared. But even if he had been, would it have made any difference? Maybe not but at least he'd have felt he'd done his best, been professional about it, taken the threat seriously instead of pompously dismissing it. He'd been so sure of himself, hadn't even had an alternative up his sleeve. The world out there had changed and he'd failed to understand that. That it hadn't been his fault; that few had known this agency would still be applying for the licence, let alone would drag up the spectre of human rights legislation to prevent Amos from even speaking, didn't alter the fact that he'd failed.

He felt physically sick that such rail-roading could happen here, in his patch, in so-called sleepy South Warwickshire. On top of which he felt as guilty as hell.

Amos hauled himself up the stairs to John Wilkinson's office. 'They were relying on me, John and I've let them down. How come I wasn't allowed to speak? Can you explain that to me? Why didn't somebody tell me?'

John came round his desk, opened an antique break-fronted

cabinet in the corner and extracted the brandy bottle and a glass. Aware Amos would be driving he poured a small measure and handed it to him while Amos spilled out the gist of what had transpired in the committee meeting.

'I guess your best hope is that the Phillipses clear out before the concert. With any luck the new owners might not be so keen on the idea.'

Amos sank again. 'No, because they'll be too busy building hundreds of houses on the site instead.' His face lifted a fraction. 'Unless, with their parents gone, the Phillips brothers get cold feet and just hightail it out of here – like they did out of South Africa. Without selling it I mean.' In his despair Amos had overlooked this new possibility – relevant only since Sonia's arrest. 'Though goodness knows what happens when somewhere like that is abandoned? Would the estate go to Gervaise's next of kin?'

'Not while she's alive. Don't forget she'll be tried for murdering Richard, so if she's convicted his share will go to the sons, not to Sonia – but she will still have her own half. Of course if they all disappeared it would eventually go to some obscure relative ... or to the Crown.'

'And the Crown would build all over it. So we'd be back to square one.'

'Not to mention the trouble you'd have while they sorted everything out. That land would be prey to every concert holder, rave stager, motorbike jamboree promoter and traveller you can imagine! With no visible owner the law could do little to prevent it.' He paused. 'And according to the will the Phillipses would still own Marston, whether or not they'd fled the country.'

'So still our only hope is to get Crispin back here to challenge that dodgy will.'

John looked awkward. 'You should know something else. I've been in touch with the London solicitors as you asked.'

Amos leaned forward, this was what he'd been waiting for.

'Don't get your hopes up, it's not good news. For a start, Gervaise had fallen out with the firm who used to do all the estate work, but they put me on to another outfit.' John opened a small folder on his desk. 'Here they are, Harrison, Stokes and Harrison. So I contacted them and' – John came round the desk to sit beside Amos – 'they say they have no instruction to do anything about Gervaise's will.'

Amos was puzzled. 'What sort of answer is that?'

'It means, amongst other things, that they are evidently not Gervaise's executors. They told me off the record that they had reason to believe there was a later will than the one he lodged with them anyway.'

'So they do have his will!'

'They have *a* will.'

Amos couldn't believe what he was hearing. 'You mean ... you mean they're not doing anything at all?'

'Not without an instruction they won't. Neither would I in their shoes.'

'So who's putting the will through probate then?' Amos asked.

'The Phillipses solicitors I presume.' John stood up. 'However, Harrison and Whatnot did confirm that the authorities are actively looking for Crispin.'

'Authorities? You mean the Probate Office or whoever administers hereditary titles, people like that?' John wasn't looking as pleased about this as Amos imagined he should. Surely the more people who were looking for Crispin the better – unless of course it enforced his resolve never to return, before Amos had the chance to talk him round. 'That's good isn't it?'

'I mean Interpol.'

Amos was puzzled. 'Do they usually get involved in these cases then?'

'No. Not unless they suspect foul play.'

Then Amos realized what John was trying to say, 'You mean they're worried like us that the Phillipses may have murdered

Crispin as well.' The full force of this probability engulfed Amos as he realized that if Interpol were looking for Crispin then this horror was more than a mere suspicion. 'Oh no. It had crossed our minds but ... oh no.' He put his head in his hands. 'I didn't really think ...' he couldn't say any more. All along he'd believed so strongly that Crispin was alive – because he wanted to. Not only because of their past friendship but also because of the unspeakable consequences if he weren't; the villagers' powerlessness without him having been only too well demonstrated that very morning.

John said gently. 'There is another possibility, which I hardly dare voice.' Amos looked up at him. 'Perhaps the police aren't completely sure that it was Sonia Phillips who murdered her husband.'

'They think it might have been Crispin?' To Amos this was immeasurably preferable to believing Crispin was dead. 'Where there's life there's hope' had never seemed so true to him as it did in that instant.

'From what I can glean from the prosecution lawyer ...' John paused. 'Don't ask, Amos, and whatever you do don't breathe a word of this to anyone else, OK?' Amos nodded. 'Well, from what I can gather, the case against Sonia Phillips, whilst compelling, is largely circumstantial. For instance they've found her fingerprints – on a petrol can.'

'I see. My fingerprints must be on lots of petrol cans.' Amos looked at the ingrained muck in his fingers and caught John stifling a smile. 'You mean it was Sonia Phillips who set light to the walled garden?'

'One of the differences between you and Sonia Phillips is she wasn't in the habit of mowing lawns or lighting bonfires or filling cars with petrol when they'd run out ... so, her fingerprints on an empty petrol can at the scene of a major unexplained fire are suspicious ... but they're not conclusive.'

'And why would she do *that*? To annoy Richard? Surely that cannabis was for her precious sons?' Amos was thinking aloud.

'I assume to cover her tracks. Draw attention to herself in that place at that time and so create an alibi. Remember it was Sonia whom Betty saw running down the slope from the garden, making Betty notice which direction she came from – the opposite one from the ruins. It was Sonia who rang the fire brigade – who would have recorded the exact time of the call. She wouldn't want to burn the house down but the cannabis field couldn't have been better as it pointed the finger at certain locals who might have had a motive.'

Amos took up the supposition. 'And it caused a diversion too of course. Who knows how long Richard's body might have lain in the ruins if it hadn't been for Terry. Maybe she intended to go back later and bury it – in the hope the fire would be so intense everyone would think Richard had perished in his beloved walled garden.' Amos scratched his head. 'That might explain the fire, but you said the police had a witness to Richard's murder.'

'That's the part they're being very cagey about.'

'Thank God for that. I know who it is John, and the person would be a sitting target for the Phillips brothers so I'm mighty pleased to hear even you can't find that one out.'

Another thought struck Amos. 'You don't think it's Terry do you? I mean he did hang around Marston church a lot.' Amos wasn't going to tell anybody, not even John, that Terry had felt there'd been somebody about in those ruins the day before the murder. Anyway, Terry hadn't known who it was – or if he had he hadn't said. 'Is that why he's disappeared I wonder, doesn't trust the police to protect him? No one's seen him for days.' Amos drained the last of his brandy. 'Can't say I blame him if he is the witness, it's not a position I'd like to be in.'

'So now we've got two fugitives by the sound of it, Crispin Thimbleby and Terry Finn. I'm not at all sure I know where all this is going Amos.' John looked as worried as he sounded.

'Jack Ashley reckons they're one and the same.' Amos hesitated. 'Personally, I don't think so. It is just possible I guess but ...' He rubbed his eyes. 'I suppose I can't understand why he'd keep the fact from *me*. Doesn't he trust me? Which makes me biased, I don't really want Terry to be Crispin.'

John tapped his pencil on the desk in front of him, turning it through his fingers between each tap, evidently now even more perplexed by this new possibility.

'Well, if he is Crispin he's hiding for a reason isn't he? Whether to protect himself from attack or now to escape arrest for murdering Richard or he's met a worse fate. Thinking about it, if it is Interpol who are looking for him, then the police must think Crispin is abroad. So if Terry is Crispin, how did he get into this country without the police being able to trace the entry record? On a false passport? Is that where the name Terry Finn came from? We could do some searches, see what turns up.'

The irony of it was not wasted on Amos. It had been Terry himself who'd performed some initial searches on Crispin.

The black mood returned as soon as he left John's office and faced the prospect of explaining to the people of Weston Hathaway how he'd failed, that there was therefore every likelihood that the concert would indeed go ahead as planned – and by the way, the expected number of attendees would be around the 50,000 mark. Focused on these unpalatable consequences of his failure, for the second time in as many weeks, he again missed the turning for Weston Hathaway.

He'd heard of people having murder in their hearts and wondered what it meant – now he felt he knew; if he could have seen off the Phillips brothers at that moment he wouldn't have hesitated. Just as dusk was approaching he automatically took the next turn down Featherbed Lane and, still on autopilot, gunned the Land Rover down the incline. There were no other vehicles in sight.

Near the far end three hooded figures leapt deliberately from the hedgerow into his path; their intention clear, to force him to swerve violently into the hedge. Instead he accelerated.

He could hear the breaking branches as the boys leapt for their lives. There had been no thuds against the panelling, no tell-tale hump of running over anything. He hadn't touched any of them but hoped their narrow escape would encourage them to abandon their lethal games.

Later on, the atmosphere was subdued as he opened the door into the bar. 'Ah, here he is,' Jack said, with more than his usual joviality, handing Amos a pint of beer.

'We think you've deserved that today.'

'You've obviously not heard then,' muttered Amos. Did they know the application had been tabled after all, and assumed it had been refused – as he'd promised?

Marion came from the kitchen and others who'd been sitting by the fire or playing darts gathered round, now he'd have to tell them. Instead Jack spoke up.

'We want you to know how disgracefully we think you were treated – which means us really, since you are our representative – and we're wondering if we can appeal against this injustice' – here Jack lowered his voice – 'or if not, how we can make sure the concert doesn't happen?' Several shook Amos's hand, others patted his back, more pints were left in the pipe for him. He was touched, they were being so kind. John Wilkinson must have rung Jack and warned him.

Amos felt much better – there was after all more than one way of stopping a concert. He was well into his third pint when the door shot open admitting the Sanderson parents, patently upset. They marched up to Amos at the bar. 'We've just come back from the hospital. Our Kevin thought his arm was broken.'

Pity it wasn't his neck. 'And is it? Broken?'

'No, but it's no thanks to you. He's got big cuts down his face. He said you tried to run over him.'

'I assure you I did not, Mrs Sanderson. As I was driving down Featherbed Lane he and his pals jumped out at me in an attempt to force me off the road. My livelihood depends on that vehicle being roadworthy, I can't afford it to be broken up in a hedge – I wouldn't be able to go out and feed my sheep.'

'He was nowhere near Featherbed Lane; he was walking along our road by those big bushes!' She turned to her husband for support.

'You've not heard the last of this, Cotswold, I shall report you to the police as soon as I get home.' With that they both turned and marched out.

Marion came up, glancing at Jack she said: 'This is our battle you know, not yours. They've picked on you because you came to my, or rather Lucy's, rescue when they tried to intimidate me. Now they've set their parents up to ruin your reputation, all incited by the Phillipses because Jack banned them from here.'

Jack took over from Marion. 'We've had an idea how we can stop this Amos – if you're game.'

Amos kept replaying in his mind what Betty had said when they'd heard about Richard's murder. Namely, that other than the rightful heir, anyone attempting to take Marston would meet with disaster.

He pulled himself back up in his chair. He wouldn't be surprised if there were similar sayings spread about many of the large old estates – just to frighten any would-be usurpers. Such stories had provided an obvious deterrent for a superstitious society. If he were to let it be known that any youngsters found loitering in Featherbed Lane would break their arms within a week perhaps he could stop their nonsense too. It would have to actually come true a few times mind – just to prove its veracity, give it real impact. Is that what Jack had in mind?

As far as he could remember, the rest of the legend recounted the fate of the two brothers who'd murdered the Baron. At any rate, the prophesied disaster hadn't come true this time. Richard had perished yes, but it hadn't altered the course of things – if anything his death had made any possible restitution of the estate more remote. Nor could Amos remember what had happened in the end. Had the Baron's son ever retrieved Marston? And why should it matter, 800 years later, at one in the morning?

The clock chimed the half hour – and still he sat there. Something was going to happen, he felt it strongly. It must be all this dwelling on legends and curses after an extremely stressful day though such things used not to affect him. Like most small boys, he and Crispin had revelled in them; they'd even dared each other to stand alone in the churchyard at midnight on a moonless night just to see what might result. He chuckled as he remembered catching Crispin out. Against the rules, Crispin had taken a torch ... but never understood how Amos had known. There were no windows on that side of the church so he'd accused Amos of hiding in the churchyard, which he hadn't.

At two the phone rang, the noise shrieking through his now cold sitting-room, shattering his peace.

CHAPTER TEN

'I didn't tell you this mind.' It was Sergeant Wilson. 'Mrs Phillips committed suicide in her cell in Warwick, two hours ago.' He paused, obviously waiting for Amos's reply. 'Councillor?'

'Are you sure?' Amos had difficulty assimilating this news. 'How did she do that?'

'Strung up by her belt apparently. I'm just glad she wasn't in one of our cells – all those reports we'd have had to write.'

'I thought you people removed belts to prevent this sort of thing happening.' Amos heard himself say, consciously playing for time by asking questions about procedure, when all he really wanted to know was: *What the hell does this mean?*

'These things happen, I'm afraid. Save us a lot of trouble though, won't it, councillor? Talking of which, I've had a complaint about you this evening.' Sergeant Wilson carried on as though suicide were an everyday occurrence to him. The attitude was catching. Fleetingly Amos wondered how it must feel to be as unmourned as Sonia Phillips.

'Mr and Mrs Sanderson think I tried to run over their Kevin. Tell me, Sergeant, how busy are you?'

There came a sigh from the other end, the unmistakable sound of a man with so much to do he didn't know which job to do first and who feared he was just about to acquire another. 'Up to my eyes, councillor – as usual.'

'Cheer up, all I'm going to suggest is that you leave this complaint in your in-tray for a week or two – I think you'll find it'll solve itself.' He rang off. His false ebullience cut off as he replaced the receiver.

He couldn't understand it. Admittedly he'd known little about her and met her only a handful of times, without exception acrimoniously, nevertheless he would not have said Sonia Phillips was the sort to commit suicide – whatever that sort is. She'd always appeared to him as a driven personality, scheming, grasping, caring nothing for the suffering of others, out to get what she wanted regardless – with the possible exception of those sons of hers. She didn't seem the type to be tortured by remorse, worried, depressed or to feel victimized ...

The more he thought about it the more puzzled he became. He would certainly have described her as someone unaccustomed to losing. Maybe that was why she'd done it – because she'd feared she'd be convicted and couldn't bear to lose. Amos shook his head to clear it, no, that didn't ring true either. She was a fighter, she'd have fought.

Early the next day, Amos collected Jack's paper at the shop and wandered up the lane with Napoleon to tell him the news.

'Perhaps she found out that Richard had no lover after all and couldn't stand the guilt,' Jack ventured, lamely. Then he brightened. 'I know! That tribal chief in South Africa – the one who threatened to get her sons – maybe he put a curse on her and sent her a voodoo symbol in prison. Isn't that how they do it? The victim sees the symbol, knows what it means and instantly drops dead through fear.' Jack was off. 'Then of course he'd have to remove the symbol, in case the authorities guessed, but it could have been something quite ordinary – just as long as it had the association with his curse. I mean when we hear of people being given bloody chicken feathers or hen's teeth or something we think it's really weird but to a native in an African village those would be everyday objects. It's likely to have been a common or garden item.'

'Yes, thanks, Jack – I think we can leave that to the police don't you. I'm much more interested in how it leaves the situation at Marston.'

He followed Jack into the kitchen at the Hathaway Arms. Jack put the kettle on.

'Hey! I've just had a thought. You know that thing you usually see in wills about "… if my heir predeceases me or survives me for less than twenty-eight days …" then some other things happen with the property?' Jack nodded. 'Well if Richard and Sonia Phillips both died within twenty-eight days of Gervaise then Marston may well go to someone else!' He slapped Jack on the back. 'Our troubles may be over! Who cares why she did it.'

'I hate to tell you this, Amos, and I know time means nothing to you, but I'm afraid Gervaise died a lot longer than twenty-eight days ago.' Jack looked sadly at his friend who subsided into a chair, deflated.

What confounded Amos as much as anything was that Sonia must have known much of the evidence against her was circumstantial, which meant she had some chance of getting off. So what on earth had she stood to gain by taking her own life? He stiffened. 'The only thing I see it changing is she can no longer be tried for the crime – as far as I know anyway. If that's so, then it means she won't ever be convicted for it.'

'I give in,' Jack admitted. 'I can't for the life of me think why she of all people would commit suicide but I'm perfectly happy to accept that she has and be grateful for small mercies. She sure as hell won't be missed around here.'

Jack poured the tea and handed a large mug to Amos. Now he looked serious. 'Don't think this is my idea because it isn't, but Marion has decided' – he glanced balefully at Amos – '… and you know what that means.'

Amos sat down. 'Go on.'

'Today's Tuesday, the day Marion goes to see her mum. What are you doing say about four o'clock? No, better make it three-thirty, because we need to set up and then hide before they get there. The school bus gets back about quarter to four doesn't it?'

'Set what up? What are you planning to do?'

'Will you help is all I want to know?'

'I haven't heard what you intend to do yet. I might not—'

'Oh, get on with you. We'll see you in Featherbed Lane about three-thirty.' Jack walked away leaving Amos staring after him, perplexed and not a little dubious.

Busy with council meetings for the rest of the morning, Amos had no time to give the Featherbed Lane Mob, as he'd taken to calling them, any more thought. He still didn't know what harebrained scheme Jack and Marion had cooked up between them except that they'd gone to some lengths to keep it from him, presumably because they expected him to disagree with it. The way they saw it, they'd got him into this problem – having his reputation threatened because he'd tried to help them – so it was up to them to get him out. Which meant he'd have to go along with it if only to make sure it didn't backfire.

He met Jack at the end of the lane where it joined the road to the pub. 'Where's Marion?'

'Oh, gone off to see her mother as usual.'

Amos guessed the rest. 'I don't like it, Jack; you're going to use Marion as a stalking horse, aren't you? I don't like it at all. What if it goes wrong somehow, Marion could get hurt.'

'We knew you'd say that which is why we didn't tell you. Don't worry, I'll be in the back of the car under a heap of jumble – so even if they do get into the car, they've got me to contend with.'

'I still don't like it, Jack – all sorts of things could go wrong.

You didn't hear the language last time and I only caught a small part of it.'

'Don't worry. Marion's heard a great deal worse than that in her career as a landlady. The difference here is, unlike poor Lucy, she won't be taken by surprise, and she won't be alone. Now come on, you've an important job to do.'

The boys arrived about half past four, from the Marston direction – they were still getting 'fuelled up' there then. The Phillipses must have the stuff stock-piled. He started to record the sound; they were talking about Marion and how they were going to stop her.

At 4.45 exactly, Marion turned off the main Stratford Road into Featherbed Lane in her blue car. Amos saw the lights about a mile away. He was sitting on the leeward side of the blackthorn hedge near the bottom of the lane – as close to the spot where Lucy had been ambushed as he could remember – on the fishing stool Jack had thoughtfully provided. A camcorder rested in his lap.

The boys had seen the car; of course, they didn't know if it was Marion or not, but from what Amos could hear they were going to give whoever it was the same treatment. They flattened themselves against the hedge, cursing the thorns as troopers might; Amos could easily have touched one of them if he'd leaned forward.

Marion drove steadily down the road, not fast, not slow – just as she normally would. They'd agreed not to use the mobile phones to communicate with one another after four o'clock for fear they'd be heard, so Amos couldn't tell them the boys were in position in the hedge.

Amos could imagine how nervous she and Jack must be feeling. It was all very well dreaming up these brave schemes over a few glasses of wine, but when it came to carrying them out ... More than once he'd had the jelly knees, the emptiness in the pit of the stomach and that nagging voice which asks you what on earth you think you're doing in this situation anyway. Oh yes, he knew how they felt, much the same as he did. Not that he feared the boys – only what might happen to them, accidentally – it was so tempting.

As the car drew alongside, Amos timed the switching on of the camera to coincide with the attack, so as to hide the whirr. One of them moved quickly to the far side of the car but two stayed on this side. Jack also had a microphone in the car so the sound should be OK.

What on earth…? Marion was winding her window down! 'What do you want, boys?' she was asking, as nice as anything. Then it came. He saw Marion blush scarlet and start to drive on, but one boy dashed in front of the car so she'd have had to mow him over. Go on, Marion, go on … drive! Amos willed her.

Then one opened the back door. As Amos stood up, holding the camera over the hedge to catch the action, the boy shot backwards out of the car, his neck jerking on his shoulders and landed hard on the tarmac. Scrambling to his feet he made off after the other two who had spotted Amos a second earlier.

Amos half ran, half hopped across the furrows to the field gate, stool in one hand, camera in the other. Jack and Marion were standing in the road, throwing the old clothes Jack had dislodged back into the car.

'So are you going to give this to the police, or do you want me to?' Amos asked, proffering the camera.

'Oh no.' Jack said, snatching it from him. 'We've got a much better use for it than that.'

*

The letter lay obtrusively on the kitchen table. Not that it took up much room but it certainly got in the way, obstructed his every move in the little cottage. Wherever he went there it was, looming up at him, daring him to approach. At one stage he even put the newspaper on top so he wouldn't have to keep seeing the envelope – then thought better of it, afraid lest the letter be swept away with the paper to light the fire or clean up after Napoleon. He daren't lose such a precious object. He just didn't want to open it – yet.

Because then he'd have to decide what to do next. What was he going to do if it simply had 'Return to Sender' scrawled across the inside? Where could he look then? Should he photocopy his enquiry and send it to every aid agency in the world? Yes, maybe. Worse, what if it was from Crispin, or on his behalf, saying please don't bother him he was far too busy doing important things on a world scale. Or even worse, '… we regret to inform you that Mr Thimbleby died twenty years ago in an earthquake/uprising/civil war … we didn't realize he had any family.'

Lindsay popped in that evening. 'You still haven't opened your letter, Amos,' she sang up the stairs. As if he could forget! With any luck she'd grow tired of her one-way conversation in a minute and go away. 'It's got a very pretty stamp.'

Now the letter had taken on an altogether different imperative. He came reluctantly down the stairs. Susan, Lindsay's daughter, collected stamps. Lindsay handed him the letter-knife for the operation, as a theatre sister would pass a scalpel to a surgeon. She'd bought it for him one Christmas, tired of the ruined stamps which resulted from the way he ripped open his letters – those he did open that is.

Out fell the envelope he had addressed to Crispin – unopened. Amos caught it before it hit the floor and put it down carefully on the table, smoothing it out as he did so. Lindsay tactfully left the room.

Oh well, he'd been foolish to expect to strike gold on the first foray, he knew that, but he was disappointed all the same. What an anti-climax after he'd built up his hopes. He'd put so much faith in something coming of this initiative … still, never mind. Then he noticed he'd screwed the accompanying letter he held in his left hand into a tight ball – unaware he'd been clenching his fist.

It came from a lady. She explained that their records were incomplete and only dated from two years ago when they'd managed to computerize them – before that they were often lost or burnt or both. They didn't have any mention of a Crispin Thimbleby on the computer now, she was sorry she couldn't help.

When Amos considered it, he wasn't surprised. Many of their helpers might be people running away from something at home. Maybe aid agencies filled the gap the French Foreign Legion had left – somewhere to run to, something honourable to do when all else failed. If so, those people would avoid being on any database. He could picture Crispin standing beside the lady while she typed the letter – helping fugitives flee their persecutors being all in a day's work for her. She wasn't about to tell some old buzzard in England where Crispin was if he didn't want her to.

Had he really expected to find him just like that – with one letter? If it were that easy the authorities would have found him by now. Mind you he hadn't known Interpol were looking for Crispin when he'd written that letter.

The downside was he may have alerted Crispin before he could get to him, explain how much he was needed. This abortive attempt may have done more harm than good – forcing Crispin into even deeper cover.

To stand any chance at all, someone was going to have to go out there, ask around, ingratiate themselves with the locals, befriend those who know all. Where the hell was Terry when he needed him?

If he couldn't find Crispin quickly, what then? He refused to contemplate it. Richard had been weak and Sonia grasping, but they'd begotten real evil when they'd had Colin and Paul. He felt sure Sonia had curbed the worst of their excesses by appealing to their greed – that they could succeed beyond even their wildest dreams if they just toned it down in the short term whilst the relevant paperwork, licences, acceptances were acquired. Amos thought that likely – she'd been shrewd – would have realized it was better not to stir things up unnecessarily.

What were the police going to do? Raid the premises for illegal substances? Unlikely these days, they'd got too much else on. Even if they did it would be ages before the case went to court and for what – a fine, community service, Ha! Here was one community who'd be far better off without their services.

And what if the villagers did set out to thwart the rock concert? That worried him too; the villagers were normal, decent folk, with jobs and families – and scruples. It would be a bloodbath.

He knew he wouldn't sleep again, for if he did he'd have to face Gervaise. Gervaise mocking him for failing. Gervaise goading him for his inaction. He could still feel him clutching his arm despairingly and dreaded having to gaze again into those reproachful sockets.

*

Saturday night was scheduled as Race Night at the Hathaway Arms. Jack had held the event for the first time last year, very successfully, so he'd agreed to hold another, this time for charity.

Because it was in aid of church funds, tonight Jack's bar was graced by the great and the good from the surrounding area as well as his regular customers. Bunting flew from the beams and an atmosphere of gaiety and excitement pervaded the scene. Looking around, Amos reckoned most of Weston Hathaway were there. Alan and Madge were beside him with their three grown-up sons. In front of them sat Lindsay, Ted and Betty – over to the left he spotted the Sandersons and their next door neighbours and then the reverend and the church wardens.

The 'races' came as films in sealed cannisters. Jack had rigged a large white screen at one end of the long room and the projector at the other, volunteering to be chief technician.

At eight o'clock sharp, Jack rang his bell and dimmed the lights. Together with the usual whirring and crackling, upside down numbers sped down the screen then the sound track cut in and a familiar local scene exploded onto the screen in sombre colours. Not Stratford Racecourse but Featherbed Lane on a late autumn afternoon.

A few shouts of 'typical', and 'get the right film, Jack', quickly subsided as the appalling language followed by the identity of the boys and their ambush of Marion unfolded in seconds. The expressions on Diane Sanderson's face ranged from slight irritation at the race not coming on, through indifference to what she evidently took to be an irrelevant piece of home movie, to shock as she recognized her son, turning to abject horror as she realized what the boys had done; the whole culminating in shame and flight. Other people's reactions followed the same trajectory, except theirs altered course at shock to go through outrage instead of horror. The Sandersons stumbled their way out of the bar, unable to look their neighbours in the eye.

Yet for Amos the victory felt hollow. As though he and Jack had taken their revenge on the innocents whilst failing to catch the real culprits – the Phillips brothers.

*

He was sure John's stairs were getting longer and steeper by the week. The bannister trembled as Amos strained its fixings in levering himself up the incline, plastering with mud the edge of each linoleumed tread as he went.

John was engaged in printing something off his new computer. He retrieved it from the tray with the flourish of one who has accomplished a technical feat he'd thought forever beyond him. 'Here we are, it's not much, but at least it's something – if we've got the right Terry Finn of course. Do you realize how many there are? Guess, go on, guess.'

'How should I know – two dozen?'

'Well it depends if you count Ireland – which I daren't – but even without that, in the rest of Britain, there are five thousand and some odd.'

'Yes but they won't all be his sort of age and not many will be card-carrying vicars.'

'Very true. Which is why I'm, what do they say, cautiously optimistic.' John read from the paper. '"Born Terence Finn …"' he broke off to look at Amos over the top of his reading glasses. 'That narrows it a bit in that there's no middle name, but it still leaves hundreds to go through I'm afraid. Anyway …' He returned to the piece of paper. '"On tenth February 1948 in Bristol."' John stopped again to seek confirmation. 'That would be about right, wouldn't it – puts him in his late fifties?' Amos nodded, wondering where this was going.

John resumed: ' "To a Florence Courtenay and a John Finn." Interesting, they weren't married. The man I use checked the local school registers and so on from about 1953 onwards. He found young Terence registered at the infants' school in Downend.' Amos looked puzzled. 'Part of Bristol. But then no trace of him in that area after 1956.'

'The only other interesting thing is a death certificate for Florence Courtenay dated July 1956, so maybe she died and the father took the boy to live with his mother or her mother or some other relative. We're trying to trace her family to give us a clue where else to look.'

'But how does that help us find him now – or know who he is?'

'Patience, Amos, patience. With so many Terence Finns we have to start right back there to make sure we've got the right one – we may find we have to follow the trail of dozens more born around that time before we find the right one in today's census information or today's register of ordained clergy. Then we can find his marriage certificate, assuming he is married to the woman he calls his wife, and then we can try and find her; hopefully she'll know where he is. Of course if we find a death certificate – then we'll know our Terence Finn isn't who he claims to be.'

Amos frowned.

'If you want it done quicker go to the police, they can open all sorts of doors we can't.'

'No, I don't want to make it any worse for him if he's already in trouble.'

She was lying in wait as he came out of John's office, talking to Napoleon, fondling his ears through the open window of the Land Rover. She smiled as she saw Amos approach.

Of all people he'd have wanted to bump into in a Stratford street she would have been high up on the list at any time. Right now the encounter was as welcome as it was surprising. She was the one person who could answer his questions about the ruins. She must know what Gervaise had been after ... and that had to have a bearing on what had happened since, it had to.

'Is there somewhere we can talk? Have you got time?' she asked.

They walked in silence, as comfortably as old friends might, Amos wondering what had brought her here. The town was bustling with traffic, overburdened shoppers bustled past them, barging their bags against any impediment, harassed looks on their faces, anxious hands guarding purses against pickpockets.

He was relieved to make the comparative haven of the Mason's back parlour in one piece. Still she smiled but said nothing. Waiting to be served he looked back at her from the bar. She had about her the confident air of someone used to command, but in an understated way. He'd seen compassion and curiosity from her and guessed she must have determination, too, to have risen so high in her career. He wondered idly what Mr Mainwaring did – retired stockbroker, or fellow academic? Amos returned with the drinks.

'I went to Weston Hathaway to find you, but the lady at the pub said you'd come into Stratford to see your solicitor.'

Then it wasn't an accidental meeting; even better.

'So I came on to Stratford and saw your Land Rover parked down there. I remembered it from that day at the church.' She grinned and, before Amos could register his amazement at a woman who could remember licence numbers, added: 'There aren't too many festooned like yours,' referring to the red binder twine he kept handy on the front bumper.

'I heard about the Phillips family being left the estate and then about Richard's death of course ... and now Sonia's suicide.' She sighed as if to suggest it was all too much for her. Amos knew how she felt. 'Funny, I wouldn't have said she was the type. Not that I knew her that well. I'm sure she resented me being there.'

Amos realized Annabelle was one of the few people who might know what Gervaise had thought of the Phillipses, particularly Sonia. His actions over the will would suggest it had been a great deal. 'Was Lord Marston fond of Sonia Phillips, would you say?'

'Odd, isn't it?' she mused out loud. 'He never mentioned her, but I always had the impression he disliked her. He would stop talking if she came into the room, leave her out of any conversation we might be having – that kind of thing.' She smiled. 'But then, he seemed to dislike most people.'

'So tell me, how did Lord Marston come across you in the first place?'

'Because no one else specializes in architectural archaeology. Plus of course Oxford was his Alma Mater.'

In the back of Amos's mind another question had formed and then gone; he couldn't recall it now. Instead he asked: 'So why did you do it? Why take the job?'

'Oh that's easy – money. He offered my college a very large sum which he paid up-front. The college desperately needed the funds, so I had to do it.' Fortunate he paid in advance, Amos thought to himself. It was almost as if Gervaise had known.

She looked down at her hands – clean, lined, with short fingernails. 'I never actually finished the work I was doing at the Old Manor.'

'Because Gervaise died. You said he wasn't clear on exactly what he wanted anyway, so, I supposed it was finished with him gone. Why did you think he wanted you to work out the original design?'

'As you can imagine I gave that considerable thought, seeing how unusual his request was. Frankly I was disinclined to believe him, kept thinking he had some ulterior purpose – some quite different aim he neglected to tell me.'

Amos thought back to the day of the funeral. 'But you said he'd been excited when you told him you'd located the Great Hall?' For some reason he didn't tell her what the gardener had said. He didn't know why; maybe he was reluctant to put ideas into her head before he'd heard her views.

'You've got a good memory. Yes, he was excited. Maybe that's where whatever it is was buried?' She'd used the word 'buried' for the first time. Did she mean physically?

'So you do think something was buried there?'

'I don't know, but I admit I'm curious. What was so interesting about those ruins that a distinguished elderly gentleman like Lord Marston should suddenly go to all that trouble?'

She looked at her hands again, twisting the intricate band on her wedding finger, 'I never found out ... neither did I finish documenting what I had done. So now you will understand why I want to go back.'

'You do know Richard was murdered in those ruins don't you?' He watched her reaction closely.

'Yes, or at least the newspaper said something of the sort.' Amos had forgotten Richard's death had made the nationals, albeit only a column inch or two.

'And you still want to go back there?' Her answering look was such as to make his query seem a rhetorical question even though he hadn't devised it as such.

He'd pried too much, he didn't want to upset this lovely lady who was making his day with her presence. 'Sorry we've digressed. Yes, I see you'd like to go back – if only to complete the commission you've been paid for.' She smiled, looking relieved that he'd understood. 'Forgive me, but what's that got to do with me?'

'Because I heard you could fix anything.' Amos groaned then frowned in incomprehension, so she continued. 'I'd phoned several times to no avail, so the other day I called at the Manor – still no reply.' She looked sheepish. 'I drove back down past the Old Manor and well ... I couldn't resist making a start. I didn't think the Phillipses could really object. But I'd only been there a short while when one of them came down on a motorbike, he must have watched me leave the house. I tried to explain but he wasn't interested – said I was trespassing and I wasn't to come back.' She leaned forward eagerly. 'Can you help?'

'I doubt it sweetheart, they're not very fond of me either.' He watched her face lose its light, move from up-curves to down-curves with one movement.

'I'll gladly try for you though, I just don't want you getting your hopes up that's all.' Her face regained its equanimity. Thank goodness for that and anyway, why should they refuse; he was sure if he talked to them, man to man, they could come to some accommodation. After all it was a generous proposition – a search by the country's expert, to find whatever might or might not be worth finding, with all expenses already paid; and obviously anything she might find would be their property. No one in their right mind would pass up a deal like that. In fact he couldn't see why they'd turned her down anyway – maybe she just hadn't asked them the right way, pointed out the advantages. He sat up straight, squaring his shoulders, raising his chin; the more he thought about it the more he thought he, Amos Cotswold, could succeed in persuading the Phillipses.

'That's unusual.' His gaze had followed hers to the wedding ring she kept twisting.

'Yes, isn't it – it's African. I grew up there, my father worked for one of the big coffee companies in Kenya.'

Maybe it was the second pint of beer this early in the day, or the congenial female company, or both, but something triggered the floodgates. 'You don't have any friends in aid agencies out there, I suppose?'

Taken aback but obviously sensitive to his change of mood she said: 'Er, possibly, why?'

So he told her. Told her about the excesses of the Phillips brothers, about Tom Dutton's horse, about the rave and how Tom Dutton had died and the livestock had been petrified. But then she'd witnessed the scene at the graveyard for herself so she knew what they were like. 'I think they've tricked their way into the estate.'

She looked shocked, horribly shocked, turned quite white.

'Are you all right? Can I get you anything?'

She rallied. 'No, no. It's just such an awful story.'

Amos waited in silence while she recovered completely. 'I don't suppose Gervaise ever said anything to you that might...?'

She shook her head. 'Not that I recall.' Then, more forcefully: 'But surely, if the will is wrong ...or a forgery, you should challenge it.' Now she sounded as keyed up about it all as he was, bless her.

'Ah well, you see,' he subsided back into his seat. 'The only person who can really do that is the rightful heir – Gervaise's son, Crispin Thimbleby, the current Lord Marston. Last seen in these parts forty years ago and last heard of by the friend of a friend over twenty years ago. We can't find him Annabelle! Can you help us? We think he's probably in Africa – if he's still alive that is.'

Now very subdued she said: 'Let me think about it Amos, I'll certainly try.'

In a hurry to retrieve her car before the parking wardens discovered its time had expired, she said as they parted: 'I don't know if it's relevant, Amos, but I think there's been some recent plastering in the Old Manor.'

CHAPTER ELEVEN

Amos tied Napoleon to a tree in the Bancroft Gardens and continued a few paces upwind to a bench.

Why had she come? Did she really think he could get the Phillipses to agree to her continuing her work? They'd be bound to want to know exactly what she was looking for.

What was it about her he couldn't quite catch hold of, couldn't express – even to himself? Something hidden. Yet she seemed natural enough. She was a very intelligent, well-travelled lady – he'd wager highly respected in her own circles – who needed him to intercede for her. Whereas in other circumstances the vice-chancellor or other worthy administrator might have written to the landowners requesting permission, she'd had the sense to realize that that approach would not achieve the required result with the Phillips brothers. Who knows, perhaps the college had already tried the usual channels and failed. And besides, maybe this had more to do with professional secrecy than Amos had appreciated; he'd heard of fierce rivalry between archaeologists – which sometimes led to theft, even murder. Perhaps she was reluctant to broadcast her interest in the Old Manor.

More importantly he wondered if she could help find Crispin – she'd looked thoughtful when he'd asked. But then she'd said it. That bit about recent plastering. An afterthought left hanging there, subtly disturbing. He didn't want to follow that train of thought, but he was being pulled along it, every bit as strongly as Napoleon had just dragged him down Sheep Street. What other explanation could there be?

She'd said: 'If it's relevant …' straight after they'd been talking about Crispin. What else could she have meant? Only she hadn't wanted to think that either, or be alarmist – she was far too level-headed for that. So she'd said it lightly, as a parting shot – something for him to consider along with everything else.

Amos's imagination began to somersault. Theirs was a powerful motive – the most powerful of all; Crispin was the true heir. Is that what had happened to his friend? Was that the explanation for the magnetic hold the ruins had had on the young Crispin – they were to be his final resting place? Was this another instance of the vindictiveness of those Marston ghosts?

Amos shuddered as a boy ran past him on the towpath, stopping to pat Napoleon – a boy about twelve years old.

The only other person he knew who might possess more knowledge than she realized was Betty Summers. He'd no one else to ask. He went straight round to Lindsay's. 'Is Betty still here?'

Betty appeared from out back, wiping her hands on her apron. 'Aye I'm still here, Amos Cotswold. I'm not going back to the Manor while them's there.'

'I wanted to ask you something. About what you said when we heard about Richard's death.'

Betty sat down beside him and eased her foot out of her slipper, bending stiffly to rub her toes, as though she'd been standing up too long.

'You mentioned the old legend. You said, "anyone who gains improper ownership of the manor will meet with certain disaster".'

'Aye, and now she's gone too. Just shows you, don't it?'

'But they were likely to say that about any big estate surely?'

'I don't know nothing about no other estate. All I knows is my old ma always told us kids that.' She looked mischievously at Amos out of the corner of her eye. 'And I don't think it were because we'd shown signs of mounting no take-over bid at the Manor neither!'

'I suppose by our time it had just become a local saying, lost its original purpose.'

'Oh I don't know about that – it's coming true now right enough. Pity them Phillips parents didn't say it to their children!' She attended to her toes again. 'It were all to do with that Baron who were murdered in the Old Manor.'

Although Amos had always known the outline of the tale – just recently he was finding its parallels with recent events uncanny.

'You'll have to ask Reverend Whittaker if you wants to know more.'

Amos wished he'd thought to ask Annabelle Mainwaring about the legend – wondered if she'd researched it in an attempt to piece together the history of the Old Manor. The more he thought about it the more he thought it likely.

'Lord Marston mentioned the legend,' Betty suddenly volunteered.

Amos leaned forward and put his hand on her arm encouragingly. 'When Betty? Can you remember when he mentioned it? What did he say exactly?'

'Oh I remember when right enough. It were the day the archaeologist lady told him she'd found out where the Great Hall used to be. He were that excited, I told you, started scratching around for his boots wanting to go down there straight away. Kept muttering something like, "… now I know where he died. And now we know where the Great Hall is." something like that.'

Amos scratched his head, he'd missed something. 'So how do you know he was referring to the old legend?'

'Well it's obvious, isn't it? I mean he couldn't be referring to anyone else who'd died in the Old Manor, could he? It ain't been lived in since the eleven hundreds.'

Amos went cold – deathly cold. Had Crispin died a long time ago? Was that what Gervaise had been trying to tell him? Was it Crispin's body he'd been searching for? And how had he known? It might explain the will though … if he'd known Crispin was dead. But why hadn't he told anyone? Why had he not called in the police to dig over the old ruins? Why hadn't there been a proper funeral? Had Gervaise been somehow complicit in Crispin's murder? Enough! This was ludicrous.

But was this the answer to why Gervaise had recruited Annabelle Mainwaring to help him, because he'd been looking for Crispin – thought he was buried in the Old Manor? There seemed only one way to find out.

The morning was crisp and bright, the frost sharp enough to break down the turned sods on the furrows. Pheasants picked their dainty paths across the fields like Victorian ladies out for a walk in the wrong shoes. Amos could smell snow in the air.

Telling himself he was only carrying out Annabelle's request – see if he could persuade the Phillipses to let her continue at the ruins – he steered the Land Rover into the front drive of Marston Manor and alighted. Everywhere seemed unnaturally quiet, only a flock of lapwings and a jackdaw or two disturbed the silence. The place looked deserted. Since Richard had gone and the rest of the staff had either been fired or fled, no one had even cleared the leaves from the drive or given the hedges near the house their winter trim. A sad atmosphere of decay and neglect permeated the grounds, it was much more than the annual cycle of birth, bloom and death … followed by rebirth. This was a more profound change – and it was going in only one direction.

Amos pulled the bell and listened to it ring throughout the house – down in those deserted servants' quarters. It didn't surprise him when no one answered. He tried again – still nothing. He should try round the back, but dreaded being cornered, the stable block was a cul de sac.

He gave the bell one more tug for good measure, but instead of waiting any longer, he climbed back into his Land Rover and crawled down the drive. Compelled to enact the second part of his plan, he chose to appear extremely submissive whilst in full view of the house ... like a cat creeping with exaggerated slowness from its antagonist. That way they might just ignore him.

In the past twenty-four, mostly sleepless hours, he'd moved from the strong belief he'd previously held without any proof, that Crispin must be alive – to the unavoidable conviction that the reason Crispin hadn't been seen was that the Phillipses had indeed murdered him – possibly even before Gervaise's death. Driving past the ruins without parking at the lych gate and walking back was not an option.

Even in the sunlight, the north side of the ruins cast a foreboding shadow. Its craggy topstones, crenellated by age, leered over him, ready to spring should he falter. Amos shook himself. 'Keep away you, Marston ghosts,' he whispered. 'I'll have none of you today.' Nevertheless he felt an awesome loneliness – as if on a bleak moor hundreds of miles from civilization, rather than a couple of miles outside Weston Hathaway. As if he'd stepped into an alien world.

He refused to hurry, refused to indulge those old childish fears that if he failed to round the corner into the sun within a count of ten, the hidden rock demons would drag him down into their lair. His mobile phone rang, heralding the welcome return of shrill reality.

'You were spotted driving up to Marston Manor. What are you doing up there?' Jack sounded peeved.

'Well I'm sitting on a boulder in the ruins of the Old Manor, nattering to a friend. Oh-o ...' Amos heard the Harley before he saw it. Then he heard the second. A younger man might have had an evens chance of sprinting back to the Land Rover but the odds on Amos achieving it were a hundred to one against and he knew it. 'I've got company – don't hang up, Jack.'

Amos slipped the phone back in his pocket and stood up. He looked quickly around him, no sign of any activity where he was standing. Damn, if only he'd had time to penetrate further he might have discovered where they'd put Crispin's body. If only she'd been more specific about that new plastering.

'What the fuck are you doing on our property, old man?' Colin and Paul Phillips drove their bikes straight into the ruins braking at Amos's feet, showering him with dust and stones. If the ghosts hadn't moved him he was damned sure these two pieces of excrement weren't going to. Nonetheless he hoped fervently that Jack was this moment phoning the police.

Paul was riding his motorbike in a circle around Amos while Colin sat astride his machine, hissing. Amos could see his mother in him, that same reptilian cast to the complexion and the features. For a change they both seemed relatively in charge of themselves, relatively inside their own skins.

'What do you want then, old man? We might as well hear it before we decide what to do with you.' It was Colin who spoke.

'I came to make you a proposition.' At least he had been, but not now. He was no longer prepared to plead Annabelle's case for her, she wouldn't be safe out here. It would look as though he'd failed – again. Then let it, for once he wanted to fail. He must have been mad to countenance the idea in the first place. He'd been carried away with bravado, machismo, had enjoyed being asked to help. He hadn't wanted to disappoint her or look like some weak-kneed apology for a man. So he'd puffed himself up and said he'd do it. Well he wouldn't. The sooner everyone realized how truly dangerous these people were, the better.

'But since you're obviously in no mood to be spoken to civilly – I'll bid you good day, gentlemen.' The hardest part was in turning his back on them to walk away.

'Not so fast old man,' Paul Phillips almost ran over his toes.

Amos stopped. 'What are you doing snooping around out here eh? Shacked up with that woman we caught out here yesterday, are you?'

'Hey, Paul, this is the geezer who was spying on us that Sunday afternoon and brought the coppers down on us. And the one who tried to stop the concert.' He turned to Amos. 'So, answer my brother. What are you doing out here?' He looked around him, as if in search of a clue to the answer.

'I have every right to be here.' Amos said it automatically, just came out with it. He'd known his impetuousness would land him in trouble, well he'd done it now. The curious thing was they didn't dispute his remark – or even question it.

'What's this proposition then?' Why had his rights led them back to that? Unless they thought he was trying to blackmail them? How could he get them to tell him what he wanted to know – what they'd done with Crispin. He knew it was dangerous, but in a moment of bravery he realized whatever they said would be heard by Jack at the other end, even if something happened to him. He had to provoke them into telling him.

Colin began to crack the joints in each of his fingers, slowly, one by one. Then he reached into his jacket and produced a gauntlet, studded with vicious spikes across the knuckles. Amos had to keep the conversation going.

'You know the police are looking for Lord Marston's son, don't you?' He needn't tell them why yet, let them surmise what they liked. That's what he wanted to see – their assumption.

Paul muttered something like, 'I told you so', and shot an angry, worried glance at Colin. Turning to Amos he said: 'Because of the title.'

'Exactly, and if they can't find him' – Amos left a significant pause – 'then they have to look for the next in line.' Paul looked worried, Amos played on it. 'With a title like that which goes back hundreds of years there's bound to be a male heir somewhere, they'll trace the family until they find him.' He stopped again and looked pointedly at Paul, wishing the police would hurry up. Amos wanted to add *Because you can't inherit the title no matter how many murders you commit* but for once allowed discretion to win.

'Then, of course, when they find his son or the next in line, whoever it is will probably want to claim the estate too, after all what use is a title if ...' Too late Amos realized it might not have been wise to tell them this.

'He doesn't have no son,' Colin snapped.

'Oh?' Amos said, hardly daring to breathe. 'What have you done with him then?'

They all heard it, the familiar wail of a police siren. Jack had not only rung them, he'd obviously moved heaven and earth to get past their answering machine and achieve swift action. But the timing was unfortunate. Amos had openly held the Phillips brothers responsible for Crispin's disappearance, without learning any more from them. Now they would be gunning for him, to stop him spreading any more of his theories.

They revved the bikes and started to move as Jack's car sped round the corner, several hundred yards ahead of the police jeep. So much for believing that even if he'd copped it, Jack could have testified at their trial, having heard what they'd said through his mobile. Jack had obviously decided rescue took priority over corroboration or witness.

'You haven't heard the last of this, old man. If you so much as put one foot on our property again we'll blow you away. You savvy!' Colin yelled above the noise of the bike and the siren. 'We've killed men for less.' He wheeled the bike and collecting his outrider, sped back the way he'd come. Anyone overhearing him would simply have assumed Colin Phillips had employed that last remark to embroider his threat, a boast to frighten – we've done it before, so it makes no difference to us, we'll kill without blinking. Except now, Amos believed McKenna.

As his legs gave way beneath him, Amos stumbled to the nearest rock and sat down.

Jack came running across the grass at full tilt, closely followed by a single young policeman. Jack dashed round the corner but slowed as he saw Amos.

The policeman turned to Jack: 'If you think he's all right, sir, I'll go on up to the house, speak to the owners.'

Amos spat on the ground. 'Ha! If I were you, young man, I'd get some reinforcements before you go up there. They won't be complaining to your superior officer about your not apprehending their trespasser if that's what you're worried about! They prefer to do that themselves.'

Unacquainted with Amos, the young constable looked uncomfortable; evidently unsure whether or not to take his advice. The last thing Amos wanted was for this young whippersnapper to get hurt because of something Amos had done. It sounded absurd in rural Warwickshire, but Amos no longer doubted what the Phillips brothers were capable of.

'Why don't you ring your Sergeant Wilson – tell him what I've said. But meanwhile I'd stay away from that house if I were you.'

Feeling stronger, Amos rose. 'Guess we'd better get off their land before they come after us again.' They set off towards Jack's car.

'The minute I heard Colin I got onto the police. Luckily that young constable was at Alan's for the renewal of his gun licence, otherwise I don't know what we'd have done.' As he said it, Amos could see Alan pulling up by the church with his largest son.

'It's all right,' Jack yelled across to Alan. 'He's OK.' Then to Amos, 'We didn't know how many we'd need.'

'Thanks, Jack. I don't mind telling you I was bloody scared. They don't have the same rules as normal people – in fact I don't think they know any rules. The more I think about it, the more I reckon she took them to South Africa to get them out of trouble in the first place.'

Jack dropped Amos back at his Land Rover. Alan had already departed again with a smile and a wave. The constable finished his telephone conversation and drove over to them. 'Thank you, councillor. The sergeant says you're right, I'm to get on with my next call. Good morning to you both.'

They watched the constable drive off. 'So are you going to tell me now?' Jack had clearly been containing himself.

Amos climbed into his seat still feeling shaky. Jack leaned with his back against the bonnet, one leg crossed over the other, arms folded.

'Marion told you Annabelle Mainwaring was here yesterday, looking for me?'

Jack nodded impatiently.

'She wants to finish her work here. She's curious to know what it was Gervaise had really been looking for. So she wanted me to talk to the Phillipses for her – explain it would be a good deal for them if they let her continue ...' Amos trailed off as he registered Jack's pitying expression.

'Turns out her dad was in the coffee business in Kenya – she grew up there so I told her how I was trying to find Crispin and asked if she could maybe use her contacts out there to help. Well, immediately after that and just as we were parting she said a strange thing.' Jack was motionless. 'She said: "... if it's relevant, I think there's been some recent plastering in the Old Manor".'

Jack let out his breath in a long slow whistle. 'You think it's Crispin. That they've killed him and ... why don't you go to the police?'

'And say what? I think there's a body buried in the ruins of the Old Manor? I need to find some evidence. And that's why they've plastered him in, so digging won't find him.'

Amos bent his head to negotiate the low beam into the Reverend Whittaker's sitting-room cum study and made himself useful coaxing some life into the fire.

'I came to ask what you know about the old legend, Reverend. I can't help but see a parallel with what's going on here now.'

'You mean that the will was witnessed by the priest who daren't get close enough to detect it wasn't the Baron in the bed for fear of the plague. Doesn't reflect very well on my profession does it? I assure you I haven't witnessed any wills, forged or otherwise.'

'That's not the parallel I had in mind, reverend. I just wondered if you knew any more about those times at Marston? It might help us be prepared if this whole thing is following some sort of pre-ordained pattern – the forged will, the brothers from hell and ... well, I don't want to say this, but what if Gervaise's son did come back after his father's death, and they killed him and plastered him into the Old Manor? Is that what occurred before? What happened when the son came back from the Crusades? Did he come back?'

'They've done what, did you say?' The reverend was on his feet, understandably horrified at the thought of Crispin's murder – or was it more than that?

'I don't know about your parallels, Amos, but the rest of that story tells how the two brothers, like many criminals before and since I daresay, boasted in the tavern about what they'd done and, on their way home, fell out and one brother killed the other.' Amos opened his mouth to speak but the reverend motioned to him to wait. 'That wasn't the end of it. The survivor was tried for the murder of his brother. In those days if you pleaded guilty you were hanged and your estates forfeited. If you pleaded "not guilty" but were then found to be guilty, your end became vastly more gruesome – you were pressed to death – but the estates could be kept by your family. So the surviving brother was walled up – in the Great Hall at Marston.'

They came back that night. Only this time they had different faces. Gervaise was still there together with several older ones.

But now Amos discovered what happens when the rock demons get you; the Phillips brothers had tied him down so he couldn't run. He couldn't get away before the count of ten ended. Then a repulsive reptile opened up its mouth and swallowed Amos down into a vast dripping cave where other morons were doing unspeakable things in the darkness. He thought he saw....

Then it all changed, everywhere was white. The spectres were barely visible against the transparent background. The light was ethereal, shifting, but light always light – and soundless.

Amos opened his eyes. Through the open curtains he could see them floating past the window to settle on the world below and reflect their icy whiteness back into his bedroom. Beyond them the white was tinged with grey as it mixed with the inky blackness of the night sky. It was snowing.

Half past four. He might as well get up. An early morning was vastly preferable to returning to the nightmare of his sleep – and he knew he would return to it if he dared close his eyes again. He peered through the old bottle glass windows of his bedroom which produced their own distortions. He had no idea how long it had been snowing, but a few hours judging by the drift he could see nestled against the step. Just as well he'd woken, he'd better go and check the ewes, make sure they hadn't slipped over in it or been buried in it; carrying lambs they'd never right themselves again.

He put on an extra layer or two – his only concession to the difference between the seasons – extra socks, an extra shirt and his thick jacket. Downstairs he grabbed a torch and a broom, told Napoleon to stay put, and opened the door gently, careful to let little of the drift tumble into the house. The Land Rover fired first time.

Cutting his engine as he came down the hill so as not to wake the Tregorrans if he could help it, he parked at the edge of the field and stood on the bottom rung of the gate, to count. It was easy when they were all sitting down. All present, all the right way up, good.

It was a beautiful night, the whole panoply of the heavens papered the ceiling above him and he could see his breath form tiny icicles as it hit the air. Wide awake now, he glanced towards the tow path and felt compelled to walk as far as the church. He wasn't going onto Marston land, he'd be very careful to stick to the path. And he certainly wasn't going anywhere near those ruins tonight – not after that dream. So where was the harm?

In ten minutes he reached the lych gate. Even with its icy mantle the graveyard looked as dark and threatening as it had all those years ago on nights when he and Crispin had dared one another to stand there alone in the dark. He wasn't going on that side, the side which faced the ruins; he'd just keep to the path and sit in the porch for a few minutes – get his breath back.

As he reached the porch he saw them, leading out of the church and round the corner – footprints in the snow.

CHAPTER TWELVE

An animal? With shoes on? Of course – Terry! How singularly appropriate he should turn up now. What was it Amos himself had said to Betty: 'There have been as many sightings of Terry as there have of the abominable snowman.' Wasn't it here he always appeared, like some wandering ghost inescapably drawn to the graveyard? But where had he gone?

If only the church hadn't been locked these days, he'd have had a quick way of finding out. Just in case, Amos crunched across the porch floor and, not expecting it to give, turned the ancient ring latch in the studded oak door. It opened. Perhaps the reverend had forgotten to lock it after him, or Terry had borrowed a key and decided to shelter inside when the snow started.

The door creaked on its hinges as Amos pushed it forwards and went in. The starlight reflected huge shadows on the nave floor, unnerving shadows. They had never connected electricity to the old church, making do with candles for evening services; he cursed himself for leaving his torch behind in the Land Rover.

As Amos's eyes grew accustomed to the dark, he headed for the hagioscope in the south wall – the side which had no windows because it had been walled up when the adjoining chapel had been destroyed during the Reformation. The hagioscope had permitted the celebrant at the chapel altar to co-ordinate his actions with the ceremony taking place at the high altar; its secret was that because of its slant it functioned almost as a horizontal periscope. Amos could use it now to see round the corner where the footsteps had gone, see if he could spot Terry.

He walked through the church until he was positioned directly in front of the gap in the wall, he had to stoop slightly to see through it – men had been shorter in those days. There in the darkest part of the graveyard, with the falling snow doing its best to alleviate the blackness, stood a figure with its back to him, carrying a torch. He was dressed in jeans and a large duffle coat with his collar turned up against the weather. Then the figure turned and smiled at him, knowing it was being watched.

There in the graveyard, with the snow rapidly whitening his hair and shoulders, stood the spectre Amos had dreaded seeing. The one face he had never wanted to recognize in those awful dreams, the face he daren't look for because it would have meant.... The man he'd spent every waking hour for weeks hoping to find. Amos wiped his eyes and looked again – but the apparition had gone. Its footprints already obliterated with fresh flakes.

Seconds later a whirlwind of white burst through the door and bounded up the aisle. 'I worked out how you did it! All those years ago, how you saw I'd got the torch!' He enveloped Amos in a snow-covered bear hug – warm, solid and real. Amos couldn't speak for shock. He'd been so sure he'd come back and then so sure he'd been killed. He staggered into the nearest pew, gripping the end-post lest his knees give way, whilst he stared at the man and grinned inanely; unable to comprehend, afraid to believe.

Crispin was actually an inch or two taller than Terry but yes, much the same build. His once blond hair had greyed with age, his tanned skin was deeply lined and his eyes wore a permanent squint against the sun – otherwise he hadn't changed at all.

The years fell away as though they'd never intervened. Once

Amos recovered, words tumbled from both of them like an avalanche, their syllables cascading over one another in their eagerness to communicate. Questions swirled in eddies, gaining momentum as they fought to escape but with no chance of completion.

'I never thought I'd see....'

'When did you come back, Amos?'

'How long's it...?'

'How come you've let them...?'

'You know she killed...?'

'Was it you that day...?'

'How long have you been back? Why didn't you tell me? And what the hell are you doing here at this hour?' Amos felt his relief – at finally finding Crispin, alive, and returned to Marston – changing to anger as his anxiety melted away.

'I could ask you the same question. Look, I've got a flask of coffee and some sandwiches stashed behind the font. I'll go and get them, then we can start at the beginning.' Crispin set off down the church with his torch and soon reappeared bearing an altar candle, matches and a bag of sustenance.

'You'd planned a siege then,' Amos commented.

Crispin poured coffee into the two plastic cups which he'd unscrewed from the top of the flask. 'I've been here quite a bit, yes. I saw you the day of my father's funeral.'

Amos remembered the figure at Holy Trinity. 'It was you! At the far side of the churchyard in Stratford. I thought it was another chap I know. So exactly how long have you been back?'

'Since the day he died.'

'You mean you were actually here?'

'I saw you look out of Father's bedroom window a few hours before he passed away.'

'It was you by the gate! You stopped to talk to my pig.' Amos was kicking himself for not realizing. 'No wonder you looked familiar.'

'At the time I didn't know he was yours – I should have guessed though.'

'Near the end your father asked the doctor to send for me, but the Phillips woman ignored him. By the time the doctor realized and called me himself it was too late; Gervaise kept trying to tell me something but I couldn't understand him. I think he wanted me to find you. It's time you explained why you stayed away, particularly after his death? And why you've been loitering like some local tramp.'

Crispin took his coffee and a sandwich and settled himself at the opposite end of the pew behind Amos. Propping his back against the peeling musty wall, he stretched his legs out along the seat. 'After Mother died I couldn't get away fast enough. I hated Father as you know – that never changed. But he didn't want me to go. Goodness knows why, he'd never had any time for me. In fact I always thought he preferred you to me. You stood up to him more, he admired that.'

'That's rubbish. I saw you stand up to him – more than once. What about that time over the runaway orphan boy? If that wasn't standing up to Gervaise ... And anyway he wasn't my father, it's always easier then.'

'Yes, but I only did it if I had to – for someone else. I couldn't be bothered on my own account, never could see the point. I'm sure that's the real reason he sent me away to Winchester, wanted me out of his sight.' Amos could hear the bitterness, the disappointment of an unloved child, still there fifty years on. He was sure Crispin had been sent to Winchester to be well educated – but to Crispin it was one more illustration of his father's rejection.

'Anyway, I joined an outfit called UAA who were an aid agency based in Africa.'

'Yes I know, I met a friend of yours.' Crispin swung his feet off the bench and leaned forward, interested. 'Week or two ago, man named Ian McKenna.'

'McKenna, McKenna ... ah yes, I remember, Sudan. It must be twenty-five years ago! How extraordinary, what a small world.'

'Not really no. He came here specially – because of you.'

'What?'

'Oh yes, it seems our Mr McKenna took his camp following a bit too far. It made him feel good, boasting about how he knew a member of the aristocracy. He envied you, couldn't understand how you could turn your back on all this and never return.' Amos looked at Crispin who had a puzzled expression on his face. He went on. 'Which would have been OK except he happened to tell a certain Richard Phillips about it.'

Crispin listened spellbound.

'So he came here to visit Richard but instead, and to his amazement, found Richard had acquired your very own estate – and been murdered. He even thought for an hour or so it was an elaborate hoax and then that he could find you and somehow make amends for what he'd done. That's why he came to see me. He's gone back to South Africa now, afraid the Phillipses would kill him as they had some poor unfortunate over there.'

Crispin was quiet, obviously struggling to assimilate this new information. 'So the Phillips family came here deliberately – with the intention of somehow getting their hands on the estate – knowing I probably wouldn't show up?'

'Looks that way, yes.' Amos looked round at his friend. 'And I daresay they might have got away with it if they'd behaved more suitably. After all you'd not been seen for over forty years – lots of people round here weren't aware Gervaise even had a son.' Amos's own view of Crispin's continued absence was evident in his tone.

'What do you mean "might have got away with it". As far as I can see they have. I thought it was Father's way of getting back at me, leaving it to people like that.' Crispin looked down. 'Father considered me unworthy because I showed no interest in my inheritance. Well if it meant being like him, I wanted no part in it. When I said I was going he tried to bribe me to stay. Said if I left he'd write me out of his will, that I wouldn't deserve to inherit the estate.' Crispin raised his eyes up to Amos. 'So you see I wasn't surprised when he kept his promise.'

'But these people are con-men ... murderers Crispin! They killed a man in South Africa and Sonia Phillips was arrested for killing her own husband.'

'I know, I saw her.'

'What?'

'I told the police – well, sort of. I did it anonymously but I would have testified. I knew I had to. I was just afraid they'd blame me for his murder since I was in the vicinity – and I had an obvious motive.'

So that's why the police were being so cagey about their witness. 'What do you mean you saw her?'

'That's what I was trying to tell you earlier. I finally realized how you'd seen me with a torch out there, when we were boys: you'd used the hagioscope. I couldn't resist it when I saw you coming down the track tonight. It reminded me of that night years ago.' Crispin grinned at Amos.

After all the worry since Gervaise's death, Amos was not to be so easily mollified. 'Took you long enough. But what's that got to do with Sonia Phillips?'

'I was in the ruins, the day Richard was killed. I saw him set off in my direction so I whisked out of his way sharpish and hid here until he'd gone. But I was curious, wondered what he was up to – if anything, and as you know there aren't any windows on that side. Thinking about it since, the poor chap probably only wanted some peace and quiet. Anyway, it was then that I rediscovered the hagioscope and sure enough I could see him sitting on a rock just inside the north entrance.'

Crispin paused. 'I couldn't believe it. This woman just walked up behind him carrying a boulder in both hands and hit him hard over the head with it. He hadn't even turned round, must have known it was his wife. They were probably talking.' He looked at Amos. 'As soon as I saw her leave I ran over there to see if I could help but he was already dead. And no, I didn't report it because as I said, I was afraid they'd accuse me of it.'

'So how did you know it was Sonia?'

'I didn't – well, not straight away, I mean. I saw her picture in the paper.'

Crispin was hiding something but Amos had far more pressing questions than that one. Finding Crispin had been only the start, now he had to get him to act. 'So you're telling me you haven't challenged the will because you think it's genuine?'

'Put it this way, nothing about my father would surprise me.'

Disappointment replaced the elation Amos had felt at Crispin's reappearance. He wasn't the only one who'd been looking forward to the heir's return – the hopes of the villagers were pinned on the thirty-ninth baron seizing back what was rightfully his. They saw him as the answer to their prayers – their saviour. Were they to discover he had feet of clay?

'Do you realize the people around here have been desperate to find you? You're the only one who can stop the Phillipses. You must have seen what's been happening, the death, the destruction – now they intend to hold a concert with fifty thousand people attending – and then I expect they'll sell Marston and thousands of houses will swamp our way of life. How can you just sit there and pretend it only affects you? What's happened to you?' Amos stopped for breath but only momentarily.

'We thought you were dead. But I kept faith, I knew you wouldn't ignore your duty, I knew you'd come back. So when you didn't it meant either you'd died some time ago or the Phillipses had murdered you. Don't look at me like that – that's what I thought. Instead of which you were here all along, skulking around with a defeatist attitude.' Amos subsided. 'By the way, did you know Interpol are looking for you?'

'Yes. That's another reason why I've been keeping out of the way.'

'What do they want you for?' Amos was beginning to feel uneasy. He hadn't seen this man for over forty years.

Crispin viewed him with his kindly eyes and mild manner. 'Don't worry Amos, I haven't hurt anybody. Truth is I don't know. All I can think is I was an obvious suspect when Richard was killed – and their interest increased when they couldn't find me.'

'But there must have been entry records – when you came back into Britain. Or don't they bother any more, what with the European Union, open trade and all that?'

'I came in on a friend's boat from Trieste, he's a good man who's helped us a lot in Africa but if the authorities got hold of him ... I've got a place about thirty miles south of here, had it some years. I often used to pop back when I could hitch a lift. But the day Father died was the first time I'd been back to Marston since I left, so you'll understand what I mean when I say I felt drawn ... for the first time ever. Of course I'd no idea *you* were back; I don't know why, but I thought you'd probably done something like me. I couldn't believe it when I saw you at the window. I'd have recognized you anywhere – you look just like your old man, Squire Cotswold, or at least how I remember him.' Crispin craned his neck to study Amos. 'Except you're not so clean. You always were an untidy beggar!'

Amos had held off asking the obvious until now but he had to know. Had Crispin thought so little of his childhood friend he couldn't be bothered to look him up? 'So why didn't you come and see me – after Gervaise was dead? Anyone around here could've told you where to find me.'

Crispin looked down at his feet. 'Believe me, Amos, I really wanted to talk to you.' The warmth in his words was certainly convincing. 'But I was afraid.' Amos looked incredulous.

'I thought you'd make me do something about the estate.'

'I should bloody well think so.'

Crispin held up his hand. 'Then when I heard these Phillips people had inherited it, I obviously realized they wouldn't be pleased to see me and ... because you'd been there when he died, I thought you must be pretty friendly with them.' Amos tried to speak, but Crispin put his hand on his arm and left it there. 'No, hear me out. Then as things got worse and I fervently hoped you weren't part of it all, Richard was murdered and I was afraid I'd be blamed. So it wasn't until ... well, anyway that's the truth.' He sat up, releasing Amos's arm.

Amos was silent for a minute, while he weighed up how he might have felt had he been in the same situation and had the same information as Crispin. He came to the conclusion he, too, might have held back from his old friend – especially if he'd suspected he was involved with the enemy.

'So what changed your mind?'

Crispin walked along the pew he'd been sitting in and came to sit next to Amos. 'Annabelle – the conversation you had with her. I actually hadn't realized you were looking for me, thought you would have given me up for dead by now. So yes, I was going to come and see you tomorrow but then you walked in here.'

'Ah, so you know the professor.' Was there no end to the night's surprises?

'Annabelle's my wife, Amos.'

Amos stared at him, opened his mouth to say something, then closed it again when no sound came out. He ran his hand through his hair, opened his mouth again, cleared his throat and then Crispin spoke.

'And now you want to know why she didn't say so?' Amos could only look at him in astonishment. 'For the same reason. We weren't sure whose side you were on; forty years is a long time.'

Amos was dumbfounded. Why hadn't it occurred to him? Why should it have?

'Did Gervaise know who she was?'

'We don't think so – she never told him and he certainly never enquired about her background or her family.'

'One hell of a coincidence though.' Now it was Amos's turn to assimilate this new shower of information, analyse its effect, go back over his conversations with her. 'So ...' No, that couldn't have been, he tried again. 'So ... the day of the funeral when she was sitting in the porch ...' Amos could vividly recall his first meeting with Annabelle Mainwaring. Of her sitting there, waiting, holding the single red rose for Gervaise ... and how she wouldn't go into the church to keep warm and had seemed concerned in case the funeral party did. 'You were in here all the time.'

'I tolled the bell. After all he wasn't just my Father, he was a Marston. It was only fitting that his passing be properly marked.' There it was, that chink, that link to history, that morsel of chivalry which Amos had to nurture.

'I still don't understand.' He didn't know what to say, felt deflated, used. 'You knew she was coming to see me.' He stopped. 'You knew she'd been up to see the Phillips brothers, tried to get back into the ruins – didn't you realize how dangerous that was? Is she here, with you?' Amos twisted around in his seat expecting Annabelle to emerge from the shadows at any moment.

'No, no, she's not.'

'And that's how you knew the woman you saw was Sonia Phillips – you described her to Annabelle who of course would have known instantly.' Amos was piecing it together, slowly.

He moved along the bench, away from Crispin, and turned to face him. 'Why have you been sneaking about in the church here? How did you get in anyway?'

'I knew there was a key which always hung inside the old stable door. It has probably been hanging there since they built the new manor – it was never used. So the other week, when I found the church locked I remembered and went up and fetched it.'

Amos waited, sipped his coffee and kept his eyes on his friend. Finally Crispin said: 'I couldn't sleep. What brings you here?'

'I was checking the sheep ... you know, the snow.' Amos faltered, what had brought him here? What had made him walk the mile in the snow from Alan's to here. Had he known he wouldn't get back to sleep? Still, he could have sat by his nice warm fire with a glass of Scotch and caught up on his council papers. He could hardly admit to Crispin that Gervaise kept haunting him. He shivered involuntarily.

'Why are we sitting in here like this, freezing to death? I'm going home – are you coming?'

Crispin moved to let Amos out of the pew. 'Amos, could we meet tomorrow?' He looked at his watch and smiled. 'Today now. Only I can't afford to be seen around here – especially now I know they've killed before.'

'How did you get here?' Amos had only just thought to ask.

'Oh, along the towpath from Stratford, left my car at the other end.' Crispin returned to his planning. 'Look, why don't you come over to my place when you're ready.' He scribbled down an address in Woodstock. 'We've got lots of talking to do.' He touched Amos's arm. 'I'm frightened, Amos – of lots of things. I need your help.'

Amos stood beside him while Crispin locked the church. Outside in the crisp sharp air he still couldn't believe he'd found him – but here he was after all those years, and still the same old Crispin by the looks of it. They parted at the lych gate.

Amos trudged back to his truck with his head down against the blizzard but otherwise heedless of the weather. At least Crispin was back. All Amos had to do now was persuade him to fight for what was his. 'I'm doing my best, Gervaise,' he muttered. The weight may have shifted but the onus still bore down on him.

Aware that news of Crispin's return would be widespread in the time it took to say, 'Hallelujah', for Crispin's safety, Amos realized he'd better not mention their meeting to anyone for the time being.

Crispin hadn't pursued the subject of what Gervaise had been trying to tell Amos – any more than he himself had pursued it when his sisters had told him something similar of his own father. Neither of them were under any illusions on that score. To others it would have seemed sad and somehow wrong – Amos inside with Gervaise, and Crispin outside alone. But Amos understood. He had avoided his own father's deathbed because he'd still craved consolation, a rapprochement even at that late date, and had feared – no, known – he wasn't going to get it. He guessed Crispin had felt the same. Why volunteer to be kicked in the teeth yet again.

Amos stopped on the path and lifted his head. The snow stung his face as he thought of all those sightings he'd had. And what Betty had said about seeing someone who looked a lot like Terry leaving the ruins before Sonia got there. Amos now knew that too had been Crispin.

Speaking of Terry – where the devil had he got to? Jack had thought Terry was Crispin, solely because Terry was new to the area, about the right age, and kept quiet about his past. What if the Phillipses had come to the same conclusion? What if that new plastering was for Terry? That would explain why the Phillipses thought they'd got their man. What had Colin Phillips said to him only yesterday? 'He doesn't have no son.' Amos leaned against the fence, horrified.

He'd been so relieved when he'd discovered Crispin was indeed alive – not only for Crispin's sake, but also because it was terrifying to think that the Phillipses, people living so close to Weston Hathaway, could murder so readily. Was that really why Terry had disappeared? Surely not. What was the matter with him lately? He was getting like Jack, always thinking the worst instead of hoping for the best. There'd be some perfectly logical explanation for Terry's absence.

The snow had largely melted away by the afternoon so he took the old route down from Stratford to Woodstock, through the Cotswolds.

Annabelle opened the door. If Amos had been apprehensive at meeting her after last night's extraordinary revelations, he needn't have been. She welcomed him with a bear-hug similar to that which Crispin had given him, took his hand and pulled him into an elegant entrance hall. We're through here – in the kitchen. She showed him into a vast high-ceilinged room at the back of the house where Crispin stood waiting.

'I'm so glad it's out in the open now, I hated not telling you,' she said. 'But we didn't understand what was going on and when Crispin saw you up in Lord Marston's room with the Phillipses running the household – and then the Phillipses inherited – well, we naturally thought you were well in with them. That's why I came to ask for your help to persuade them to let me carry on my work. But then when you quizzed me about Sonia Phillips I began to realize how little you knew her – either that or you were playing some elaborate game, which seemed unlike you.'

Crispin laughed. 'Oh, I wouldn't say that, Anna, he's as crafty as a desert fox, you watch him!'

'Then when you said they weren't keen on you and proceeded to tell me all the disasters they'd caused and asked if I could help you find Crispin....'

'When Anna came home and told me that, I knew you hadn't changed.'

Annabelle produced tea and biscuits and they sat round the table.

'I tried to help you, you know. I went up to Marston yesterday morning.'

Annabelle and Crispin both leaned forward. 'And?'

'Well, as with you, they didn't answer my knock so I too went on down to the ruins and unfortunately they came after me. It was a good thing my friend Jack had seen me heading in that direction. He had to call the police.'

'But what were you doing in the ruins?'

'Because of your last words to me. Immediately after I'd asked if you could use your old contacts to help me find Crispin, you said you thought there'd been "some recent plastering done in the Old Manor". Those were your very words I think. I couldn't get them out of my head – I thought they'd killed Crispin and walled him up in the Old Manor.'

Annabelle held her head in her hands. 'Oh dear, I didn't mean …' She looked up. 'You see "recent" to me means anything less than a hundred years old. I was referring to some plastering I noticed when Gervaise was still alive. It just wasn't ancient, that's all I know.'

'Terry was very much alive some time after Gervaise died so it can't be him then. Mind you they could still have killed him.'

'Who's Terry?' Crispin asked.

'Terry Finn. He arrived in the village the day Gervaise died. He's about our age and never talked about his past. So some folk thought he might be you … which is why it's possible the Phillipses have killed him. Colin Phillips said to me yesterday: "Gervaise doesn't have no son".'

There was a silence no one seemed to want to break. Crispin got up and paced the room. 'So now some other poor bastard has been killed in my place. I should never have come back.'

'That wouldn't have made any difference, they don't know you have, remember.' Amos went on. 'It seems to me this business of the ruins all started when Gervaise, quite out of character, commissioned an expert to determine the lay-out of the original manor.' For confirmation Amos looked at Crispin who merely shrugged.

Crispin took Annabelle's hand. 'I know I waver on this,

believe me I find it as confusing as you do, Amos, but well, we knew he was getting on a bit. We guessed he was still alive because we thought someone might have been enquiring for me if he weren't, as indeed they have been recently. I wasn't sure if I ought to come back but in any case you don't walk back in after forty years without seeing how the land lies. I'd been pondering it for a while.'

Annabelle took up the story. 'So when Lord Marston wrote to the college, it seemed a heaven-sent opportunity to get to know him and understand how things stood.' She looked at Amos. 'I'm sorry I was a little less than straight when you asked me before why I'd taken the commission but you'll understand now – I couldn't tell you that without revealing Crispin's presence. But I was telling the truth when I said Gervaise hadn't been clear about what he was really looking for. He didn't confide that in me. Nor did he ever mention his son – not once. Crispin forbade me to tell Lord Marston who I was because he thought his father would say he'd come crawling back to watch him die. Crispin was only prepared to return if his father appeared to want him.'

Same as me Amos thought, just the same. That craving to be loved – or even needed – by one's father, even if it's only on his deathbed.

'But he was excited when you located the Great Hall.' Amos muttered then jumped out of his seat. 'Christmas, why have I been so slow. It was Gervaise who'd been plastering! One of the under-gardeners told me he'd carried some tools and a heavy bag and big container of water down to the ruins for Gervaise and when he was told to go and fetch the tools back the container was empty and so was the bag.'

'Did he bury something? What was in the bag?' asked Crispin.

'It could have been plaster, couldn't it? That would explain why the bag and the jerry can were empty when the lad went to fetch them back.'

'But my father never did anything like that in his life – well, not when I knew him at any rate.'

Amos turned to Annabelle. 'Did you mention this recent plastering to Gervaise?'

'No, it was quite a small area, very small in the scheme of things, so you shouldn't worry, Amos, it wasn't body-sized. It was pretty dirty. I spotted it, but it would have been much less obvious to an untrained eye.'

'Truth is, Amos, there's something damned important about those ruins for Father to have taken such an unprecedented interest in them. And yes, I believe whatever it is belongs to me.' Another chink in that armour Amos thought. 'I've been back a few times – when I've thought I wouldn't run into any Phillipses.'

'So that's why you've been spending so much time there – even in the middle of the night, with just a torch mind, not an arc light! And that's why you needed Annabelle's help there.' Amos arched his eyebrows at Crispin.

'All right, I know. I didn't want to admit it to you because I know what you're like. You think I should go marching in there don't you? You think I should go and stake my claim. Well I'm not so sure – and until I am....'

Crispin got up and fetched a wine bottle and three glasses. 'Yes, all right, even after all these years I feel a sort of pull towards the place. I can't describe it – maybe it's because I grew up there, it could even be because it still holds memories of my mother, I don't know. I find myself going there – to be close to it.'

'I think that's perfectly understandable, I wouldn't expect you to feel clear about it – you'd have been back long ago else. Yes, I have an ulterior motive – I care about the estate, and the people who worked there, and the people in Weston Hathaway – and yes, we need you to do your duty. Call it pressure if you like.' Amos looked at the bottle. 'Are you going to open that some time soon?'

Amos understood very well about the pull – he'd experienced

it several times himself lately, last night for instance – and he had far less justification than Crispin for feeling that way. The ghosts wouldn't leave him, an outsider, alone. He dreaded to think what hold they must be exerting over Crispin.

'Annabelle, did Gervaise ever talk to you about the history of the Old Manor, the legend as the locals call it? I imagine you researched it anyway to give you some clues?'

'Lord Marston told me how the estate had been wrested from that early Baron, but that was about all and of course Crispin told me the legend. There's nothing written down anywhere though – not that I could find anyway.'

'Well, don't think me quite barking but there are certain parallels with what's been happening lately. The locals have always quoted a saying that anyone taking over the manor who wasn't the rightful heir would, well basically, come to an unfortunate end. We've had Richard's death and now Sonia's. Then there's the parallel of the "brothers". It was two brothers whom the Baron employed who murdered him – and forged his will,' Amos explained.

Amos was surprised when, far from considering him mad, Crispin too had been pondering his family history. 'The thing I've never understood is, are the Thimbleby Marstons, my family, descended from the original Baron … or from the family who took over? And I'm not sure I want to know.'

'At the least we've got to find out what this plastering was about, particularly if it was done by Gervaise.' Amos turned to Annabelle. 'Could you draw us a diagram, so we can find it quickly?'

'It's in what was the Great Hall – which actually isn't where you might think because it's in the middle of the building. I can take you straight to it.'

Amos and Crispin looked at one another. 'It's too dangerous, Anna. Amos and I will go. Just the two of us. Tomorrow night.'

CHAPTER THIRTEEN

Had he properly considered their expedition he might have questioned their chances of uncovering the mystery in pitch darkness and without being able to make much noise – versus the daylight sorties others had already made, including Crispin himself. But he refused to consider it – because he needed to encourage Crispin in any and every way he could think of, lead him back to Marston. If that meant midnight marauding on a wild goose chase, so be it.

What Amos daren't admit to himself was that the attraction for Crispin seemed to be solely in the riddle of the ruins. If he solved it – or worse, if he decided there was nothing there to be found – would he go away again?

From what Amos could gather in the conversations he'd had so far with Crispin, he hadn't even seen his father's will. He was so ready to accept that Gervaise had deliberately disinherited him, he wasn't prepared to fight; but he did have this nagging compulsion about the ruins.

Amos had to dig further – find something about the will to attract Crispin's attention. He must expose it as a forgery because he still couldn't believe Gervaise would have left the estate to the Phillipses. He pulled the Land Rover onto the verge as a fresh thought struck him, one he'd never really considered. What if Crispin was right and Gervaise had indeed cut him out of the will. That was certainly possible – Gervaise had not been a man you crossed lightly. But what if he'd then bequeathed the estate to the Red Cross or the Battersea Dog's Home or English Heritage – as people do, and the Phillipses had exploited that fact. Doubtless Sonia had typed the will so she'd know what it had said, then, trusting their faithful friend McKenna that Crispin would be unlikely to resurface, they had hijacked it.

As far as Amos and the villagers were concerned, just about any owner would be preferable to the Phillips brothers. He turned the Land Rover round in the next field entrance and headed back to Weston Hathaway, to where Betty Summers had now been installed – the kitchen of the Hathaway Arms. 'Is Betty about Jack?'

'In the back.' Busy filling the till with change, Jack indicated over his shoulder with his chin. 'And don't go poaching her, Amos, there's a good chap, you've already got her sister.'

Amos propped himself against the work top. 'I wanted to ask you about Gervaise's will again. Did you see the will itself, Betty? I mean, for instance, was the document typed, do you know?'

'The paper were long, like. Longer than papers are usually.'

Amos thought back to the few wills he'd seen in the past and other documents such as the title deeds to property. They too had been written on thick legal paper, foolscap size or larger. It sounded like a will then. He'd just wondered if it might have been something else.

'Who else was there, can you remember?'

'She were, Sonia Phillips, and the estate manager. That were it I think.' Betty recalled. 'That other chappie had gone, I seen him drive off down the track. You remember that, what were he called, flor-ensic is it? Yes, he were a florensic man. You met him afore that, Amos, the day the master sent for you, but then had some urgent business crop up that stopped him seeing you. That florensic chap were there that day an all. You both ended up in my kitchen, drinking tea and kicking your heels. Don't you remember?'

He remembered, it had been the day he'd had a message from the estate manager saying Gervaise wanted to see him. He never had found out what about. It occurred to Amos now, that when he hadn't gone to see Gervaise on his deathbed – or at least not until later – Gervaise had probably thought Amos was paying him back for that previously wasted trip.

Betty was right, Amos had sat in the kitchen eating her fruit cake and drinking tea while he waited. Then the bell had jangled on the board summoning her to Gervaise's study, and a few minutes later she had returned with a young man whose appointment with Gervaise, it seemed, had also been thwarted by some more urgent business. Betty'd been asked to give him a cup of tea before he went and he'd opted for the warm kitchen rather than the impersonal drawing-room.

'He used to help the master with his cases. You had a chat with him while I went to get some more cake.'

'Not for long I didn't – my phone must have rung or something – whatever it was I had to go so, no, I didn't get much chance to talk to him.'

Disappointed he had failed to fathom from Betty's account how the Phillipses might have accomplished their misappropriation, Amos left Betty to her baking. He'd have to think of some other way to get Crispin interested in challenging the will. At the very least Crispin should contact Gervaise's solicitors. Then after tonight he could go away for a time so the Phillipses would pose less of a threat to him. It was only while he insisted on trespassing – no that wasn't right – 'approaching' Marston that he was in such danger.

The Reverend Whittaker was cycling along the road, bicycle clips restraining his trousers, cassock screwed up in the basket in front of him. To supplement the brakes, he extended a leg and dabbed at the pavement with his foot several times to slow himself down before squeaking to rest beside Amos.

'I've been thinking about our chat the other night, Amos, did you get what you wanted?'

'I don't know the answer to that, reverend, since I don't know what I'm looking for exactly.' Amos thought back to that night in the vicarage, remembering what the reverend had said about the surviving brother.

'What I don't understand is why the surviving brother was pressed to death in the Great Hall of the Manor, reverend? Why there?'

'Oh I daresay the Manor was the only building around made of stone, the rest would have been wattle and daub cottages or wooden lodges except for the church of course.'

'Yes, but why the Great Hall? Why not the dungeon – I bet there was one. It couldn't have been very nice for the family, having to live there knowing he was buried in the wall. Gruesome I'd call it.' Then Amos realized. 'Of course, it was done purposely – to punish them all, so they couldn't enjoy their ill-gotten prize! I wonder if his family did keep Marston after that?'

'If it happened at all,' the reverend replied, sceptically.

Ignoring the implication, Amos tried a long shot. 'You don't happen to know what the brothers' surname was, do you?'

'That's a bit like asking me Peeping Tom's surname! Lots of these legends had bits added or changed centuries after they were alleged to have happened. If you want to study medieval history you could do worse than start with the heraldry, the coat of arms. You've seen the Marston Arms many times I'm sure, there are several examples in Marston church.

'For instance, do you realize that some of the coats of arms in the church differ from one another? That wasn't unusual when different generations married into different families and decided to amalgamate their arms, but of course at Marston they might have decided to change the arms for another reason; the executed brother's family, who took over, may have wanted a different version. But there again, if you're going to steal someone's lands and titles you might as well go the whole hog. If their intention was to supplant the Marstons, it doesn't make sense to alter the arms. It'd be an immediate give-away, wouldn't it?

'So, if these usurpers did adopt the Marston Arms as they were, and at some point the true Marstons won back the estates – then the genuine Marstons would have wanted to differentiate themselves from the pretenders but without losing their heritage. After all a coat of arms was like your name and similarly very precious to you.'

'So, you think the Marstons may have won the estate back and then changed the coat of arms?' Amos said.

'It's possible.'

The telephone cut through Amos's thoughts. 'Amos, I hear you've been having more trouble with those buggers at Marston – been rampaging around, holding raves, into drugs, the wife murdered her husband. What on earth's going on over there? Can we help?' It was Marty Singleton, his biker friend.

'It's true, Marty. Trouble is we're pretty sure the Phillipses killed a man in South Africa. They're completely ruthless. That's why I haven't rung you before. They're in a different league.'

'What are the police doing about it?'

'Not a lot. Prevention isn't easy for them these days – all they can do is pick up the pieces afterwards.'

'Isn't there an heir to the estate then? How come these people have got it?'

'Yes there is but he's been away for forty years.' Amos was thinking, quickly. Everything depended on finding an answer tonight – if there was one to be found in the ruins. 'I'm hoping we might get a breakthrough tonight but if not, perhaps we could have a chat ... because I don't know which way to turn.'

'Any time, Amos, any time.'

No give-away footsteps in the snow this time. Amos was both excited – and nervous. So much hung on this escapade for persuading Crispin to stay but, after his taster the other day, Amos feared any fresh encounter with the Phillipses. He felt alternately foolish, chastising himself for behaving like a schoolboy, and foolhardy, realizing they were in all likelihood heading for real trouble.

Avoiding the larger puddles, Amos walked carefully up the path and pushed on the door. It swung open and without thinking he gave a low whistle – a calling signal unused since childhood. It was answered from the front pew, accompanied by a downcast torch beam to light his path. After his conversation with the Reverend Whittaker earlier in the day, Amos was impatient to examine the Marston coats of arms on the windows but realized that would be impossible tonight. Flashing torchlight around the church would be tantamount to a neon sign advertising their presence. He'd never looked closely at all those shield shapes – if as children they'd noticed any differences, he'd forgotten; perhaps their very familiarity had rendered them invisible.

'Our past comes back to haunt us, doesn't it?' Crispin said thoughtfully.

'You've not changed your mind have you – you still want to do this?'

'I see no alternative, Amos.' Crispin turned to look at his friend and smiled warmly. 'I've been wanting to have a better look in those ruins all this time. All I needed was a little moral support – and some physical reinforcement.'

Amos smiled – this from a man who, by McKenna's account, had spent a lifetime running the gauntlet between rebel forces and sundry vagabonds in order to bring emergency supplies to people otherwise doomed. A man whose courage couldn't be questioned when it meant running risks for someone else, but for himself ... that was another story.

'What's our plan then? I think we should go around the back of the church, where you stood the other night, and approach from there – less chance of us being seen from the road that way. Seems silly to expose ourselves unnecessarily.'

'Agreed. So we'll go in by the furthest side and keep walking straight through until we come to the Great Hall.' Crispin brought out the map Annabelle had drawn.

Studying it, Amos said, 'OK, so that takes us past where Annabelle dug, looking for the original walls, along here.' He pointed. 'And down, past the paving, to the old walls in this corner. And that's where she noticed the recent plastering?'

'Yes it is.' Crispin noticed Amos's expression and raised an enquiring eyebrow.

'I'd better tell you now – I think I've jumped to conclusions over that. When I think about it I can't really believe Gervaise had been plastering.'

'I see what you mean. After all, what could he have been doing, being a belated Canute – trying to hold back the tide of the ruins' disintegration? A bit late for that don't you think!'

'There again he could have been trying to stem the tide of Marston's disintegration,' Amos replied shortly.

Crispin gave him an old-fashioned look and put the cups back on the flask. 'Let's go before you talk me out of it.'

They doused the torch, crept out of the church and Amos waited while Crispin locked the door behind them. They turned right, in the path of Crispin's footsteps of two nights ago, and crossed the dark graveyard keeping close together.

If it had been lighter they'd have seen him sooner, but they were almost up to the old boundary marker when they initially sensed rather than saw the figure sitting on it.

Thinking it was Annabelle, Amos cursed softly; he thought she'd accepted her exclusion from this expedition rather calmly for the strong-willed woman she obviously was. Too late, he realized it was a man.

Crispin and Amos stopped in their tracks not twenty feet from the stone. The years regressed like the 'fast backwards' feature on a tape. The darkness became fog, the icy mist hadn't changed – their breath was still balled in front of them; a frame frozen in time from which they'd never moved on. Amos must have jumped visibly.

The figure lowered his hood. 'Amos, I'm sorry, I didn't mean to startle you. You looked so furtive I feared if I called I'd upset something.' It was Terry Finn.

Amos recovered first, hiding his shock in a mild reprimand. 'Any further into the graveyard and I really would have taken you for a spectre this time! What the hell are you doing out here at this time of night ... and where have you been?'

Terry rose from the rock and turned. 'You must be Crispin. Am I glad to see you!'

Crispin stared at Terry. Yes they were similar to look at but by no means *doppelgangers*. Could it be that he felt he was staring at his own alter ego? Judging by Crispin's rigidity anyone could have been forgiven for assuming so. Amos looked at his watch – not yet one o'clock. 'Why don't we go back into the church – we can't talk out here.'

Having steeled themselves, this early set-back, if that's what it was, was disappointing, even irritating, but he couldn't just go and leave Terry sitting there – especially not after what he'd just said. Once back in the church with the heavy door closed behind them, Crispin switched on the torch training its beam on the floor to allow just enough light by which to see one another.

'So where have you been, and what were you doing sitting out there like that? I sometimes think you can't have a home to go to.'

'And why so pleased to see me? Do we know one another?' It was the first time Crispin had spoken since they'd met Terry.

'I'm sorry, Crispin Thimbleby – Terry Finn.' Amos belatedly introduced them. 'Terry's the man I told you about who people thought might be you.'

'And whom you feared had been killed by the Phillipses because of it – yes, I guessed that.'

'Oh goodness, I didn't realize it had come to that.' Terry turned to Amos. 'I still can't explain, except I found myself in an unreal situation and I didn't know why ... or what I was supposed to do about it, so I ...' Terry took a deep breath, swallowed and began again in a lower key. 'I knew some people thought I was Crispin – and of course I knew I wasn't – then I had this growing feeling they thought me an impostor, come to claim the estate. At first I took no notice, thinking Crispin would appear and the problem would go away, but then Richard was killed – and I think some people thought I'd done it. So I wondered if any of my clerical friends in Africa might know where Crispin was.' Terry looked at Amos who nodded in acknowledgement of that conversation.

'To cut a long story short the Mission, who set up this agricultural scheme you're helping me with, they fund a "look see" trip to give people a chance to grasp what they'd be taking on. So I used that to go over to my friends in Kenya and see if I could trace Crispin. You'd said yourself it would be better done by somebody on the ground.'

Amos scratched his head. 'But why didn't you tell me?'

'Ah, that's where it gets complicated.' He looked at both of them. 'That first day I arrived, well I thought I'd seen you somewhere before.'

'That's funny, I did too but I put it down to your being similar to Crispin.'

'Then when I saw the manor and the church, and that old stone, then I knew. But I didn't know why.' He turned to Amos. 'It looked as though the Lord had sent me back here, sent me at this precise time – for a reason. But how could that be, I'd turned my back on Him so how could God be using me?'

He looked at the floor. 'And I didn't know what to make of you all. I knew nothing about you so how was I to know what part I was meant to play. Was I supposed to help you ... or not? I could only trust my own judgement on that.' He looked up. 'Anyway that's about the sum of it.

'So not knowing what to do I thought I'd better try to find Crispin. I knew Amos couldn't go over to Africa and desert the animals – or leave the village to the mercy of the Phillipses, so I thought that's what I was meant to do.' He turned to Amos. 'I'm not sure exactly why I didn't tell you – except I was reluctant to say anything until I'd understood what I was doing here.

'I'd been thousands of miles in search of God knows what in the past – and failed. Just seems I'm meant to spend my life searching. So I decided to say nothing, but I never dreamt you'd worry about me.' He looked genuinely amazed that anyone would ever concern themselves over him.

The last people to do so had been Crispin and Amos. They realized at the same moment. 'You're the boy, aren't you – the boy who ran away from the orphanage?' they chorused. 'The one who was sitting on the marker stone in the fog that day.'

Terry beamed. 'Yes, I was, am. But I'd no idea where that place was or who the people were who'd helped me. Now perhaps you can understand my perplexity when I found myself back here. Why? What was I here for?'

'And now you know?' asked Amos.

'No, but I know whose side I'm on. I learned about you while I was here, and when I heard what Crispin had done over there, well, all I can say is – count me in.'

Amos looked at his watch, 1.30. He took out his mobile phone and handed it to Terry. 'Crispin and I need to go and satisfy ourselves about something in the old ruins. I can't tell you it all now, but things have moved on while you've been away. The Phillipses are ... let's just say we'd rather not run into them.'

'I'll come with you.'

'No.' Amos glanced at Crispin who shook his head; the last thing they wanted was to put anyone else in danger. 'It would be very useful to have a back-up who can call the police if something does go horribly wrong.' It was all Amos could think of to make sure Terry agreed to stay put and not insist on accompanying them to the ruins. But it made Amos feel more comfortable too – and since Terry was already here....

Then they led him up the nave and let him into the secret of the hagioscope like two schoolboys initiating a third. 'You'll be able to watch the ruins from here.'

Amos and Crispin crept out of the church and skirted around the back of it for the second time that night. As they passed the marker stone, Crispin said: 'What do you make of it then, Amos? We all end up in the same place, all inextricably drawn. What is all this about?'

Amos didn't answer. As they approached the ruins he concentrated on negotiating the memorized route in the dark; one false move could mean a sprained ankle or for him a dislocated hip. Higher up in the outer walls, the blackness turned to darkest grey, the looming sightless eyes of the old windows admitting enough starlight by which to navigate. In daylight the realization of their history, the centuries upon centuries of lives they'd sheltered and the waves those lives had left behind, made the ruins eerie. But on a winter's night, with no outside factors to deflect the senses, Amos could smell the roasting ox, hear the clashing swords as the young men practised in the courtyard, follow in the wake of the booted knight, placing his own feet in the same place on the same stone floor seconds afterwards, and pet the man's hound.

Amos felt better being swallowed up in the aura of the past than he did dwelling on his nightmares, both sleeping and waking. Though strangely, out here tonight, actively pursuing their mission, he felt less troubled by the Marston ghosts than he had been while lying in his bed. The mantle of the past helped him ignore his last frightening encounter with the Phillips barbarians – usurpers of the tradition, destroyers of a way of life. And this time he wasn't alone; according to legend he'd be treated favourably – because the man by his side was indeed the true heir.

Together they entered the Great Hall and crept very slowly and very carefully along its eastern wall, shining the torch on the patches of disturbed earth, looking for they knew not what.

'I've been all along here in daylight, no obvious sign but then I had to be so careful, so I could easily have missed something,' Crispin whispered.

They kept going, spanned out like police at the scene of a crime, though woefully short in number, and unsure of what they were searching for. They would have welcomed anything which might give them a clue. As they turned the corner of the old chamber onto the northern side, Amos experienced that familiar shiver. Although everything was in shadow tonight, this part of the ruins still held a special menace.

'The plastering Annabelle saw is supposed to be over in this corner.'

Amos realized why it hadn't been immediately visible, a pile of boulders created a diagonal room divider, partially cutting off that corner. Crispin scanned the old wall with the torch. It was more intact that many others, protected as it was from the elements by outer walls. Between the stones lay rubble and rudimentary infilling, and gaps, then the torchlight picked up a change in texture – and colour. There were other tracts of plastering, or was it painting, both between and across the stone, but nothing like this. Like the entrance to a tiny tomb. An area no more than four inches square had been roughly covered over; as though the space behind had lost the stone which once filled it and someone had decided to use the vacuum it left as a wall-safe. A sealed wall-safe.

'I don't remember this being here when we were lads,' Amos said. 'And we knew just about every square inch of this place.'

'Now you know why I have to find out. If anyone knew the Old Manor it was you and me. How come we missed whatever it was my Father suddenly realized?'

For answer Amos extracted a selection of chisels and a small hammer from the pocket inside his jacket and from another a thick piece of old towel with which to muffle the sound. Crispin held the torch steady. Inexpert masons as they were, to them the plaster was either very old or very new because it crumbled easily. 'Wrong proportions in the mix I'd say,' muttered Amos, using the cloth to clean away the plaster rubble from the entrance to the hole. Then he stepped away from it, and looked expectantly at Crispin.

Crispin shone the torch inside, put his hand in and extracted two large Manila envelopes inside a plastic bag. A crude attempt to protect them from damp? To Amos they didn't look as though they'd been there long. He had a fleeting thought they might be nothing to do with the Marston family at all but the hiding place of some lover's poetry or messages left by a cold war spy.

Crispin gasped. 'It's addressed to me. What the...?'

Struggling with the torch and the envelopes, Crispin replaced one of them just inside the hole and tucked the torch under his arm while he took the first document out of its envelope. Amos rescued the torch and trained it on the paper.

It was a handwritten letter dated three weeks before Gervaise's death. Crispin read it aloud with trembling hands.

> Dear Crispin,
> I write this letter to prevent a miscarriage of justice which recently I have begun to suspect may result from my death. As a precaution I have enclosed a copy of my will with this letter, the original of which is lodged with Harrison, Stokes and Harrison at Lincoln's Inn in London.
>
> My fear is that after my death, knowing of your continued absence – though how she heard of you at all I do not know for it was not from me – my secretary, Sonia Phillips will forge a will which leaves the Marston Estate, the manor, all my investments, in fact everything, to her and her husband Richard, my head

gardener. If you do not appear and challenge that theft then this could be easily accomplished.

I have two choices; I could fire them both now, but as I am an old man they may seek a swift solution to that dilemma. Or I can trust you will return and do your duty after my death. I have decided to trust you.

For many years I have known of your whereabouts – and of your marriage. Wishing to determine your wife's suitability without alerting either of you to my intentions, on discovering her profession, I lit upon the idea of commissioning her to study these ruins. In so doing I was reminded of the old legend and realized the parallel I was envisaging would transpire. When she found the Great Hall I thought it a most appropriate hiding place wherein to inter this precaution … and my last letter to you, my son.

You may wonder why I have not taken my suspicions to the police? One answer is they are only suspicions and hence impossible to substantiate – but should my fears prove founded, perhaps for once I want you to fight for what is rightfully yours. For that reason I have not alerted my solicitors either.

As a fail-safe I feel that even if you do not wake up, Annabelle will find this and do the right thing. You have chosen wisely there – I congratulate you. If indeed she discovers this before my death then maybe so much the better. I leave that and what follows in the hands of God; may He guide your decision.

Believe me,
Yours very truly,
Gervaise Thimbleby-Marston

They both subsided onto the rocks piled behind them, facing the hiding place in the wall, their backs to the room. Amos held the torch on the letter and they re-read it, this time each to himself, slowly and silently.

Choosing the least painful part, finally Crispin said: 'So it was my Father who did the plastering.'

'Yes, and he knew who Annabelle was all along.' Then Amos remembered, that day in the Mason's Arms when they'd been discussing why Gervaise had come to her specifically to do the job; the thought which had flitted across his mind had been that maybe Gervaise had selected the lady – then chosen a job which only she could fulfil. 'Gervaise wasn't interested in the ruins at all. It was a ruse to get to know Annabelle!'

Crispin stared at him incredulously, having difficulty taking it all in. 'You mean there wasn't anything hidden here – no treasure, no archaeological find?'

'I wouldn't say that. Why did you feel so drawn to the place?' Amos didn't add *and why did I*? 'Maybe it was her infectious enthusiasm which made him remember the old legend. Was it that which alerted him to the Phillipses in the first place I wonder? You have to admit there's a similarity!'

Now he knew – this was what Gervaise had been trying to tell him. Gervaise's increasing certainty of the Phillipses intentions had meant he no longer dare leave the finding of the real will to chance. Too frail to travel to London, and knowing Sonia Phillips would overhear any phone call on another extension, when at the last he needed to, he'd been unable to alert his solicitors. Who else could he have trusted who was strong enough to do something about it, but his son's childhood friend. It certainly explained why Gervaise had been so very agitated that last day when he couldn't make Amos understand ... and so very angry when Sonia Phillips had entered the room.

'So what had Richard been looking for?' Crispin still didn't want to consider the real meaning of the letter, he'd rather stick to the surface than plumb the depths.

'As you said before, probably after some peace and quiet poor man. Or he might have remembered seeing the under-gardener either taking or bringing back the things for Gervaise a few weeks before and wondered what he'd been up to.'

They were so absorbed in the letter, so wrapped up in their

own thoughts, their own understandings, their attention so locked into what it meant, that they dropped their guard, forgot to train their senses on survival. By the time they heard a noise and powered up their reflexes – it was too late.

The Phillips brothers leapt from behind them yelling and shooting into the air. The letter fluttered away into the darkness as Crispin and Amos jumped forwards together, away from the onslaught, then turned their backs against the wall, to face the pair who had deposed them and who now stood in their places – atop the heap of stones.

'What did I tell you, old man?' yelled Colin Phillips. 'Don't let me catch you back here, I said. What's so effing important in here, eh?' He pointed the machine-gun into the air and fired for effect, his curiosity outweighing his bloodlust – for the moment. Amos prayed Terry would hear it inside the church and tried not to think about the odds at this hour of Terry having the same luck Jack had had in finding the police so near at hand. And also realized that a hapless night-duty constable would be more of a liability than a help.

'Who's the geezer with him?' Paul asked.

'A friend of mine from Stratford,' Amos said quickly.

Turning slightly Amos caught sight of the second envelope just visible inside the hole he and Crispin had exposed – presumably Gervaise's will. He started to shuffle to his left to block the site with his body before the Phillipses spotted it and went to investigate. Nonchalantly he shifted his weight, drew up his other foot, inched his left foot out again ... too late.

'Keep still, old man!' Colin Phillips loosed a round of machine gun fire to the side of Amos's foot where he'd been about to tread.

There must have been a weakness in that part of the ancient wall unable to withstand the onslaught of lead. Whatever the cause, with a deep rumble and a gurgle of rubble, part of the wall caved in, cascading its load of stone and mortar down beside them in a shower of dust and ancient particles ... along with its macabre burden. Each of them watched transfixed as the trussed skeleton of a man rolled out onto the floor at their feet.

CHAPTER FOURTEEN

Slivers of flesh and clumps of wire-like hair still garnished the torso. Its limbs were unnaturally folded beneath it, like a giant roasting fowl which had been force-fitted into a space no more than three feet square.

While the Phillipses recoiled from this loathsome sight, Amos covered the extra yard needed for him to block the will from view.

'What the f—! I don't like this, Colin.' Paul was trembling all over and the hand holding his gun shook violently. Amos and Crispin looked at one another as Crispin began to edge away.

'You stay where you are!' Colin spotted him but this time refrained from shooting. Maybe he feared another cascade of dead bodies.

'You know who this is, don't you?' Amos asked, indicating the skeleton.

'It wasn't us, we never—' Paul started.

'Shut it.' Colin swung his gun towards his brother who relapsed into a lethal state of snivelling and shaking – irrational with fear and, Amos judged, likely to shoot at the slightest provocation.

'In the twelfth century two brothers murdered the lord of the manor here and forged his will to get their hands on his estates.' Amos paused – a mistake.

'And you shut it old man, you hear?' Colin pointed his gun at

Amos but kept one eye on his brother who had grown even more agitated, hopping from foot to foot and whining.

'I told you, we shouldn't be here. I told you! But no, you're always right. Why do we always have to do what you want?'

Amos looked pointedly at the dead body then at Paul directly. 'The brothers fell out – and one killed the other.' Colin fired at Amos – and, whether by design or not, a bullet hit the wall beside him and ricocheted back towards Paul. Amos kept on. 'It happens you know. When one brother gets greedy.'

Paul had required little prompting. 'You did that on purpose, you want it all, don't you?' He was scrambling backwards across the scree, dislodging boulders, stumbling and cursing, visibly undecided whether to shoot, or try and escape from his brother. Crispin moved smoothly back into the shadows, circling behind him.

One second Paul was perched on a slab, drunkenly waving his gun, first at his brother, then at Amos – even at the trussed corpse, as if he thought it a decoy which would spring to life and fly at him any moment. Then came the sound of trickling stones. The boulder next to him moved. The slab tipped and, flailing his arms in vain to regain his balance, Paul plummeted down into the dark brown depths of the earth. The ground had very literally opened and swallowed him up. Amos's nightmare had come prophetically true – though not for him.

There was nothing they could do – except listen to his screams for what seemed like eternity, or was that their echo? Fifty, sixty, seventy feet, maybe a hundred. No splash – was it so far down they couldn't hear it?

One minute he'd been there in front of them, a foolish, easily led young man, high on drugs, uncomfortable in his brother's skin, ignorant of his own, not knowing which way to turn, besieged by devils, and the next – nothing. A literal void had opened up where a life had been. Amos was stunned. He hadn't liked him but given different circumstances he could have felt sorry for him as he had for Richard after his death. A man was dead, a young life had been wasted, gone in an instant. And for what?

Amos looked for Crispin, frantic lest he too had fallen into the abyss. Then it came, the whispered whistle which signalled Crispin's survival and his obvious desire to retain the distance he'd gained in the diversion. Some diversion.

One remained – and that one had a gun trained on Amos. Colin's demeanour had crystallized into ice. He stood immobile, displaying neither surprise nor sorrow at his brother's demise. Amos thought again how much he resembled his mother – whereas Paul had been more like his father, possessed of a conscience. Colin looked almost pleased – as his mother might after she'd killed his father and for a similar reason. Perhaps he now had one less problem. Then Amos realized why the reptilian smile. The opening up of the ancient pit had provided the perfect repository for another corpse or two – his and Crispin's.

'Before you make any rash decisions, let me tell you the rest of the story.' Colin continued to stare at him. It took all Amos's concentration to keep his tone tempting, hypnotic, while all he could think was: *Any minute could be my last.*

'In those days if you pleaded guilty to a crime you were hanged and your estates were forfeit. But if you pleaded not guilty and were found to be guilty, you were pressed to death but ... your family could keep the estates.' Amos moved his head slowly to look at the trussed corpse. 'That's what happened to him.'

'What's your point, old man?'

'We know you didn't kill your brother, it was an accident but ...'

'They won't find you two neither.' Colin must have cat's eyes, for suddenly he shot over Amos's shoulder into the darkness. 'You come out here where I can see you,' he yelled at Crispin.

'Or your friend gets it.' For good measure he illustrated the last point by a further shot or two around Amos's feet.

'Run, Crispin, run!' Before he'd even said it he knew it was hopeless. Crispin would no more run and leave him, than he would have left Crispin. He emerged from the shadows on the far side of the rocks. He'd been half way to freedom. And now Amos had given away his name; Colin Phillips must surely have picked that up.

'I thought as much,' was all he said, clamping his mouth in an even thinner line and waving Crispin to the edge of the opening in the floor.

They had to play for time. Terry would do something to bring help he knew he would – they just needed to keep Phillips talking. 'Why do you think your mother committed suicide?'

Silence, Amos dared not breathe. He went on, 'Because she loved you.' He'd done it, he'd finally gained Colin's attention. He saw the eyes change, saw the mouth unclamp, saw the fingers fidget on the trigger. Colin moved his weight from one leg to the other. Was he weighing up the words – coming to terms with them?

'You see, she knew if there was a trial they'd examine that will carefully and then it would all come out about the forgery – and you would lose Marston.' He wanted to add *that she had lied and cheated so hard to win for you.* 'So she chose the second option from that old law – the hard death – so that you and your brother could keep the estate.'

He'd said it to find a topic Colin would want to talk about but, having expounded the theory, he realized how near the truth it must be. There was no other explanation for her uncharacteristically sacrificial act. Her weakness had been her sons. By taking her own life the forgery would remain undetected and the sons could inherit the estate. Now they'd finally established Gervaise had not bequeathed Marston to the Phillipses – a possibility which had obscured his thoughts before – now it was obvious. And there was that parallel again. Amos shivered, if only he knew what the end of that legend had been ... or was it better that he didn't?

'And that's exactly what I'm going to do.'

'Colin you're not a stupid man. If we disappear people will come looking for you.' Amos looked towards the pit. 'Even if you do manage to conceal the bodies.' Amos took a breath. 'You don't think we've come here tonight without back-up do you? The police will be here very soon. If you kill us they'll come after you. Believe me.'

'It'll be too late for you by then.'

This was the opening he'd needed. 'But it needn't be too late for you. Give yourself up – plead guilty to your part in the deception.' He looked at Crispin who nodded in understanding – and agreement with the tactic. 'You've no family to be thrown out of their home or their inheritance.' It took a lot for Amos to put it like that – what inheritance! Ha! They were usurpers and deserved to hang. 'Remember the old legend, Colin, plead guilty.'

Colin changed. 'I've heard enough of this.' It had been a mistake to mention the police were on their way; whereas he might have taken his time, now he was in a hurry to finish and be gone. Then they heard them, the unmistakable sounds of powerful motorbikes in the distance – approaching fast. Colin Phillips heard them too. Their noise polluted the night, masking other sounds.

'You ain't the only one with back-up, Mister Toffee-Nose.'

Nose ... that's what Amos could smell. Inured as he was to most noxious smells, he thought he recognized this one, it was fear – the smell of fear – but it wasn't only that. Crispin seemed to have noticed something too, but he wouldn't realize what it was. Amos looked at him, willing him to understand what he was about to do and why.

Abruptly, Amos switched from his conciliatory tone and started shouting as loudly and furiously as he could – as though he were the one holding the gun. 'They'll get you, Colin. If you kill us they'll get you – and wall you up in a prison for the rest of your life.' He looked pointedly at the body. 'How dare you threaten us, hold us at gun point. What do you think you're playing at! They'll get you! Get you!'

Crispin joined in. 'Put that gun down now and get off my land!'

He came barrelling through the north entrance – two hundredweight of black camouflage at the gallop – incensed. His master's shouts had registered a distress signal in his porcine brain. He was being summoned to charge. Phillips was wrong-footed. By the time he realized what was happening it was too late to shoot; as the boar growled and reared Colin Phillips fled through the gap in the wall, and raced across the grass to the security of his friends.

Outside the noise was deafening as the bikers roared up the track at break-neck speed and fanned across the grass followed by Land Rovers, trucks ... With the boar behind him and blinded by the bikes on each flank, Phillips veered into the path of the first Land Rover – its black bodywork festooned with red like a medieval warhorse – and went down. The driver had no choice; the vehicle went straight over him. Napoleon reached him first, sniffed and trotted away triumphant. Colin Phillips was dead.

Marty wheeled his BMW to a stop beside the body. He dismounted and felt the man's pulse then shook his head. He straightened up as Amos hobbled across the grass to him, followed by Crispin. 'I won't say I'm sorry, Amos. Good heavens, man, you look as white as a sheet. Come over here and sit down.'

'Thank God it was you, Marty. He thought it was his pals – so did we!' He turned to Crispin. 'Crispin, this is Marty Singleton, veterinary surgeon, biker and friend indeed. Marty, this is Crispin Thimbleby, Lord Marston – returned.'

It was Amos's Land Rover which had run over Colin Phillips

– ably driven by Terry Finn. Terry had since alighted but was having difficulty walking; one of the bikers stopped to help him. Pulled up behind, were Jack Ashley in his Jeep, and Ted, Lindsay's husband, in his truck; behind them, in the fourth vehicle, came Alan Tregorran and all three of his sons.

Assisted by one of Marty's giants, Terry was half carried across to where Amos and Crispin were trying to make sense of what had happened. Meanwhile Marty was on the phone to the police.

'I'm sorry, Amos, I saw them sneak in after you and I couldn't get the police to answer the phone. So I rang Jack and I rang Alan – since they were nearest,' stuttered Terry in shock.

Closely followed by the Tregorrans, Jack came running up, relief showing in his annoyance. 'What the hell do you think you were doing out here at night – without telling any of us?'

'I couldn't, Jack, I'm sorry. Let me introduce you all to Crispin Thimbleby, the new Lord Marston – the man we've all been waiting for.' All eyes turned to Crispin, while Amos continued. 'He was obviously in great danger if the Phillips brothers caught him so we had to keep his return a secret.' Amos saw Jack's incredulity. 'Don't give me that look, Jack, I knew myself only the day before yesterday!'

Amos looked round. 'Where's Napoleon? I reckon the old boy saved our lives.' Alan found some left over sandwiches with which to encourage him and the pig emerged from the shadows to flop at Amos's feet.

'So how come you and the boys were out here, Marty?'

'It was that phone conversation we had. You said you were expecting a breakthrough tonight ... and you'd told me how rough these people were. I just had this premonition we ought to ride over here.'

'The best part of a hundred miles or more!'

'Well that's why we were a bit late – by the time we'd rounded up the gang and set off. You'll be glad to hear we were very quiet when we got to Weston Hathaway, dismounted and pushed the bikes to your cottage, but you weren't there. Your wagon was but not you. Then we saw Napoleon wandering around looking agitated. That worried us. Then he disappeared at the trot so we went up to the pub and knocked up your friend here,' he indicated Jack.

Jack picked up the story. 'It was a good thing we'd met before is all I can say – otherwise I'd have bolted the doors and stuck my head under the duvet.' Everybody laughed, keen to release some of the tension the evening's events had engendered. 'We were standing in the yard debating what to do – and where you could possibly have gone without the wheels, when Terry rang.'

Terry's colour was seeping back now. 'As I said, I rang Jack and told him I couldn't raise the police – but there was no time to lose. Then I crept up to the ruins to see what I could do but when I heard the guns I thought I'd only make it worse on my own.'

'So you would have. Paul Phillips was crazy, high on something; he'd have fired at anything if he'd heard a sound,' Amos said.

Jack looked around, a worried expression on his face, 'Where is he by the way?'

'He's dead, fell down an old pit in there – it's at least sixty feet deep, probably more.'

Crispin added, 'I'd heard stories about there being a pit here somewhere but I'd never known where.'

Terry went on. 'So I ran back along the track to meet up with Alan and Jack and the next thing I see is your Land Rover turning up the lane from Weston Hathaway.'

Marty continued. 'I don't know why but we thought you might be needing it, Amos, so Guzzler hot-wired it and Odd-job tossed his bike in the back and was bringing it over ... when we met Terry who said he would drive.'

Terry hung his head. 'I thought you'd be dead by the time I'd found help. I thought it was too late. Somehow I felt it was the least I could do – bring your Land Rover.' He shrugged, unable to explain what had obviously been an impulse. He caught his breath in a gulp. 'He came straight at me, I couldn't stop that quickly. I felt the bumps.' Terry sat down on the grass. 'But they did do it, you know.'

'Steal Crispin's land, yes, we know.'

'No, I mean they killed that man in South Africa – in cold blood. After you told me about McKenna and his story I e-mailed my friends over there. It's true and he had fifteen children to support – his own and some of his neighbours. You see he wasn't the first man they'd—'

Amos remembered the will. 'We've left the other envelope in there, and the letter.'

Crispin was on his feet. 'Anybody got a torch?'

'I'll go first, sir, you just show me the way.' The aforementioned Odd-job, six feet ten with hands like hams and tattoos up to his widow's peak, had stepped forward, surprising Amos with his sensitivity. Not, 'would you like some company' or 'let me go for you' ... both of which Crispin would have refused either through habit or form. The man-mountain gave him no choice. Right now it was the last place on earth Amos wanted to go back into.

A flashing blue light on the horizon heralded the arrival of the police. Amos turned to Marty and Alan, Jack, Ted and the Tregorrans – 'I don't know how to thank you all – you've been marvellous – talk about knights errant.'

They all shuffled their feet in embarrassment. 'You've done the same for us in the past Amos ... least we could do.'

The police were considerate, aiming to ascertain only the bare facts – the rest could wait until the morning – then they let everyone go. There were so many witnesses to Colin's fate, all saying the same thing: 'he just threw himself in front of the Land Rover', that Terry was completely absolved of any wrongdoing.

There would be an inquest of course. No one mentioned the loose pig.

Marty and the boys retrieved their machines and set off with Alan who'd offered them all rooms for the night in his holiday cottages, it being out of season. Ted went off home to tell Lindsay the news and Amos drove his own Land Rover back down the track with Crispin beside him and Napoleon in the back. Terry went with Jack. All five piled into Amos's cottage.

While Crispin phoned Annabelle to give her an abridged version of events, Jack found the Scotch bottle and Terry stirred the fire into life.

'The old saying was right then – they did all meet with disaster,' Amos mused to no one in particular. 'One murdered, one committed suicide, two met with horrible accidents.' The Marston ghosts had indeed been malevolent, he'd felt it the night Gervaise had died; at the time he'd attributed it to the strangeness of the day, later he'd put it down to his guilt at not getting to Gervaise earlier.

Now he realized Gervaise hadn't been the only one disturbed when Sonia Phillips had entered his chamber when he lay dying. The spirits too had fluttered in the shrouds of the four-poster, the ghost ship they sailed ready for its cargo. Amos hadn't wanted to admit it but he'd sensed them. He wondered what he'd feel like now, if he went back into that room. Were they finally at peace, could Gervaise lie content at last? He hoped so – for his own sake as much as Gervaise's.

Crispin came off the phone. He too had begun to relax. Amos caught the twinkle in his eye, saw a man thawing with the warmth that came from having a troubled soul soothed – for the first time in forty years. Eschewing the other armchair he pulled a stool up next to Amos's and sat warming his feet in the blaze Terry had enticed.

Jack handed round generous measures of Amos's Scotch and held high his own in a toast. 'To the new Lord Marston, welcome home … and what kept you!' They all laughed and drank.

While they had been waiting for the police to complete their preliminaries, Amos had answered as many of Jack's questions as he could, explaining about Annabelle being Crispin's wife and the documents they had found plastered up in the ruins. But Jack's curiosity remained unsated. 'So how did Sonia Phillips do it – I'm guessing it was mostly her doing?'

CHAPTER FIFTEEN

Amos shot a glance at Crispin. He'd been about to say, *let's have a look at the will then* but was sure Crispin would want to read the will himself rather than make its contents public. 'My guess is it was Sonia Phillips who typed the real will and that gave her the idea. It was a gift which landed in her lap. Gervaise might have made his will decades before she arrived and never wanted to change it.'

'You mean they didn't come here planning to forge the will?' Jack asked.

'Who knows but my guess would be, not necessarily. Yes, they knew about the Marston Estate and the absentee heir. Maybe they just thought they could siphon off the wealth from a senile old man who wouldn't notice.'

'Some hopes – knowing my Father!'

'So how did they find Marston when they were up in the north west was it?' Jack looked to Amos for confirmation. 'There must be lots of places called Marston or something Marston, or Marston something, I can think of three or four myself.'

'Oh that's not difficult, Jack.' Terry had woken up. 'You can do a search on the name on the Land Registry website or various other websites, it wouldn't take long to come up with a shortlist; then all they had to do was drive round and have a look. I'd like to bet, with what they already knew from McKenna, they had it pinpointed first time.'

Jack couldn't restrain himself for long. 'So how did she do it? How come they've had their hands on some of the money at least; were able to fire all the staff; give permission for events to be held – and God knows what else that we don't know about yet. I mean, they may even have sold it for all we know.' Jack realized his mistake the minute he'd said this. 'Oh, Crispin I'm sorry, I didn't mean....'

'Don't worry, Jack. If they've sold it without having legal title then it will soon be unsold.' Crispin sounded just like his father. He turned to Amos. 'Go on, how do you reckon she did it?'

'Well she knew the construction – the layout and the legal language – from typing the real will.' Amos stopped, wondering why Gervaise had written a new will at all not long before his death. Had he wanted to add or delete one or two of the legacies customarily given to staff ... or maybe the estate had changed in some way? Maybe he'd bought or sold some properties? With even Amos's scant knowledge of wills it still seemed unnecessary – weren't codicils designed to cope with small changes? And the estate would be constantly changing in minor ways, surely wills were written to cater for things like that. He frowned, had Gervaise made a major change to his will then?

They were all looking at him, waiting for him to continue. He went on, 'So she knew what it should look like, even down to that phrase about revoking all previous wills I'll bet, and I daresay Gervaise had copious supplies of that foolscap size lawyer's paper lying around.'

'But what about the signatures?'

'Well the only one they had to forge was his, Gervaise's – and she had months in which to practise. Hell, she could even have traced it.'

'Or done it electronically. It's not difficult you know. You just have to take a photograph of the signature and then scan that on to the document say in some light colour – then go over it in ink.' Was there no end to Terry's technical know-how?

'What about the witnesses?' pursued Jack. 'She must have forged Betty's signature because Betty is adamant she only witnessed one document – the one which Gervaise himself signed in person.' This had clearly been the subject of much debate in the Hathaway Arms; Amos suspected the 'Marston Puzzle' had supplanted *The Times* crossword in Jack's routine for the past couple of months.

'Isn't that the whole point of having witnesses anyway – in case there's some doubt about the will? So they can ask the witnesses if they actually saw it signed? Isn't that the main safeguard against something like this happening?' Terry had to be right.

'Yes, you've put your finger on it ... "if there's some doubt". Nobody was challenging that will. Even when our friend McKenna made the connection for us between Marston and the Phillipses no one could be sure the will was a forgery.' Amos turned to Crispin. 'You yourself said nothing your father did would have surprised you. No one here could afford to start a legal action on that flimsy a basis, even though deep down we knew it couldn't be right.' He had the horrible feeling he was trying to justify his own failure to grasp the real situation earlier and act as he should have done.

Amos paused and held up his hand to stop Jack jumping in. 'And to answer your question, Jack – they obviously got some new witnesses. They couldn't use their own family because I don't think you can be a beneficiary and a witness, can you?' Amos gave a hollow laugh at the irony of this. 'They either paid some people who were prepared to lie if necessary – but that would have been risky, left them open to being blackmailed over it later – or, my guess is, they invented the witnesses and banked on the fact no one would challenge the will.' He sipped his drink. 'Sonia Phillips knew that if the case against her for Richard's murder went ahead, the will was bound to be examined ... and it wouldn't stand up to that much scrutiny. Which is why she took her own life, to prevent that happening.'

'But all wills are published anyway, you can send for them,' Terry said, puzzled.

'Yes, according to John Wilkinson, but only after probate is granted,' Amos explained. 'And then, how many people know that you can do that ... and how many of those would actually do it? No, they assumed no one would bother – I mean you've got to have some brass neck to do what they did in the first place.' Nevertheless he felt guilty. Guilty at his own idleness or, at the very least, reticence.

'So how did they get their hands on the money to run the place before probate was granted then? Did he keep a lot of loose cash?'

'That's easy,' Amos said. 'All they'd have to do is make themselves the executors of the will, the trustees if you like. They are the people entrusted with carrying out the wishes of the deceased, and I think I'm right in saying they have various powers to pay people – for instance the funeral expenses and so on – anything which has to be done in the best interests of the beneficiaries. If you think about it that makes sense. Otherwise an estate could go to rack and ruin if probate is delayed.' Amos wished he hadn't said the last bit but no one picked him up on it.

'What I still don't understand is why she murdered Richard,' Terry said.

Jack answered him. 'Oh I think he'd served his purpose. I mean it would have looked even more strange if Gervaise had left the estate just to her, wouldn't it? But then Richard probably got the jitters about it all and she was afraid he'd give the game away. But how come she was so careless as to get caught?'

'Well I saw her from the church. She wouldn't have considered that since there aren't any windows on that side,' Crispin explained.

'And Betty saw her going down there from an upstairs window in the manor,' Amos added. 'I think it was typical of her and her eldest son. They did exactly as they pleased, saw no moral boundaries, recognized no laws ... and woe betide anyone who tried to point them out. They just took what they wanted and assumed they'd get away with it. Sonia Phillips banked on the fact her staff would be too scared of the consequences to report anything suspicious to the police.'

'OK – so what was all that about the doctor writing a note to verify that Gervaise was in sufficient control of his wits to be able to make his will?' Jack asked. Betty had certainly kept the Hathaway Arms Debating Society busy.

Amos shrugged, conscious that Crispin must be increasingly keen to read the will his father had left for him. 'I think it's time we turned in, don't you? You staying here, Crispin?' As Jack opened the front door to let him and Terry out, a hooded figure was coming up the path towards them. They all stiffened – except Napoleon.

The reverend shed his cloak and propped himself against the edge of the table. 'So the story about the brothers and how the surviving one was executed turned out to be true after all – not an embellishment as I'd suspected.'

'You know, I'd always hoped it wasn't true – because now it must mean we Marstons are descended from those brothers. His being executed that way means his family kept the estates, doesn't it?' Now Crispin looked thoroughly miserable – like a man who'd won and lost an estate in one night. 'It means that wretch was my ancestor, not the real Lord Marston.'

'Not necessarily,' said the reverend thoughtfully. He turned to Amos. 'You were asking me the other day if I knew what had happened after that.'

A horrible thought struck Amos, though he didn't voice it. Was the trussed skeleton really that of the true heir? Had the family meted out to him the same punishment their father had received?

'All I was going to say was you could pursue that idea about the coat of arms. It's one of the best ways of tracing a family's history back that far.'

After the reverend had left, Crispin and Amos were sinking back into the two armchairs when a car drew up outside.

Annabelle stood on the doorstep, beaming. 'I couldn't stay at home – I've been up all night.' Here, at last, was the genuine excitement and pleasure the occasion deserved and Crispin threw off his melancholy of the previous ten minutes to share in the euphoria with his wife. He and Amos, and to some extent the others, had been too close to the action and were now too tired to fully appreciate just how momentous all this really was. The usurpers routed, and now all dead. The true heir returned. Gervaise had done the right thing after all. And now they knew why he had seemed so interested in the ruins. All was solved.

'So there wasn't any burning secret about the ruins after all!'

'Not initially, no. He wanted to meet you, my dear,' Crispin replied, putting his arm around his wife. 'But he still couldn't bring himself to send for me – pride I suppose. So when he suspected the Phillipses might try to seize the estate, instead of warning us or the police he decided to play games. Said for once he wanted me to fight for what was mine.'

'But why was he so excited when I determined which was the Great Hall then?'

'Because of the parallel with the legend,' Amos answered, keeping quiet about pressure from the Marston ghosts. 'Those medieval brothers had forged the will, too, and the survivor had been walled up in the Great Hall. So that's why Gervaise thought it would be fitting to put his fail-safe device there ... for the rightful heir to find. I wonder if he knew about the pit, too?' He told Annabelle how Paul Phillips had died.

She smiled. 'Some families kept a pit of lions or vipers into which they tossed their enemies.' Seeing Gervaise's letter open on the table she read it through.

'The real reason I wanted to go back was I felt there was

something there he wanted me to find ... but I had no idea it was this. Neither did I realize he knew who I was. But why did he never speak of you, his son, as anyone might – even if only in passing?'

'I might have been his son – hence this letter – but it doesn't mean he liked me. I'm quite sure the bad feeling between us was quite mutual. I went away when he believed it was my duty to stay – unforgivable in his eyes.' Crispin stopped. 'You know, I've just thought. I wonder if that's what happened to the early Baron Marston's son? Perhaps his father was furious with him for going off to the Crusades.'

Annabelle turned to Amos. 'He wasn't exactly a conversationalist was he, but he mentioned you a couple of times I remember.'

'It's only thanks to Amos we've still got the will.' Crispin interrupted. 'We'd just read the letter and were about to get the will out of its hiding place when the Phillips brothers arrived. If they'd seen it, well, I think the outcome would have been hugely different. Can you imagine what they'd have done instantly if they'd realized what we'd found! Anyway, Amos risked his life to inch his way in front of the hole in the wall so they couldn't see it. They were shooting at him! That's why the wall crumbled and the walled-up body fell out. And it's only thanks to Amos's quick thinking that I'm still here at all.'

'Oh nonsense,' Amos said. 'You saved my life. You had the chance to run and you didn't take it. You drew his attention to you and away from me.'

'No, you saved mine. You tantalized Colin with fresh information about his mother – that was clever, guaranteed to get to most men – and it bought us time until Terry could fetch help. Then you shouted so that Napoleon attacked. For sure he'd have shot us otherwise.'

Crispin pulled the second envelope, bent double to fit, from his coat pocket and opened it. Inside were two documents. He examined the smaller one. 'This looks like the letter from the doctor.' He handed it across to Amos.

Amos unfolded the letter. 'Yes that's what this is. Hang on, there's a note written on the top.' Amos scanned it. He looked up and smiled. 'We were right. It says something about how the requirement for such letters has become important for wills made by the elderly.' Amos paused and looked at the note again. 'So he included it here, just in case there was any dispute.' How could a man as meticulous as Gervaise have left the succession of his estate to chance – gamble on his son's return after forty years? He must have had an amazing faith in the pull which Marston exerts. Then Amos remembered the nightmares and understood. Had Gervaise been thus visited all those years for letting his heir go?

Crispin scanned the outside of the other document and then opened it up.

'Just out of interest, who were the witnesses?' Amos asked. Crispin turned to the back and read aloud: 'Elizabeth Jane Summers and Gordon McDonald.'

'Betty and the estate manager,' Amos said. 'So this is indeed the will that Gervaise made shortly before he died.'

CHAPTER SIXTEEN

'There's the usual legal preamble and so on, ah, here it is: That's interesting.' Crispin looked up. 'You and I are his executors and trustees, Amos ... which explains why he was trying to tell you about it on his deathbed.' Crispin went back to perusing the will. 'Good, he's left legacies to the individual staff and to Marston Church – that'll please the vicar – and to his staff in London, ah, right, here we are ...' Crispin read aloud: ' "And the residue of my estate, to include all my lands, Marston Manor, my property in London and elsewhere, shall be divided equally between my son Crispin Thimbleby and one Amos Cotswold." '

Amos was speechless, but quickly realized his mistake. 'That's all that legal stuff about leaving everything to the trustees who then pay all the expenses and legacies out of it and then they hold the remainder in trust to be paid to the beneficiary. That's all that means.'

Crispin read the passage again, this time silently with Annabelle reading it over his shoulder. 'You're right about how the trusteeship works, but, no, Amos, he's split his estate between the two of us!' Crispin lowered the document and beamed at Amos. 'I couldn't be more delighted. For once in my life I couldn't agree with him more! What a sensible old sod he was after all.'

'He can't have done! What on earth for?' Amos had had too many shocks for one night.

'Well, I guess in case I didn't turn up. He wanted someone he could trust to look after things, someone who would respect the staff and the local communities – not do anything to upset them. And who better to choose than the man elected year after year by the local populace. Oh yes, I know all about you, Jack filled me in.'

'But you have come back so there's no need for it now. I couldn't possibly accept it. It's yours. That would be like stealing. No way, Crispin, the estate is all yours!'

'I don't think you have any choice in the matter, Amos.' Crispin went back to the document. 'Here we are ... "if either of them should predecease me or die within twenty-eight days of my death, then the property shall go to their heirs." It couldn't be clearer – it doesn't all revert to the surviving beneficiary or anything,' he grinned at Amos. 'Just in case we felt like bumping each other off. Here, look for yourself.' He handed the will across. 'And that must have been the real reason he went to the trouble of getting that letter from the doctor. In case anyone thought you'd pressurized him.'

Amos sat down and read the document through carefully, while Crispin and Annabelle chatted quietly in the background. He couldn't believe it. No wonder Gervaise had tried to tell him. He chuckled, he couldn't help it. 'I can't take this in you know but it's funny isn't it; there was Sonia Phillips throwing me out of the barn which I'd rented from your father for fifteen years, and those brothers telling me to get off their land – which I always knew was yours – but it never occurred to me it might be mine too.'

Amos ran bewildered fingers through his hair. 'Now it begins to make sense. That's why the London solicitors failed to receive any instructions: Gervaise had made us his executors all along – but decided to keep it a secret.'

'Yes, and as you said earlier, Sonia Phillips probably typed that will for Gervaise ... so she alone knew who the executors were.

No wonder she declined to send for you when the doctor asked her to. She was banking on your ignorance of the executorship – you hadn't been close to him and you weren't acting as though you had any authority there. She hardly wanted Gervaise spoiling everything by telling you with his dying breath.'

Amos was pensive now, thinking aloud. 'But why didn't he send for me earlier – at least ask me to be his executor?' He shuffled his feet. 'Just think, if only I'd known, I could have stopped this Phillips nonsense before it started ... and saved their lives.'

'Or lost yours,' Crispin added. 'It's probably just as well you didn't know. You'd have been their prime target.'

'I suppose you're right. I just don't see why he didn't....' Amos shrugged and gave up on the sentence.

Crispin clapped him on the back. 'Look, we're all whacked. Annabelle and I will go home so you can grab some sleep and I'll come back up here after lunch. We can start talking about what to do then.'

Amos dragged himself up the stairs. Crispin was right, he couldn't think about it now; he was just too tired and too bowled over with all that had happened. When he felt better he'd get on to John Wilkinson and see how he could get out of this. It was all very well for Crispin to appear so pleased about it – that was the measure of the man, to be kind and generous. But what must he be thinking underneath? In a remote corner of his mind he must believe Amos had engineered this – deliberately offered to help Lord Marston in the hope of material gain.

Why on earth had Gervaise done it? Why couldn't he have just made Amos an overseer – a trustee. Wouldn't that have been sufficient? He could even have given him a small legacy if he'd felt he needed rewarding for his labours, to encourage him to care for the place diligently. But this? This was way out of line.

'Lord Marston's just arrived so I thought I'd better wake you up.' Lindsay put the mug of tea by the side of the bed and stood arms akimbo looking down at him. 'At least you won't have to waste time getting dressed.' She beamed. Jack had obviously imparted all the news.

Beneath the smile Crispin looked miserable. As soon as they were out of the cottage he said: 'I know how you must feel, because you see, I feel the same.'

'I knew you must, so would I in your shoes. Don't worry, I'll speak to my solicitor, we'll get this changed. I don't want half of your inheritance, Crispin. I hope you know that.'

Crispin caught Amos's arm and turned to face him. 'No, you don't understand, Amos. I'm not the rightful heir either.'

'Of course you are!'

'No, not now that legend's been proved true. That robber's family inherited Marston. We've all been usurpers ever since.'

'We certainly don't know that. No one seems to know whether the real heir ever came home or what happened to him if he did. But even if it is true, how can it matter now, eight centuries later?'

'It does to me.'

'Just think about it for a minute. Your family has the title. The family of that walled-up brother wouldn't have had that now, would they?' Amos sighed, relieved. At least he'd quashed that one. The last thing he needed was Crispin dredging up yet another reason why he couldn't come home. Amos dreaded yet more nightly visitations from an unhappy Gervaise because he'd failed to persuade Crispin to stay.

'Oh I don't know. All they'd have had to do would be to lend the king a lot of money. I expect it was quite easy to get a title in those days.'

'Yes, but not this title. You're the thirty-ninth baron. I'm sure we can easily trace the records to see when the first one lived and hence prove your title dates right back to then.'

'Yes, but they still could have bought that particular title. If they kept the coat of arms and wanted people to believe they were the real Marstons then they'd have bought the real title too, wouldn't they?

Without any further conversation they climbed into the Land Rover and drove up towards Marston. Amos couldn't avoid noticing the police cars, the tents, the bunting and other paraphernalia which decorated the sward around the ruins, but felt unwilling even to glance in that direction. Instead they swept on up the hill, coming to a halt in the kitchen yard.

'I saw the smoke from the fire that day but I didn't know then it was the walled garden burning.' Crispin strode up the incline and poked his head through the entrance where all that remained of the gate were the blackened hinges. Amos joined him. 'My mother loved this garden.' For a man who'd just inherited a small fortune there seemed no consolation. Crispin was sinking further and further into a mire which was partly of his own making; though Amos had to admit the sight of that garden – now black, barren, destroyed – was enough to depress the liveliest of souls.

They crossed the bottom meadow into the field where the barn stood. 'This is where they held the rave and Ted and me came and cut the cable to the generator – but not before the damage had been done.' The great swathe of mud across the field, where hundreds of feet had destroyed the grass, was now ridged and solid with frost. Inside, the barn still held the debris of that night: scattered glasses, bottles, cables, clothing – discarded needles sticking vertically out of the ground to catch the unwary, as deadly as the landmine antennae they resembled. Amos turned away, more disgusted by this human detritus than ever he was by animal excrement.

Once over the five-bar gate into the field by the river, they struck out as one towards the church without another word. How long was it since he and Crispin had last walked the fields like this – forty-four, forty-five years? It must be. They hadn't always talked then, either.

Although they seemed to have been in the church a lot lately, they hadn't been in daylight. They both knew what they'd come for.

'We should take a look at those old coats of arms. As the reverend said, they might tell us more about what happened in the aftermath of the death of those medieval brothers.' Amos tried the handle on the door as Crispin, who'd come prepared, produced the key. But the door was already unlocked. Maybe one of the village women was doing some cleaning.

As they stepped inside, Terry Finn strode purposefully down the nave towards them, notebook and pen in hand.

'Thought I'd make a start for you,' he beamed. 'The Reverend Whittaker mentioned you'd been asking about what happened to the crusader. Said he'd pointed you to the different shields in here – said they might shed some light.' He looked modestly down at his wellingtons. 'As it happens I know a bit about heraldry.' Was there anything Terry Finn didn't know a bit about?

Amos turned to Crispin. 'I'd never really noticed, or if I had I'd forgotten, but apparently the Marston coat of arms must have changed, some of the ones in here differ from one another.'

'I think I had noticed, yes, but I didn't think anything of it – I've never understood what all the parts represent anyway. The one I remember is the one over the arch into the stables, which is the same as the one on my father's stationery.'

'Come and look at these then.' Terry led the way up into the chancel where the older brasses lay in the floor. 'What about those?'

In turn, Crispin crouched beside each of the brasses Terry was indicating, both of which depicted a warrior carrying a shield with a coat of arms etched onto it. The escutcheon was in red and black with a wide diagonal band dividing the field from top left to bottom right and a pelican repeated both above and below the band.

'They're similar, but they're not the same as the one on the stable.'

'Those on the brasses date from the eleventh and twelfth centuries from what I can decipher of the Latin. But what about this?' Terry pointed to a wall-mounted monument which from the costumes looked as though it dated from the Elizabethan period. 'This one has a bend sinister instead of a bend dextra; the bend is that broad bar you can see dividing the face of the shield. In other words it goes the opposite way in these, i.e. right to left instead of left to right, and, if you look closely there's the pelican in the top left hand segment but, now there's a boar in the bottom right-hand corner.'

'Yes, that looks like the one.' Crispin peered intently at the monument. 'It's been so long since I've seen it – I'd almost forgotten what it looked like.'

Terry turned to Amos. 'Good thing there's a boar now, eh? Suits you doesn't it. Jack told me what was in the will.'

Amos was furious.

Crispin stepped in to prevent him castigating Terry. 'Hold on, Amos, it's my fault. I met Jack on my way to your place this afternoon. He asked me if I'd read the will – obviously wanted to make quite sure the place was in safe hands at last. So I told him what it says.' He raised his arms, hands open, towards Amos. 'I saw no reason not to.'

'Well the world will know by now then.' Amos wasn't pleased. He turned to Terry. 'I'm not taking it, Terry, it's not mine,' and strode off down the church.

Terry and Crispin caught him up. 'I haven't told you what the boar means in heraldry,' Terry went on undeterred. 'It's usually worn by a warrior because the boar signifies a fierce combatant which ceases fighting only with its life. I thought you'd like that after Napoleon's performance last night.'

Had it been only last night? To escape from the embarrassment of Gervaise's will Amos asked: 'Reverend Whittaker told me the coats of arms were often changed on marriage. Is that what's happened here?'

'No, or at least I wouldn't have thought so. You see in early times, the twelfth, and thirteenth centuries, they simply put the two shields together when they wanted to join two houses as it were. Later on, at the end of the fifteenth century, they impaled them – you've seen it I'm sure – where there's a vertical line right down the middle of the shield and the woman's father's arms went on the right as you look at it and her husband's on the left … but not always. It's not an exact science, you know.'

'And yet these are neither joined nor impaled.'

'Precisely.'

Then Amos remembered. 'Have you looked at the one on the bell?' They all moved into the tiny vestry at the rear which housed Gabriel.

'That's interesting,' Crispin said. 'The one here is the same as on that Elizabethan monument and the same as on the stable arch. Which would suggest that the change was made very early on. The new manor – and the bell – both date from the early twelve hundreds.' He turned to Terry. 'But what do the changes mean?'

'That's where my knowledge is insufficient, I'm afraid. You'll have to bear with me while I find out.' Terry looked at his watch. 'I'll have to wait until the morning when the library reopens, so I can use the internet.'

The phrase "find out" set Amos thinking back to something Terry had said last night, standing in much the same spot: that he'd spent his life searching. Amos had been so wrapped up in his own quest he'd paid no attention to it at the time. 'Did you ever find your father, Terry – all those years ago when you ran away? You thought he was in Portsmouth didn't you?'

'No. No I didn't. I got to Portsmouth and from there around the world, but no, I never found him.' Terry looked ruminative. 'I don't even remember him from when I was small, he was always away. Perhaps that's why I started following our Heavenly Father ... when I couldn't find my earthly one.' Amos felt sorry for him. He and Crispin had despised their fathers but at least they'd known who they were. Terry had never really known his.

Leaving Terry to his enquiries, Crispin and Amos went out of the church to find a plain clothes policeman headed purposefully towards them through the lych gate. He nodded to Amos and turned to address Crispin.

'I'm sorry to bother you, sir, but you ought to know we've unearthed several more bodies. Those ruins were quite the little killing field it seems.'

Amos and Crispin said: 'Oh no,' in unison.

Realizing the impression he'd given the inspector added: 'It's all right – they're centuries old. Just skeletons.'

'Not all buried in the wall?' Crispin was aghast.

'No, sir. We had to send a man down the pit to recover Paul Phillips's body; that's when he found the others. It looks like there are four skeletons.'

'What do you do in such cases, Inspector?'

'Well, we have to get the pathologist to verify they are ancient ... then usually they go to one of the specialist university departments for historical research. It's amazing what they can find out from bones these days.'

'I'm sure my wife's college at Oxford would be very pleased to have them, Inspector. I'll ask her to get in touch with your people.'

They went to cadge some tea from Betty who'd wasted no time in reclaiming her domain. Maybe sitting in that kitchen again, where he'd briefly met the forensic scientist, jogged Amos's memory, but he suddenly remembered that man whom Betty had mentioned last week.

Walking back round the house to the Land Rover, he broached the subject with Crispin. 'If you're worried about whether you're descended from the brothers who robbed the estate ... I was just thinking, while you're having those skeletons shipped to Oxford why don't you send the trussed man too? They can DNA test you and him – see if there's a match. Then you'll know for sure.'

Crispin stopped walking. 'That's a brilliant idea, Amos. Brilliant! In fact I could get on to the forensic service myself, no need to wait for the university.'

Amos wished he hadn't said it now. 'That's if you really want to know. Personally I don't think it matters, you'll make a perfect lord of the manor which is all we care about round here.'

'I've got to know, Amos. It'll help me decide what to do.'

'That's what bothers me.'

Crispin turned to him. 'I know you've got your own reasons for wanting me to take up where my father left off, Amos, but I've spent a long time building a life elsewhere. Oh I know we've a house in Woodstock, but that's so Annabelle can be near her work. My life is in Africa. I'm proud of what we've accomplished there but it's like a tiny clearing in the veldt. We can't stop now – I don't want to stop now. We've got to make those people properly self sufficient so that when there's a bad harvest they don't all sink back into starvation. It's what I do.'

CHAPTER SEVENTEEN

After the service at Marston church on Sunday morning, Terry kept Crispin and Amos back.

'I've taken some advice – about the heraldry. There's a man in America who's an expert, has his own website, so I e-mailed him. He's been really helpful. It seems records exist showing the coats of arms carried by the Crusaders. That's where the idea really started – so they could recognize one another even under a helmet and vizor. So this chap looked for the name Marston and guess what – he came up with two; both right at the end of the third Crusade, the late twelfth century. One was Crispin Thimbleby, whose insignia was a pelican, which fits, doesn't it – remember the pelican repeat on the old brasses over there?' Terry pointed towards the altar. 'The other was Gabriel Marston.'

'On the bell!' chorused Crispin and Amos. 'We always thought it was the name of the bell,' Crispin added.

'It may have been, of course, but that's also the earliest occurrence, in the church at any rate, of the new coat of arms. And guess what?' Terry looked from one to the other. 'Gabriel Marston's insignia was a boar!'

Amos was even more confused now. 'So what's it all mean, Terry? Were Gabriel and Crispin brothers, is that it? Why did the coat of arms change?'

'Well, of course, we can't be sure but this American thinks the same as I do. It looks as though the Reverend Whittaker's guess was right. Crispin Thimbleby did return from the Crusades to find his estates had been stolen. Somehow or other he reclaimed them but then wanted to alter the arms because he felt they'd been tainted.'

Terry propped himself against the end of the pew. 'Now, if Gabriel had been Crispin's brother, they'd have had the same coat of arms but the younger would have had what they call a cadency mark on his denoting he was the second in line. So no, I don't think they were brothers, neither do I believe they were cousins. Because the other interesting thing is that that diagonal band, or bend as it's called, altered direction. That is significant. A bend sinister as it became – denotes illegitimacy.' Terry stood up straight to deliver the punch-line.

'So we think Gabriel was a bastard brother. They met up and, when they got home, threw out the pretenders and became such powerful allies and friends that they decided to amalgamate their coats of arms.'

'And then went on to build a new manor, perhaps for one or the other of them, and donate the bell to the church,' Crispin finished. 'Well, it's a nice story but there's nothing to prove it, is there?' Doubting Thomas was off again.

Terry glanced at Amos and raised his eyes to heaven. 'I think it's probably quite close to the truth. I'll tell you something else, Crispin, do you know what a pelican means in heraldry? "Devoted and self-sacrificing charity". Because of the legend that in times of great hardship the pelican opens its own breast with its beak for its young to feed off. If you look carefully at those shields you'll see that's what it's doing.'

Amos was amazed. 'You're suggesting that's what Crispin's done with his life – and what he did for you as a runaway. You mean this self-sacrificing trait runs in the family.'

Crispin looked very embarrassed, but at least it temporarily curtailed his sceptical remarks.

Amos was becoming more and more convinced that Crispin's

increasing preoccupation with not being the rightful heir had more to do with his wanting an excuse to reject his birthright, than it did with what he truly felt. So if Amos was to fulfil his obligation to Gervaise he had to solve the problem of Crispin's unfinished work in Africa. Strange, he thought, how Terry and Crispin had both appeared back here at the same time when both were principally engaged in the same enterprise – feeding Africa's starving. Amos had the unnerving feeling that events were being powerfully manipulated around him and that soon they would all slot into place.

*

On Monday morning Crispin rang. 'Amos, would you like to come up to Marston this afternoon – the man from the forensic service has just called, he's got some results for me. Says he'll come over about two o'clock.' He said it lightly but Amos could hear the taughtness beneath the surface.

When he reached Marston Manor, Crispin and the man from the forensic service were already ensconced in the drawing-room. Amos and the scientist recognized each other from their brief encounter months ago in Betty's kitchen. After an exchange of greetings, the man opened the briefcase on his knee, extracted a thin folder and cleared his throat.

'You asked me to test five skeletons: the trussed man, and the four found in the pit – all male – plus yourself, sir,' he indicated Crispin.

'What I can tell you is all the skeletons are from the same family. The bodies in the pit are all sons of the trussed man.' He paused to give them time to digest this, then went on: 'And you, sir' – he turned again to Crispin – 'are not related to any of them.'

The silence lasted a long minute while they thought about this. Amos deliberately waited for Crispin to speak first. He wanted to be sure that whatever conclusion Crispin came to he could believe it was his and not one unduly influenced by Amos – or anyone else for that matter.

'Somebody killed them then? The surviving brother pleaded not guilty but was found to be guilty of murdering his brother ... so he was walled up in the Great Hall which option, by the law then, allowed his family to retain their estates. Except of course, they weren't theirs in the first place because the brothers had murdered the Baron and forged his will.'

Crispin didn't need any help now. 'So when the real heir, the Baron's son, returned from the Crusades and found them in possession of his lands – he must have killed the lot. That's the only explanation, isn't it?' Crispin's face cleared. For the first time since the discovery of the trussed man, he looked truly at peace with himself. Beaming, a man now sure of his lineage, he looked to Amos for confirmation.

'Absolutely. It also explains why the old manor was abandoned: you can see why he wouldn't have wanted to live there after that.'

Crispin carried on, 'And if what Terry is suggesting is true – about there being a bastard brother – well, I don't suppose the original Sir Crispin could have taken on the four sons by himself. It would also explain why the coats of arms were joined – after what they'd achieved together.'

'Funny how history repeats itself,' mused the man from the forensic service. Amos and Crispin nodded in agreement. The fight they'd had with the Phillipses, which doubtless Betty had already described to the man in graphic detail when she'd let him in today, could indeed be considered to have an uncanny parallel with the thirteenth-century restitution of the Marston lands.

'Betty's told you about the Phillipses then ... and the police will have told you how they came to find the bodies in the pit,' Amos said.

'Oh yes, yes indeed, but it's even more than that, isn't it? – with your being the bastard brother if you'll forgive the phrase.'

It was Crispin who recovered first and said starchily: 'I beg your pardon?'

The man looked shattered, flushing crimson from neck to forehead. 'Mrs Summers told me you'd inherited Marston jointly. Goodness me, I'm so sorry, I thought he must have told you. I can't believe ...' The man mopped his brow in acute embarrassment.

Crispin said gently: 'It's not your fault, just tell us what we've evidently missed.'

Calmed by Crispin's exoneration the man relaxed a little. Addressing them both he said: 'I'd done various pieces of work for Lord Marston – ever since we perfected the technique which wasn't long ago. A lot of criminal cases are won or lost on the subject of DNA now. Anyway, Lord Marston began to realize its power.

'Well, one day he asked me to come up here, said he'd got a particularly sensitive case he wanted my help on but I wasn't to tell a soul. He gave me a fair amount of work so I wasn't about to refuse. Being the clever man he was he'd also realized I was bound to put two and two together, and didn't want me ferreting around out of sheer curiosity, so he took me into his confidence.' The forensic man glanced up to see Amos and Crispin staring at him. 'He said that someone he knew had told him that his so-called son was really Lord Marston's bastard.'

Silence, utter silence.

'Without the man's knowledge Lord Marston wanted me to take a sample of his DNA and match it with his own to prove the story was untrue. He said he felt it might just have been spite – particularly as the son in question looked the spitting image of his father.'

Amos couldn't breathe properly. Neither he nor Crispin spoke, so the scientist continued.

'I'm sorry, Mr Cotswold, but I was sent to the kitchen for a reason that day.' The man took a deep breath. 'I took the DNA from your tea-cup and some hairs you'd dropped. There's no doubt: you are Lord Marston's son.'

Amos went numb. At nearly sixty he suddenly didn't know who he was; it seemed he'd never known. He felt as though one of those huge old walls had fallen down on top of him. Unable to speak, he flapped a hand at Crispin who asked, 'Can you tell us some more? Did Gervaise explain?'

'As I say, he was surprised because Mr Cotswold apparently looks just like his father ... er ... adoptive father, Squire Cotswold. But there was no mistake. All Lord Marston said was it was possible.' The man changed his tone to tread even more carefully. 'I took that to mean that Mrs Cotswold and he—'

It wasn't hard to figure out – now he knew. Gervaise's wife must have been heavy with Crispin, there were eight months between their birthdays, and Gervaise was a noted philanderer. He found it harder to believe it of his own mother – but there again her marriage to Squire Cotswold had not been a love-match but one of those prearranged marriages which still happened amongst the gentry before the war. Her father had decided whom she would marry. Amos could understand her feelings. An unhappy young woman, yet lonely with the squire away in the war ... and along comes Gervaise. And that's how the squire had known of course, he'd been away so the child couldn't possibly have been his. Presumably he'd guessed the culprit, or forced the truth out of his wife.

The squire would have gone to any lengths to avoid the cuckold's horns; so it was no surprise to Amos that he'd never mentioned it. But at some point he had apparently accosted Gervaise with it, who, just as keen to keep it quiet, had obviously been happy to consider the accusation a lie; especially since Amos looked so like the squire. But something ... or things ... must have nagged at him, so when he had the technology to finally disprove it Gervaise had used it.

It explained a lot of course. Why Amos had been constantly taken to Marston as a boy – out of the squire's sight. Why the squire had hated him. Why he'd been disinherited ... up to now that is. Maybe that's what the squire had wanted to tell Amos when he lay dying. Amos's sisters, half-sisters, said he'd been asking for Amos. Had he wanted to ask forgiveness for taking it out on the boy, the innocent party? Amos doubted that even now.

What was it Terry had said, that day: 'Your paternal grandmother was a Lawrence'? Too preoccupied to listen properly Amos had thought he meant his maternal grandmother because his mother's maiden name was Lawrence so, of course, his maternal grandmother was a Lawrence – by marriage. But Terry had meant what he said, he had been referring to Amos's grandparents on his father's side. Those were the ones Terry had found, and that grandmother had been a Lawrence too.

Now it all came back. Amos had known his mother and the squire had been cousins but never having had much to do with the rest of the family, particularly the squire's side, he'd forgotten about it. It began to make sense; the arranged marriage may well have been in order to consolidate and secure the family land holdings, prevent them being divided up when Grandfather Lawrence died. Amos looked like his father; he'd disliked that but why would he have questioned it? The squire and his wife had shared the same grandfather – that's where the looks had come from. Amos had inherited his great grandfather's looks through his mother ... not his father. He smiled wryly, the squire must have been relieved about that. While Amos looked so like him no one would ever have guessed the truth.

And now he knew what Gervaise had been trying to tell him. Yes, he might have been asking Amos to find Crispin, bring him back here, persuade him to stay – he might have been trying to tell him what he'd hidden in the ruins, what the Phillipses were likely to do – but there had been more. It had been so typical of Gervaise not to say anything, not even to explain in his will – just leave Amos half the estate, because as it happened, it suited his purpose.

So even his real father had rejected him – hadn't been able to tell him to his face except when he desperately needed to and then it had been too late. Of course! That was why he'd omitted to tell Amos he was one of his executors, afraid he might guess the real reason. But Gervaise hadn't reckoned with those ancestral voices. Hadn't reckoned with the Marston ghosts. They wanted him to claim his son. No wonder Amos had felt haunted by them. He was one of their own.

EPILOGUE

After several late nights and a case or two of claret from their father's cellar, they hatched their scheme. Amos couldn't help thinking how that early Crispin and his brother Gabriel must have made similar plans together all those centuries ago.

The people of Sudan and Ethiopia, Eritrea and Madagascar, the slums of Johannesburg and the jungle – needed expertise. Crispin wanted to continue the work he'd started there, organizing and managing the specialist aid required for the long-term solution. Yet Marston was his home – had been the home of his ancestors through eight centuries – hard fought for, too. How could he turn his back on that?

So Amos and Crispin decided to turn Marston Manor into a training centre for the African Aid Scheme. The main stables and outhouses would be converted into temporary accommodation for the volunteers and their families – making it easier for people to sign up for the scheme. Those families not wishing to accompany the volunteers could then remain at Marston at a subsidized rate. The main house would become the administrative centre plus Annabelle and Crispin's home, when they weren't out on site, ably kept by Betty Summers.

With guidance as necessary from Amos and Alan, the trainees along with a handful of experienced help, would farm the Marston lands making the centre self-sufficient. Other schemes would be adopted – such as Richard Phillips's idea for renovating the old gardens – if they added to the expertise needed out in Africa, or made money for the centre to use in Africa – or preferably both.

The pieces arranged themselves like figures in an architectural drawing, each cut-to-shape, slotting into the universal plan. Take Terry Finn, a man who'd rediscovered his faith, Amos liked to think through seeing how God had used them all to fashion His own solution. Terry would stay at Marston to run the centre – and Marston Church, and live in one of the converted barns. He was a new man. They had yet to convince the Bishop of this but Amos felt confident he could do that, especially since he envisaged the complex becoming a training centre for missionaries as well as agricultural and other teachers.

For their future rallies, Marty and his boys could use the vast pasturelands miles beyond Marston where they wouldn't disturb anyone.

The inhabitants of Weston Hathaway had gained a new lord of the manor and a new enterprise. One guaranteed not to pollute the atmosphere, terrify the livestock, disrupt the environment or threaten their way of life.

Amos climbed the stairs up to Gervaise's chamber and slowly pushed open the heavy oak door, uncertain of what he might find, of what might lurk there still. Sunbeams streamed through the lattice, dancing on the counterpane, exorcising the night. The clock ticked merrily on the mantelpiece, recycling its seconds, rejoicing in its new lease of life. The ghosts had gone, resting content now Marston was back in the right hands.